D0775935

BLOOD UPON
THE SNOW

BLOOD UPON
THE SNOW

HILDA LAWRENCE

PENGUIN BOOKS

Penguin Books Ltd, Harmondsworth,
Middlesex, England
Penguin Books, 40 West 23rd Street,
New York, New York 10010, U.S.A.
Penguin Books Australia Ltd, Ringwood,
Victoria, Australia
Penguin Books Canada Limited, 2801 John Street,
Markham, Ontario, Canada L3R 1B4
Penguin Books (N.Z.) Ltd, 182–190 Wairau Road,
Auckland 10, New Zealand

First published in the United States of America by
Simon and Schuster 1944
First published in Great Britain by
Chapman & Hall Ltd 1946
Published in Penguin Books in Great Britain 1954
Published in Penguin Books in the
United States of America 1984

Copyright 1944 by Hilda Lawrence
Copyright © renewed Hilda Lawrence, 1971
All rights reserved

Printed in the United States of America by
Offset Paperback Mfrs., Inc., Dallas, Pennsylvania

Except in the United States of America,
this book is sold subject to the condition
that it shall not, by way of trade or otherwise,
be lent, re-sold, hired out, or otherwise circulated
without the publisher's prior consent in any form of
binding or cover other than that in which it is
published and without a similar condition
including this condition being imposed
on the subsequent purchaser

Walk softly, March, forbear the bitter blow ;
  Her feet within a trap, her blood upon the snow,
The four little foxes saw their mother go—
  Walk softly.

FOUR LITTLE FOXES, Lew Sarett

CHAPTER ONE

THE snow was falling thick and fast when the last train of the day clattered into Crestwood at eight o'clock. The last bus also arrived, a split second before the train; it careered across the tracks in front of the hissing locomotive and came to rest against the station platform. The platform shuddered.

The stationmaster didn't even look out of his window. His Saturday nights were all alike and he knew what to expect. He knew Florrie was on the train with a basket of produce from her father's farm beyond Bear River and he knew he'd find a day-old newspaper in the mailbag, with maybe a picture postcard from sunny Florida for the two old maids up the lane. He knew the bus would be empty, as usual, but that wasn't his business. He suspected a new gouge in the platform, and that was. He pulled a knitted cap over his bald head, buttoned a leather jacket over his thin frame, and was well into the customary invective when he stepped out into the cold.

He looked neither right nor left, but immediately joined the engineer and the bus driver in a whispered exchange of acid remarks—whispered in deference to Florrie's presence. This, plus a little gallantry with Florrie's basket, kept him busy and happy. That was how he failed to see the stranger with two suitcases who swung down from the last coach.

The stranger was in no hurry. He stood in the shadows and watched the little group under the lanterns at the far end of the platform. The men were quarrelling cheerfully; the girl was apathetic and obviously waiting. They all

7

looked harmless and normal, even a little stupid, and he knew they hadn't seen him. That gave him an idea. Later, he called it a hunch. He deliberately stepped behind a clump of ornamental firs and waited for them to disperse.

Across the snowy lane that separated the station from the dark encroaching mountain, a private driveway yawned like an open mouth. He transferred his interest to this. He stiffened to attention when a subdued roar filled the night and the headlights of a car cut through the trees.

A long black limousine swooped out of the driveway and drew up to the station. The girl with the basket hurried forward and climbed in ; the car whirled back into the driveway, and he watched its lights as it twisted and turned up the mountain. It was a foreign car, and he told himself it looked like a hearse ; he also told himself that he'd missed a ride.

A limp sack of mail hit the platform. The train, trailed by the bus, moved off in a shower of sparks and flying snow. The stationmaster swung his lantern, clumped down the platform, and re-entered the building. The door closed behind him.

Crestwood, with its single lane of little houses, lay quiet under a white shroud.

In the third cottage from the upper end of the lane Miss Beulah Pond sat at her parlour window, enjoying the view. Like a picture, she thought, with the mountain and the trees and the nice clean snow coming down like feathers. It ought to be Christmas Eve. She rocked happily, her hands idle, her only light the glow of a dying fire.

The soft white flakes piled up against the sill and buried the little lane that wound uphill outside her gate. Mother Nature's Blanket, she said fondly. It was the last time she ever called it that.

There were no houses across the way from Miss Beulah's, only a wall of pines. It was a dark, romantic view, and somehow sad. It made her think of the poor little match girl who froze to death, and the other little girl whose cruel stepmother dressed her in newspapers and sent her out in the storm to find strawberries. Snow always made Miss Beulah think of things like that, pretty, childish things with death and tears in the background. Miss Beulah had the imagination of her century and she had read too many books when she was young.

So there she sat shivering a little and scaring herself pleasantly. She closed her eyes and conjured up her favourite pictures : a tiny bird, quite stiff and cold, undoubtedly dead ; two ragged babies huddled in the snow, most certainly dead or sure to be in an hour or so. She saw a graveyard—was it a graveyard ? No, it was a lonely mausoleum, deep in drifts, with footprints leading away from the door. Miss Beulah jumped. She was getting beyond herself. Footprints away from the door ! She called herself several harsh names and decided on a hot toddy. Perhaps, even, a double hot toddy.

Halfway to the kitchen she turned back to the window again. She never knew why, but turn she did ; and there they were exactly as she imagined them. Footprints, deep and fresh, climbing up the middle of the lane.

They couldn't be coming from a mausoleum, she told herself as she raised the window with trembling hands. There wasn't even a graveyard for miles around. At least there wasn't anything you could call a graveyard ; nothing but that old, abandoned—— She clung to the sill and peered up the lane.

A single lamp stood at the bend where the lane turned into the mountain trail. Veiled in snow, it shed a feeble light. But that was light enough to show the figure of a man. A strange man, with two suitcases, turning into the

mountain trail as if he knew his destination. But what
could that be ? The trail led nowhere, unless you counted
the observation tower three miles up. Or the hunting
lodges. That was it, of course. He was one of those
hunters.

She closed the window and sank back into her chair.
To-morrow morning she'd ask Amos all about him. He'd
probably come in on the train and Amos would know his
name and everything. Even if he'd come on the bus,
Amos would know. Summer people called Amos the Herr
Gestapo. Well, in a way . . .

She abandoned the mausoleum with reluctance. Too
bad. It was her masterpiece to date and it would have
been wonderful for scaring Bessy Petty. It had even
scared herself. She paid her imagination the tribute of a
shiver. So natural-looking ; she could remember every
detail. . . . Maybe Bessy was right—maybe she was
psychic after all. Maybe—the stranger wasn't a hunter.
Maybe——

Someone knocked at the door.

She froze in her chair and waited. The knock came
again.

She held her breath and whispered the names of possible
callers, telling them over and over with dry lips, letting
them fall like the beads of a rosary. No, it was none of
them. She knew that. And there was no chain on her
door.

She raised her eyes to the window. A man's face,
grinning, was pressed against the glass.

" Did I startle you ? " The voice was strong and
apologetic and young. " I'm sorry. I only want to ask
directions. I think I've lost my way."

That was better, much better, but it wasn't enough.
She raised the window an inch. " Where are you—
coming from ? "

He sounded puzzled. "The station. I'm looking for someone named Stoneman, and all these houses seem to be empty—except yours."

Stoneman. The old man up the mountain. The old devil, according to Florrie. But alive. She raised the window another inch.

"If he'd known you were coming he'd have sent a car to meet you," she said, peering cautiously.

"He doesn't know. I mean he doesn't know I'm coming to-night. But he more or less expects me, sometime. If you'll just start me off in the right direction.—I don't want you to catch cold, standing there."

She began to relax. "It's a long walk. You'd better let me telephone."

"Oh, no! No thanks! That would be an imposition. You see, it's my fault that I wasn't met. I forgot to let him know." He was close enough to note the weather-beaten skin of her seamed old face. One of these hikers, he decided; one of these trampers in the rain and snow. "I'd rather walk," he said engagingly. "We city people don't get enough exercise."

"Of course you don't," she said promptly. "You're the first one I ever heard admit it. Well, now, you'll never get there if you follow that trail. I mean it would be dangerous. You must go back to the station and turn into that big driveway. It's the only one there and you can't miss it. The house is about a mile up the mountain. . . . Don't you want to leave your luggage with me? You could send for it in the morning. Or come for it," she added archly.

"No." He shifted the bags and she saw that one was heavier than the other. "No, I'll carry them." Her left hand was resting on the sill; there was no ring on it. "Thank you, Miss——?"

"Pond," she said graciously. "Beulah Pond. Lived

here all my life. Come in to call whenever you can. That is, if you're staying any length of time."

" I will. Thank you again."

She watched him trudge down the middle of the lane, adding new prints to the pattern he had made before. " A nice young man," she said, closing the window and locking it. " Wholesome. I wonder what he's going to do up there ? "

She mixed her toddy and returned to the fire. Frozen children and snowed-in mausoleums dissolved in that dual warmth ; the vision of a flesh-and-blood stranger took their place.

" If he stays here"—she took a long, contented swallow— " if he stays here we may get to know him very well. And that'll be a nice change."

She finished her drink and went upstairs to bed. After she said her prayers she remembered that she hadn't asked his name.

His name was Mark East. He was short of breath and pleased with himself when he reached his destination. Thanks to that instinctive hunch, things were going his way. He had made a natural and successful contact with one of the natives and that was always good ; and he was descending on an immediate and dubious future without giving it time to set the stage.

He checked his surroundings with one quick look. No lights showing, although it was still early ; no dog, and somehow he had expected several. The architecture called for dogs, loose and chained. In the black-and-white night the house loomed like a small castle. He took a card from his wallet and pulled the bell. " Stone floor," he said when he heard the footsteps inside.

The door opened. He recognized the man who had driven the black car to the station.

" My name is East," he said, offering the card. " I
believe Mr. Stoneman expects me." He followed the
man into a wide hall. One lamp burned dimly.

Dark, quiet rooms opened on each side of the hall ;
there was an odour of flowers and cleanliness. He had
more or less expected confusion, hidden from the average
eye but visible to him, and he was disappointed. The
servant hung his hat and coat in a closet and picked up
the suitcase.

" Mr. Stoneman gave us no definite instructions, sir,
but we knew you would be coming in a day or so. I'm
sorry you were not met." No more than that ; no sur-
mise about the train or the method of his arrival.

" Have you dined, sir ? "

" Yes, thank you. Do I see Mr. Stoneman to-night ? "

The man hesitated at the foot of the stairs. " No, sir.
Mr. Stoneman is not well. I think it will be wise to wait
until morning. . . . If you will follow me."

He was shown into a large ugly room, full of heavy
furniture and red damask. " Don't bother to unpack,"
he said quickly, as the man bent over his luggage. " I'll
do that later. Is there any particular hour for breakfast ? "

" It will be served when you want it, sir. Either in your
room or downstairs."

" What is your name ? "

" Perrin, sir."

" Well, thank you, Perrin. This will be very comfortable. Good night."

He waited five minutes, then he went out into the hall.
There were other doors, all closed, and one of them was
marked LINEN. He listened carefully before he opened it.
It was a deep closet and at the far end he found a chest
filled with summer blankets and moth balls. He returned
to his room and came back with the heavier suitcase. He
put this in the bottom of the chest and covered it neatly.

" Safe until spring," he murmured, " or until to-morrow."

He undressed and went to bed, marvelling at his courage when he left the door open. But for a long time he lay awake, watching the hall.

The next morning Mark East sat before the library fire, an empty breakfast tray at his elbow. On the other side of the fire, hiding his shaking hands under a shawl, sat Joseph Stoneman. Stoneman's bloodshot eyes measured the younger man's length and breadth and he smiled as if his calculations pleased him.

" You'll do," he said. " I read your credentials very carefully. They are really—splendid."

" They should be," Mark smiled back. " I wrote them myself. I'm my own boss."

"Oh!" Stoneman looked startled. "I didn't know. This business of engaging people through correspondence has its surprises. However, in this case I am singularly fortunate." He looked as if he were begging for a pretty speech in return, but none came. He tried again. " So you yourself are the Wood Agency ? That is splendid, splendid. So many fine opportunities these days. But aren't you rather young to have a business of your own ? "

" My looks are deceptive," Mark said. " I'm very old, very mean, and suspicious."

He let that sink in while his eyes moved about the room. He looked as if he were taking an admiring inventory but actually he was straining his ears for the sound of voices or footsteps. He knew there were other people in the house, but except for Stoneman and Perrin he'd seen nobody.

Stoneman coughed. " You found your room quite comfortable ? " he asked. " I think it's a dreadful room myself and we shall change it as soon as possible. Perrin didn't know. You surprised us by arriving so—suddenly."

" Don't bother," Mark said amiably.

The old man stirred uneasily. He gave up all pretence

of hiding his shaking hands. He held them in his lap, tightly, until the knuckles showed white.

Mark thought he looked like a worn little curate with a bad conscience, so he gave him a reassuring smile. He'd used that smile with the difficult ones before and it always lulled them into saying more than they meant to.

"I'm—I'm sorry I couldn't welcome you personally last night," Stoneman said. "You must have thought it extremely odd. But the truth is—I was the victim of one of my—attacks."

In bottle formation, Mark thought. Out loud he said, "Oh that's all right."

"And I was most distressed to hear that you walked up from the station. You did walk, didn't you ? . . . If you'd only telegraphed—we're not savages here—you'd have been properly met. As it happens, the car did go down. For one of the maids. But no one remembers seeing you."

"Forget it," Mark said carelessly. "I like to walk. I always walk when I come into a strange town on a strange job. I like to know where I am. In my work we always prepare for two exits, one proper and one unorthodox."

"What an extraordinary remark ! And how unkind ! " Stoneman looked ready to cry. "Surely, Mr. East, there's nothing strange about this ! I wrote you most explicitly. I gave you all the details. It's really very simple."

"Yes. That's why I came. The simplicity got me." Mark used the reassuring smile again. Look," he said. "You're spending the winter here with some very old friends named Morey. These Moreys rent the house from somebody. They have two children, girls, and judging from the looks of the place they have plenty of money also."

"S-s-sh, not so loud, my boy." Stoneman twisted around in his chair to get a better look at the portières that covered the door to the hall. "Money—you know it's not quite nice to speak of money in connection with—possessions. Much better to say that my friends have good taste. But—you're very observing."

"Yes. I just observed you looking anxiously in the direction of the door. There's nobody out there now. I've been watching."

Stoneman looked hurt. "I only—I thought I felt a draught Really, you are disconcertingly abrupt. But I like it, I like it. Frankness is a fine thing. Now—you were saying?"

"I was saying something in bad taste about money and I might as well go on. You're offering me too much money for the work you want done, Mr. Stoneman. It worries me, it's too easy. My frankness again. I'm to live here with you and eat in the dining room like one of the family, and all I have to do is take a little shorthand in the morning and do a little typing in the afternoon. And get seventy-five a week. Does that sound simple to you?"

"My dear boy, it does indeed!" He beamed. "I shall keep you very busy, too! You won't be able to call your soul your own! And after you've met the Moreys you'll be perfectly happy, I know."

Mark's eyes were moving about the room again. He seemed not to hear.

"That's a nice portrait," he said casually. "I mean the one over the table. Who is it?"

Stoneman didn't turn to look; he kept his eyes on Mark's face.

"That's Laura—Mrs. Morey," he said. "You'll like her, you'll like her very much." He wagged his head as if it were a finger. "And she'll like you! You'll be great friends, great friends. You cheer her up and then we'll all be happy. I fear she finds country life depressing, poor child."

"She wasn't depressed when that picture was painted,"

Mark said. "She looks as happy as all get out. A Ducroix, done about three years ago, wasn't it? I know his style pretty well. Funny place to find a Ducroix, on top of an American mountain."

Stoneman blinked.

"And what's the story behind the Renoir over the mantel? That's a new one on me. I thought I could place every Renoir in the country, but I never even saw that in a catalogue. Who owns it? You?"

"I?" Stoneman looked pleased. "My dear fellow, I wish I did. But all these beautiful things belong to Laura. She paints a little herself and she loves pictures."

"It takes more than love to own that one," Mark sighed. He looked at his watch and compared it with the marble clock. Out of the corner of his eye he saw Stoneman's hands begin to shake again. He decided to cut it short. He couldn't afford to waste any more time. Either this was what he wanted or it wasn't.

"The bed and breakfast were fine," he said, "and I loved my little talk on art. My suitcase is only half unpacked and I can get down the mountain in thirty minutes. That'll put me in Crestwood in time to catch a train or bus for Bear River. And in Bear River I can find a train to take me back to New York, where nobody tries to fool me any more. Do I take it, or not?"

"But, Mr. East!" The old man's face was piteous. The blood crept under his parchment skin and stained it to an ugly mottled red. One hand moved unconsciously to his temple, as if he were in pain, and Mark saw for the first time that the skin over one eye was bruised and broken. "Mr. East, I don't understand! You have already agreed to help me out. I have your letter!"

"What did you hire me for?" asked Mark.

"My dear young man—you quite frighten me!" He fumbled for a handkerchief and wiped his brow before he went on. "You are so emphatic! And all without reason, I assure you." A little mincing gaiety crept into his voice. "I want a secretary, an ordinary secretary, but capable and wise—if possible. I made that all so clear in the letter I sent you. Didn't I? You see, I've been assembling the notes I made on various digging expeditions—with the idea of adding one small volume to the already rich fund of archæological lore—and some of them were made in pencil, on wretched scraps of paper. I want them typed, while I can still decipher them myself. Isn't that—clear?"

"No," said Mark. "Are you afraid of being overheard? I know there was someone out in the hall a few minutes ago, but he went away when I launched my lecture on art. Don't ask me who it was—I didn't see him. But it's safe for you to talk now."

"Talk?"

"That's it. And begin with the reason why a man who wants a private secretary hires a private detective."

Stoneman sat up in his chair. The curate look came back to his face, but this time it was the look of a foolish little curate—confronted with a shortage of communion wine, the bishop, and a theory on evaporation.

"Detective!" he said, in a shocked whisper. "But this is fantastic! I wrote you my requirements in good faith and you agreed to accept. You said you could do the work. I mean, the Wood Agency agreed. Mr. East, you are confusing me again!"

"I'm the confused character, Mr. Stoneman," Mark said. "I told you before—I am the Wood Agency. I bought it and kept the name. And everything I said about myself is on the level. I do know two languages, other than English, and I've even seen a few Egyptian mummies on their native heath. Now let me ask you a question. Why did you write to me in the first place?

How did you find me ? Don't tell me you thought the
Wood Agency was an employment bureau ? "

" I must have. I fear that sounds ridiculous, but I
must have. Why, of course I did ! I remember now !
Really, I must order my thoughts ! I remember now
that I checked through the New York Telephone Book,
such a very large book, looking for the number of a friend.
And I found you on the same page. My friend is Wood
also. That was shortly before I came up here. And I
remember thinking, when I saw your name, that I might be
wise to make a note of it. To have, you understand, in
case I should ever need anyone. Then I did need someone,
and I wrote you." He was out of breath by this time, and a
little pathetic. " Do you believe any of that ? " he asked
simply. " If a man told it to me, I fear I should think
him a liar."

Mark smiled in spite of himself. " Didn't it occur to you
to investigate the agency first ? "

Stoneman looked humble. " No. I—I'm afraid I'm
not very worldly. But I should call it a natural mistake,
Mr. East, really I should. If I were you I would print the
word ' Detective ' after my name. Why, you don't even
have it on your stationery ! I know—I have your letters
right here ! " He reached for the upper pocket of his
jacket and the fringe of his shawl drew back the cuff.
His wrist was bound with adhesive tape. He drew the
letters from their envelopes and held them out. " You
see," he said triumphantly. " The Wood Agency, nothing
more ! "

" I get my clients from lawyers," Mark said. " They
know who I am."

" I see." Stoneman hesitated. He looked downcast.
" Really, I'm ashamed. Here you've had this cold, long
trip for nothing. . . . Haven't you ? And all because
of a foolish old man's mistake."

" I didn't say that."

" What ? Do you mean——? "

" I mean I haven't had the trip for nothing. I mean I was interested, that's all. Also, I was curious to see this country again. I did some hunting in the next county several years ago. . . .. You'd like me to stay under any conditions, wouldn't you ? "

" Oh, Mr. East ! If you would ! Your background is so splendid—you are so exactly the type of man I need. If you feel that your other clients—if you have no more pressing affairs——"

" I haven't. . . . How long will this business take ? "

" A few weeks only. I'm sure we can finish in a few weeks. Perhaps before Christmas. If you can put up with me that long." He smiled archly. " I'm afraid I've made a very poor first impression—and after all, you know nothing about me."

" That's where you're wrong," Mark said lightly. " Maybe you didn't check on me, but I went after you. You've taught ancient history at small colleges, been curator at two museums—Indiana and Delaware—and you've done some digging on your own, mostly hampered by lack of funds. A few years ago you dropped out of sight."

Stoneman looked humble. " I hardly know what to say," he murmured. " I'm tremendously impressed. But you must put that sordid, prying life behind you now, my boy. This is vacation time ; we'll make it so. You'll —you'll stay ? "

" Yes," Mark said. " I'll stay."

Stoneman had been clutching the letters all the while ; now he put them back into his pocket and mopped his face again. He looked as if he might burst into tears.

" When do we start ? " Mark asked easily. " What about this morning ? "

Stoneman gave him a watery smile. " We won't even consider it," he said. " You've had a trying journey, and on top of that all this absurd confusion. To-day you rest. You do exactly as you like. It's Sunday, after all ! And you must meet the family, too. Laura—did I tell you— Laura is depressed these days, but you'll soon change all that."

" Isn't there a Mr. Morey ? " Mark asked innocently.

" Jim ? But of course ! My boy, I was thinking of a new face, a fresh point of view ! Jim is a fine lad—like a son. You—that reminds me of another little thing. A very small thing. I'd—I'd rather Jim didn't know about my silly mistake."

" You mean about me being a detective ? "

" Well—yes. I'm afraid he'd laugh at me. He's a merciless joker, Jim is. I'd—I'd rather he didn't know."

" I won't tell him," Mark said. " Where is everybody, by the way ? Except for you and the butler I haven't seen a soul."

" Oh, we're quite a household ! There's Perrin ; he took you to your room last night—I want to speak about that later. And the two children, Anne and Ivy. Anne is eight, I believe, and Ivy is somewhere around two. Delightful children—you'll love them."

" Looks like I'm going to love everybody," Mark observed.

" You are, you are ! " Stoneman enthused. " Although Anne is a trifle—shall I say ' womanly '—for such a small girl ? Now don't misunderstand—I like women—but I do think—well, that doesn't matter. And of course, there's Jim."

" Where are they all now ? "

" Oh, Jim is probably being very tactful, staying in the background while I interview my new secretary. Mind your little promise, now ! And Laura hasn't left her room for several days. A trifle low in spirit. The weather, you know, and the quiet. But——"

" But my fresh face is going to change all that. I know."

" You have a sense of humour," cried Stoneman. " How delightful ! . . . Well, that covers everything. I believe. The children are somewhere in the wood at present. With one of the maids. They usually observe wild life in the morning."

" Many servants ? " Mark asked casually.

" Not as many as we should have ! This enormous place—and Laura would bring her own things. I mean her linens, silver, rugs, pictures—all quite unnecessary. The house was most adequately furnished, but you know how women are. Insisting on their own sheets. And not a well-trained servant to be had. Except Perrin, of course. All country bumpkins, no manners, treat you as an equal. Democracy, my boy, has failed."

" My, my. . . . How many servants ? " Mark prodded gently.

" Perrin, Mrs. Lacey, Violet, and Florence. But why do you want to know ? "

" I don't want to make the wrong woman happy. What do the maids look like ? "

" Violet is extremely—healthy. Those very red cheeks, you know, and an abundance of—breath. Florence is a quiet child ; you'll hardly notice her. And Mrs. Lacey— now I doubt if you see Mrs. Lacey at all. She cooks, and very well, too, but the poor woman is built like a pyramid and rarely leaves her kitchen. Also, I fear, a trifle stupid. At least I've found her so."

" Very graphic," Mark said. " But there's another thing. You said something about my room——"

" Of course. But I hadn't forgotten, my boy. I have the memory of an elephant. Perrin put you in the red room last night. Dreadful room, so massive, and on the wrong side of the house. Now if you don't object, I want to make a change. I'd like to have you in the room next to mine—we'll have a bath between us—and we can work there, undisturbed. Do you agree ? "

" Certainly. Shall I move my things now ? "

" That will be done for you. . . . But you must tell me how you would like to spend your day. With books, perhaps ? And we have an excellent phonograph."

" I think I'll take a walk. I'd like to see the place by daylight."

Stoneman grew agitated. " But the snow ! It's really very treacherous ! The paths are steep, and the rocks—you might easily slip and fall ! "

" Is that how you hurt your wrist ? " Mark asked.

The dull red stained the old man's face again and he fixed his gaze at a point above Mark's head. " Oh, no," he said. " That is the result of one of my attacks. I believe I mentioned them—a sort of vertigo. I failed to negotiate the cellar stairs—so upsetting, literally—but I wisely clung to the railing, limiting the casualties to a sprained wrist. You mustn't give it another thought, dear boy."

" What about the bruise over the eye ? That looks bad."

" This ? " Stoneman felt it gently. " How observing you are ! I hoped you wouldn't notice. I don't want you to think I am the sort of person who can't take care of himself. But actually, this little bruise is my reason for discouraging your walk. Yesterday I ventured into the air and a stone, a quite small one, detached itself from a boulder and caught me squarely. I—I shall remain indoors until the weather moderates."

Cockeyed, Mark said to himself. Cockeyed when he fell downstairs, and he won't admit it. Cockeyed and a

little crazy too. I'm going to have a wonderful time.
I'll give it a couple of days and then I'll sit right down and
write myself a letter. Out loud he said, " Too bad. But
I think I'll risk a walk just the same, Unless you forbid
it. You're my boss, you know."

" Oh, no, no, I don't forbid. I want you to be happy.
But mind you're back for lunch at one o'clock. Will
you—go down to Crestwood ! "

" I sort of thought about it. Do you want anything ? "

" Nothing. There's nothing in Crestwood, as you'll
very soon discover. But take good care of yourself, and
watch your footing. Very treacherous."

Mark rose. " My coat is in that closet under the stairs.
I'll let myself out." He saw the beads of sweat gather on
the old man's brow. Sweat, and shaking hands. " Sure
you don't want anything ? " he insisted.

" Not a thing, not a thing I'll just sit here by the fire
and wait for your return. I may even take a little nap."
He closed his eyes and leaned back wearily. He looked as
if he had instantly fallen asleep.

Mark left the room quietly, making no sound on the soft
thick rugs, and took his hat and coat from the hall closet.
When he passed the library door again he glanced in.
Stoneman had turned his chair to face the hall and his
eyes were wide open.

He continued down the hall and opened the carved oak
door, closing it carefully behind him. Snow struck him
cleanly in the face. He started down the drive.

" Cockeyed and a little crazy," he said to the leaden
sky. " Or scared out of his wits. Which ? Maybe all
three. Maybe only the latter. And then again, maybe
strictly legitimate and aboveboard."

He walked briskly, remembering that Miss Pond's house
was the third from the top of the lane.

CHAPTER TWO

CRESTWOOD, lying at the foot of Big Bear Mountain and surrounded by a dark forest, is a one-lane town. It starts at the railway station and winds uphill in easy stages until it dwindles off into a mountain path. There are six brick cottages along the lane and another tucked away in a small grove behind the station.

At the time of this story Amos Partridge, representing the railroad, the United States Mail and the law, lived over his office in what he called a cosy room and Miss Beulah Pond called a rattrap.

The little house behind the station was the property of Mrs. Ruth Lacey, a widow who acted as housekeeper-cook for Colonel Davenport when he was in residence. She was now performing similar duties for the Colonel's tenants, the Moreys. The Davenport house was a mountain stronghold and much admired by summer tourists who told each other it was just like Touraine or Scotland. The road from the front door down to the station was nearly a mile long.

Mr. and Mrs. Bittner shared the first cottage next to the station. Ten years previously he had walked in front of an oncoming train to show his contempt for the schedule and lost both legs. In retaliation he bought a fleet of buses which followed the train wherever it went, enticing passengers, carrying pigs if necessary, and giving free rides to wedding parties and funerals. His slogan, decorating each bus in letters a foot high, was SAME TIME SAME STATION. The railroad never seemed to notice.

The second cottage, owned by Mr. and Mrs. Cane, was empty. They spent their winters in Florida.

The third cottage, owned by the Tait twins, sculptors, was also empty. The Taits wintered in Bear River, five miles distant, where a younger sister saw to their flannels and kept them well.

The fourth was Miss Beulah Pond's. In spite of her five thousand a year, she harboured a lending library in a small room off the front parlour. In the summer, when the mountain hotels were filled with city people, she did a brisk business. In the winter she read the books herself.

The Caldwell sisters, three of them, lived next to Miss Beulah. They were in Florida with the Canes.

The last was Miss Bessy Petty's. Miss Bessy had planned a trip to Florida with the Canes and the Caldwells but was talked out of it by Miss Beulah. She was a retired schoolteacher, and forty years' association with the fourth grade had left her looking like a fourth grader herself. She was round and sweet, with mild blue eyes ; and she believed everything she was told, provided it was told with emphasis.

Miss Beulah had told her with emphasis that Florida was full of enemy aliens looking for things to steal, and that her grandmother's pearls would vanish the minute she stepped off the train. Miss Bessy moved the pearls from the rose jar to an old missionary box and changed her plans gratefully. She didn't really know what she'd do without Beulah. Beulah always knew best. Of course they'd stay home ; wasn't home the sweetest place in the world ? And they'd read all the new thrillers, the nice English ones because they don't have the third degree in England and it seemed more civilized somehow. They stayed home, and Miss Beulah regretted it.

That was the situation along the lane on the white December morning that followed Mark East's arrival. A handful of elderly people rose late from their warm beds and set about getting breakfast. Another Sunday, exactly like the hundreds that had gone before.

Mark, turning out of the drive, looked over at the station. There was smoke coming out of the chimney, but no other sign of life. He walked up the lane, almost impassable now. The snow fell with quiet determination, veiling the neat little houses and their bleak gardens. He turned in at Miss Pond's gate and was momentarily set back by a welcoming shriek.

There was another old woman there; Miss Bessy Petty, he was told. A little simple, he decided. He made a great show of introducing himself formally and a second breakfast was pressed upon him.

Beulah's open fire winked cosily and her parlour was filled with pleasant sound : Bessy's giggle, the crackle and sputter of an occasional coal, the rattle of coffee cups. They were her best Canton cups and there had been nearly half a pound of butter on the toasted muffins that were no longer on the best Canton plate. Mark sat in the best chair with a cushion at his back and his feet on the fender.

" I never heard of such people," Bessy protested. " Making you walk all the way up from the station in a blizzard in the pitch dark when they've got plenty of gas and a sleigh too ! Beulah should have telephoned, no matter what."

" No," said Mark. " All my fault. . . . Do you mind if I have a cigarette ? "

" Oh, do," urged Bessy, " do."

" It's a mercy you saw the glow from my fire," said Beulah. " You could have perished. That butler with his nose in the air, he never sees anybody. And I can understand how Florrie missed you too. She has so much on her mind, poor girl. But I can't understand Amos."

" Amos ? "

" He's the stationmaster and the postmaster and the policeman. He always watches passengers, because you never can tell."

" Oh, the little fellow with a red cap. He didn't see me because he had his arm around a girl with a market basket."

Bessy broke in eagerly, "We called him up this morning and spoke to him sharply. We thought he'd been lazy and remiss and we told him so. An arm around Florrie is no excuse. If he'd been tending to his business you could have had a ride. It's no thanks to him you aren't dead this minute."

" I call it fate," Beulah said soberly. " If I hadn't had one of my visions I might have gone to bed and you'd never have seen me sitting here."

He looked puzzled, so she told him about the dead bird, the dead children, the footprints, and the mausoleum. " You know I'm psychic," she admitted.

" I think you are," he said gravely, " and I thank you. But here I am, alive and kicking, with two charming new friends. You both remind me of my mother."

Bessy gave him a radiant smile. " I know you're pulling our limbs," she said, " but I like it."

Beulah cut in, " That girl with the basket was Florence. Florrie, we call her. She's a maid up at the Moreys'. It's really Colonel Davenport's house, you know. They're supposed to be friends of his, but I can't imagine where he picked them up. That old gentleman drinks, it's written all over him. I can't help it if you do work for him. And the younger one laughs too much. Mr. Morey. He laughs every time I look at him. Still," she hesitated, " still I don't really know anything against them. I've tried to find out from Florrie, but she won't say a word."

" Tell me about Florrie," Mark asked innocently. " She looks nice."

" Oh, she is ! Florrie's quite a pet of mine. She reads books. She's the upstairs maid and she helps with the children too. Bear River girl. Raised on a farm. She says it's the best job she ever had."

"Like me," Mark said. "It's the best job I ever had. Florrie and I must get together."

Bessy observed that Florrie was pretty, if you cared for the delicate type. Speaking for herself, she preferred Violet, a good, strong, healthy girl.

"Violet's the other maid, although you can't really call her a servant. She doesn't work out like Florrie. She's a different type. Her mother's an invalid and she has lots of little brothers and sisters. She usually takes care of them. She's only helping out at the Moreys' because the housekeeper there asked her to, as a favour. The housekeeper is a very superior woman, a member of our church. Violet's a lovely girl. I taught her."

"Violet never reads," Beulah said. "I don't think she can. . . . Florrie takes a book every week."

Mark looked across the hall to the small book-lined room with its neat shelves and flowering bulbs. "I'll take a book every week too, if I may. I'm afraid the stuff they have up the mountain is out of my class. My new employer is something of a highbrow."

Bessy resurrected the look she used on fourth graders who came unprepared. "You mustn't say things like that, Mr. East," she chided. "We all have brains if we only use them. And I'm sure you're very intelligent or you couldn't do the work you do. . . . What do you do ? "

"I'm a secretary," Mark said promptly. "Specializing in archæology."

"Oh. . . . Isn't that digging up people who've been dead a long time ? "

"Dead cities," rebuked Beulah. "Do you like detective stories, Mr. East ? I've got a whole wall full."

"I love them. They're so true to life. What's Peter Wimsey doing now ? "

"Nothing, unfortunately. But there's a new one about —no, I haven't got it. Mrs. Lacey took it out last week.

A wonderful book, supernatural. You might get it from her when she's finished."

" Mrs. Lacey ? " fished Mark. " She's the woman you mentioned before. Housekeeper ? "

" Yes. A Crestwood woman, widow. And a great reader, too. The Moreys are fortunate to have such a woman, considering they're only transients."

" A very large woman," murmured Bessy, " if you care for that type. Very large."

One word caught Mark's attention. " I'll speak to Mrs. Lacey," he said. " Did you say the Moreys were transient, Miss Pond ? I thought they were practically permanent."

" They're renters, that's all. Renters. When Ruthie Lacey was in last week she said they were all told the family might not stay on after May. They took the house because they wanted a quiet place. But in May the summer crowd begins to come and the whole mountain is a tourist resort. I do a big business then but I don't like it. There are two hotels about a mile north of the Moreys' and I don't know how many fishing camps and clubs. People screaming all over the place."

" Men sleep in tents," added Bessy, " with the flaps up."

" Mrs. Morey seems to have brought a lot of her own possessions," Mark observed. " Some of the stuff I saw didn't look like a furnished-house decoration."

" Truckloads," Beulah said with relish. " Books, pictures, china—things like that. Ruthie Lacey says she sent some of the Colonel's things to storage to make room. I'd like to see the place now," she said wistfully. " It was beautiful when the Colonel lived there, but Ruthie says it's something to take your breath away now. They even get flowers from New York."

" Davenport ? " Mark baited his hook again. " Now where have I heard that name before ? "

Bessy had the answer ready. " You read it in the

papers. He's Colonel Davenport, the one who was sent to England on a secret mission. Ruthie Lacey cooked for him for years. But more as a friend, you understand."

Mark rose, and stretched happily. With unexpected luck and very little effort, he had learned a few things. There were other questions he wanted to ask, but they would have to wait. He classified Miss Bessy Petty and Miss Beulah Pond as a gabby pair but far from dumb. He'd be able to use them later—if he needed them.

He struggled into his coat over their protesting wails and held out a hand to each. "Give my love to Amos," he said, "and call me up if you see any more mausoleums. And thanks for the second breakfast. It's ruined my lunch."

His hostesses twittered and followed him to the door. "I'll see you both in a day or two," he added. They watched like benevolent hawks as he turned down the lane.

Five minutes later when he turned into the driveway opposite the station, he saw an elderly man behind the ticket window in the act of hanging up a telephone receiver. Mark waved an airy salute. He got a baleful glance in return. Amos had evidently just received his love.

As he neared the top of the winding drive, something whizzed through the bordering pines and neatly removed his hat. He swung quickly and saw the projectile come to rest on the gravel at his left. It was an old golf ball. As he bent to pick it up three figures came tumbling through the shrubbery on the right, and someone called his name. He stood still and waited.

Two of them were children and the other was a tall, slender girl with pale features ; obviously the delicate type, and therefore Florrie. She held each child firmly by the hand while dealing out reprimands in no uncertain terms. The children were unimpressed. When they came up to him, she spoke.

" It's Mr. East, isn't it ?   The gentleman who's staying with Mr. Stoneman ?   I'm awfully sorry, sir ; I hope she didn't hurt you."

" Which one ? " Mark asked, looking from the toddler Ivy to the self-contained Anne.

" Anne, of course. She's always throwing things. Where she got that golf ball I don't know, but she's not allowed to play with them and she knows it. She might have put your eye out ! Say you're sorry, Anne ! "

" I'm sorry," said Anne.

" She knows I can't tell her mother because it'll only make the poor woman more nervous. Don't give that ball back to her, sir ! She's no right to have it. Where'd you get it, anyhow, you bad girl ? Did you take it out of your father's box ? "

" I found it," said Anne, smiling up at Mark. " I wouldn't really have put your eye out. I only aimed at your hat."

Florrie shrugged hopelessly.   " Well, you've said you're sorry, and I guess I can't expect more. We might as well get along." To Mark, " I didn't know she had it, sir, or I'd have taken it away." She shook and pressed them into awkward curtsies and herded them up the drive and out of sight.

Mark followed slowly, fingering the golf ball. That was a good shot for a little girl who was only aiming at a hat. He hoped he wouldn't be around when she tried for an eye. He was whistling softly when Perrin let him into the house.

He gave up his hat and coat and followed the man down the hall to the library. Doors which had been closed earlier in the day now stood open, and from long habit he checked the rooms as he passed. The library, he knew, was on his right, with a wide French window opening on to the front terrace and a small card-room in the rear. The first door on the left showed him a formal little salon, full of gilt chairs and rose hangings; he saw a piano, and off in one corner a covered harp. The pink, oval rug was slightly faded and wreathed like a valentine. Aubusson, he thought, old and real. The dining room came next. Its double doors were almost opposite those of the library; he glimpsed the end of a sideboard covered with silver, and some coloured hunting prints. Perrin deftly turned him in at his destination.

Stoneman had left his chair by the fire and was standing at a cabinet, drinking sherry with the handsomest man Mark had ever seen. This must be Morey, he thought, and if so, what is the matter with Mrs. Morey? His yellow hair was thick and smooth; his blue eyes were warm and friendly. He ought, Mark decided, to wear sky blue trimmed with silver, ride a white horse, and sing songs about Vienna to the flower-throwing peasants. Mark declined the sherry Morey offered and they went in to lunch.

There were only the three of them, attended by Perrin. Laura Morey begged to be excused, her husband said, and the children only came to the table on special occasions. Mark saw the man was doing his best to make the meal a pleasant one. He kept away from personal questions and gently kidded the elderly Stoneman, who looked more ridden than ever.

" I'm glad you're here, East," he said. " I've been after Joe for months to do something about those notes of his. These old wanderers don't know how to behave in retirement. They go all to pieces. Look at him, if you don't believe me ! "

Stoneman laughed shakily. " Perhaps you're right, perhaps you're right," he agreed. " No doubt Mr. East will regenerate me. Then, with my little book out of the way, I may emerge from this—retirement—and surprise you ! " He looked suddenly pleased with himself. He beamed at Morey and batted one eye rapidly in what looked like a nervous spasm but was evidently meant for a wink. Morey gave him a sober wink in return.

" Don't let him make this book all facts," he said to Mark. " Joe's terrific when he gets fanciful. Get him to tell you some of his adventures among the dead——"

" Jim ! " Stoneman looked hurt. " Jim," he said to Mark, " is giving you a false impression. I may have been impetuous in my youth, but never, never did I desecrate a tomb—not without government permission, of course. I wish I could say the same for some of my colleagues."

" Only kidding, Joe," soothed Morey. " Mr. East understands that. By the way, we moved your stuff into the room connecting with Joe's," he said. " He thinks it's better that way, but if you don't like it, say so. . . . It looks nice in there." A wistful note crept into his voice. " Typewriter, clean paper, jar full of nice sharp pencils—looks like somebody's going to do something. . . . I don't have enough to do around here," he finished lamely.

Stoneman said nothing. He sat with his eyes downcast. Sulking, Mark thought. But why ? Morey evidently thought so too.

" Sunday ! " he said heartily. " And five miles to the nearest church. That's why we don't go. But if you feel the need of vespers later on——"

Stoneman got up from the table with difficulty, waving Perrin aside. " I think I'll lie down," he said. " Remember, you are free to do as you like, Mr. East. But if you want me, or if you care to rest after your long walk, someone will direct you to your quarters." He stalked out.

" Take the coffee into the library, Perrin," Morey directed. " Come along, East." Mark followed him across the hall.

" Did I say something to hurt his feelings ? " Mark asked.

Morey waited until Perrin had left. " No," he said. " I probably did. I keep forgetting how sensitive he is about his work." He poured coffee. " To tell the truth, I don't think he was ever very much good at it ; but he thinks he was a wonder. I guess age colours things up— he's seventy-five, you know."

" I should be so good at seventy-five," Mark said.

" Has he "—Morey lowered his voice—" has he said anything to you about his sleepwalking ? "

" No. Does he ? "

" I don't know. He says he does. That's why he keeps his door locked, even in the daytime. It's probably locked now, because he's going to take his nap. . . . It's one of the things that's driving my wife crazy."

Mark tried to think of a suitable remark and managed to say, " I'm sorry."

Morey gave him a sudden grin. " She'll be all right soon," he said confidently. " Women get nervous, and there's nothing a man can do but sit tight. She wasn't well when we came here ; in fact, we came because of her —she thought the country air would pull her together again. You see "—he spoke soberly—" she hasn't been herself since Ivy's birth. That fat little rascal has caused her mother plenty of grief. But I wouldn't take a million for her ! "

Mark recalled the rolling gait and Jovian air of Ivy and agreed.

" And on top of Laura's perfectly natural—nervousness —along comes Joe with his jitters. I asked him up here because I thought it would do him good and Laura too —he's a great talker, Joe is, when he gets going ; but I'm almost sorry, now. He told me this morning that he wasn't going to take walks any more. Do you think you can shake him out of himself ? "

" I can try," Mark said dubiously. " He looks to me like a man with—with a serious disorder. He told me he was subject to attacks."

" Your guess about the attacks is as good as mine," grinned Morey. " I'm trying to taper him off. But do what you can about the locked-door business. Sometimes the maids can't get in his room for two days. They get sore about it and you can't blame them. And they complain to Laura. . . . But he'll tell you all about it himself when he locks you in with him ! Are you going up now ? "

Mark had risen. " No, I think I'll go downstairs, if that's where the kitchen is and you don't mind. I want a little chat with one Mrs. Lacey."

" Mind ? Hell, no. But why Mrs. Lacey ? Violet's more your style."

" This is purely mental. I'm going to borrow a book." He gave a sound description of his wanderings the night before and his morning reunion with Miss Pond. " Great girls, the Misses Pond and Petty. I think they said they knew you."

" They know me because the minute we started to unload our stuff at the station they came flying down the lane like a pair of vultures. Sticking their fingers through the slats of packing cases when they thought I wasn't looking. Pretending they were looking for an oil stove. I offered the tall thin one a hammer—I probably brandished it— and they beat it. We only bow now. They don't like me."

" They love me ! " Mark said modestly.

" They probably know more about you this minute than you know about yourself. Not much those two miss. And old Bittner and his owl-eyed spouse. They, and the Petty-Pond pair, are the only ones here now, not counting the perennial Partridge. Bittner hasn't any legs but he has a terrible wheel chair, a pair of binoculars, and his Ella

May.   He navigates from window to window and rakes the countryside.   He also counts the passengers on the bus, which he owns, and heaven help the driver who holds out a nickel.   I think he beats his wife when he can catch her. Find out for me."

Mark laughed and started for the door.

"Down the hall," Morey directed, "and through the baize door ; then down the stone steps which are fit to break a body's back, I'm told.   If you want anything special to eat, tell Lacey."

Mark found the baize door and the steps, and at their foot another door of stout oak that led to the kitchen.   A long distance from the dining room, he thought ; then he remembered hearing a dumbwaiter in the butler's pantry. He knocked politely and went in.

An enormous woman sat by a coal range, shelling peas into a blue bowl.   When she saw Mark her mouth dropped open and stayed that way.   Over at the sink a strapping brunette of about eighteen was peeling potatoes and singing *Pale Hands I Loved*.   She stared over her shoulder and gave him a wide smile without losing a note.   The large woman struggled to rise.

"Don't get up," Mark said.   "My name's East.   If you're not too busy——? "

She sank back gratefully.   "Miss Pond phoned me about the book, sir," she panted.   "I'm through with it if you want to take it now."   She pointed to the book lying on the table.

Mark pulled a chair up to the stove and sat down.   "Do you mind if I stay a few minutes ? " he asked.   "I love kitchens."

She hesitated.   Then : "Please yourself, sir.   Can I get you anything—a cup of tea, perhaps ? "

"After that lunch !   Do you want to kill me ? "   He thought that would bring a smile, but the quick look she

threw him was full of horror. She lowered her eyes
without answering. He tried again.

" I'm not used to such cooking," he explained. " You
know how men are—blow all their money for steak on
Saturday night and live on beans for the rest of the week."
He was going on to say something sprightly about getting
fat but pulled himself up in time. The poor soul looked
like a beached whale. " I had coffee and muffins with Miss
Pond this morning," he finished lamely.

She responded to that. " Miss Beulah spoke very kindly
of you," she said. " You made a good impression there,
sir, and that's not easy. Miss Beulah is not one to take up
with anybody."

Mark looked grateful. " She had her doubts about me at
first, though," he said. " I don't think she likes strangers
right off the bat."

" She is very wise. But it's enough for me that she
recommends you now. We are great friends, in spite of a
slight difference in occupation." She stared over his head.
" Evil " she went on gently, " finds a rich ground here.
There's so few folks about it gets a chance to grow."

She made him feel cold. " Aren't you exaggerating ? "
he asked carefully. " Or are you just kidding me ? "

" Neither, sir."

A bit of religious mania in the kitchen, he decided.
" Miss Beulah's been giving you the wrong kind of books,"
he said easily. " No more supernaturals for you. I
recommend love stories from now on and I'll even go so far
as to pick them out myself."

Mrs. Lacey regarded him calmly. " That won't stop
what I'm thinking," she said.

The girl at the sink finished her potatoes on a sobbing
note and dumped the parings into a pail. " Pity we don't
keep pigs," she said simply. " Anything else, Mrs.
Lacey ? "

"That's all for now, Violet. You can go off for half an hour. I'll call you when I'm ready."

Violet crossed the room reluctantly and pushed open a swinging door. Through it Mark could see another flight of steps leading down and three nail-studded doors. The cellars, he decided, and probably the servants' sleeping rooms. When the door had closed behind her he turned to the other woman. What he saw startled him. She too had been staring through that door. There was a look of speculation in her eyes, but when she saw him watching her she smiled.

"I sleep back there," she said. "So do Violet and Florrie. It's dangerous going through that passage, even in the daylight. The cellar stairs go down so quick and steep. I'm always afraid somebody'll lose their footing."

Something told Mark to make no comment on that. "What's in the cellar?" he asked.

"The furnace and provisions—canned goods and such. And preserves. I have a lot of preserves I put up for the Colonel. I expect you know I cooked for the Colonel. I came here when his wife was still alive. I was sixteen then."

"That speaks well for both of you," he said sincerely.

"Yes." She stood the bowl of peas on the end of the table and folded her hands in her lap. "There's a wine cellar down there too," she said quietly. "Somebody got in a while ago and broke a lot of empty bottles. Left them all over the floor and on the steps, too."

"Children," he suggested carefully. "Probably got in a window and tore things up for the fun of it."

"There aren't any children nearer than Bear River. And Anne and Ivy don't even know where the cellar is. No, I guess it wasn't that." She gave him an impassive look. "But we mustn't bother you with such things. It's not right."

He had a pleasant but uncomfortable feeling that she wanted him to talk, to ask her questions. At the same time he knew he'd never get a straight answer. He'd seen women in that mood before, with something on their minds that they wanted to shake. They'd hold it out with one hand and snatch it back with the other. And more often than not, when it finally emerged it wasn't a pretty story. But this was a respectable soul. Probably the heaviest load her conscience ever carried weighed no more than a pilfered Sunday penny, used for candy instead of God. He was pleased with this fancy and because he was pleased with it, he believed it. No, the good Lacey's trouble was Stoneman. He'd crashed down the stairs and broken the bottles himself. Her employer's bottles. And she'd dragged him upstairs again and dressed his wounds and promised not to give him away. And now she was worried about it. Better let her work around to it naturally, he thought. There was plenty of time. Suddenly he realised she was asking him something.

" Is there anything in particular you'd like for your dinner ? " she was saying. It was a tone of dismissal. " I can't do much about the roast because that's already in, it's Sunday, but I could fix something special in the way of salad or desert."

" Thanks." He was surprised and pleased. " Anything you send up will be perfect."

" I like to cook," she said. " Maybe because it's the thing I do best. And I'd like this dinner to-night to be something you really fancy. Because it'll be the first and last I'll ever do for you."

" What ! "

" That's right," she said. " I'm leaving right after breakfast to-morrow. I sent my notice up by Florrie just before you came down."

" But why ? " She looked as if she were going to cry,

and he hurried on, "I don't get it! I thought you were a fixture here!"

"For Colonel Davenport, maybe, but he's gone for I don't know how long, and I don't really care about working for anybody else. I only came to the Moreys as a favour to the Colonel. I don't have to work for a living, you know. I've got my own little house, and my little income."

"But what'll the poor Moreys do? You'll be leaving them in an awful hole, won't you?"

"They'll make out," she said. "Violet cooks real well and they can always get somebody from the people that supplied Perrin. You won't starve, sir."

"I wasn't thinking of that," he said. "I was only thinking that if Mrs. Morey isn't well——"

"She'll get over it," Mrs. Lacey said. "I don't mean for that to sound unkind; I only mean that my leaving won't make any difference in things upstairs. I'd like to feel though that you were keeping an eye on Violet, sir. She's young, and she's only known kindness. I'd like to feel that you were looking after her, like."

He nodded in agreement. "Sure," he said foolishly. "Sure."

The armchair creaked as she heaved herself to her feet. "I wonder if you'd mind pushing that button on the wall there? It's to bring Violet. I need her now."

He did as she asked, then stood by helplessly. For some reason he did not want her to leave that kitchen where she seemed so much at home.

"I expect it was too much for you, wasn't it?"

"Yes," she said slowly. "It was. There's the book you wanted, Mr. East, and there's six cents overdue in the little envelope. I put a note inside for Miss Beulah." She lumbered over toward the dumbwaiter. "It's good-bye for the present only, sir," she said. "Miss Beulah can tell you where my little place is in case you care to drop in and talk things over."

He watched her enormous back with a kind of dismay as she waddled across the room.

Violet made an entrance through the swinging door, humming the opening bars of *Less than the Dust*. He picked up the book and went upstairs with the uncomfortable feeling of having let something escape him.

CHAPTER THREE

MARK spent the rest of the afternoon in his new room, to which, surprisingly enough, he had been directed by Violet. He'd come directly from the kitchen to find her on the second floor, flicking a duster over the hall chairs and panting a little, as well she might. She read his mind swiftly and accurately.

" Short cut," she grinned. " Back stairs behind the cardroom." Then, remembering her manners, " I thought maybe nobody had told you where to find your new room. You go straight ahead towards the front of the house and turn down that little hall on your right. There's a guest soot there and you and Mr. Stoneman have it to yourselves. It's got a lovely view too, right over a precipice."

He must have looked startled, for she added, " Nobody ever falls out. There's kind of spikes set in the sills. Do you want that I should show you ? "

He thanked her and found the room himself. And now he sat at the desk, turning the pages of the book Mrs. Lacey had given him and seeing Mrs. Lacey's face on every page. The small envelope so carefully and, he was sure, apologetically sealed over the note and the six cents was addressed to Miss Beulah in a spidery, ladylike hand. In one corner it said, "Kindness of Bearer." Apparently she'd never intended to deliver it herself, in spite of her return to Crestwood in the morning. Going visiting, he guessed ; going to put her feet up and take things easy for a few days. He looked at his own brown oxfords and decided to do the same.

Stoneman's snores came faintly through the open door into the bath which connected the two rooms ; it was a contagious sound. As nothing official had been said about locked doors when he came up he did nothing about them now. He crawled under the eiderdown with his shoes on and went to sleep.

He woke at six o'clock and took a shower, thoughtfully closing the door into Stoneman's room as he did so. The snoring had stopped and there was no other sound. No sound anywhere. He changed into a dark suit as a gesture towards the day and went down to the library. The room was as quiet as the rest of the house ; he'd never been in such a quiet house before. He turned on more lights. Eight adults, including himself, and two healthy kids, and the place was as silent as the—— He shook himself and crossed the room to a table set with bottles and decanters. Even his footsteps made no sound on the rugs. He poured himself a drink and rattled the glasses to cheer himself up. Little by little he was feeling colder and lower, and he didn't like it.

The black night crowding against the terrace window made him uneasy. After a few attempts he found the proper cord and drew the curtains over the glass. They were warm red curtains, thick as blankets, and they made him feel better. He went to a chair by the fire and sat down. A coal cracked sharply and sent up a shower of sparks. He jumped, and spilled his drink, and when he tried to mop it up his hand was shaking.

No wonder Stoneman has the jitters, he thought.

There's something wrong with this house. He poured another drink, with an extra allowance for spilling, and found that amusing. Then, after a few minutes, he began to feel normal.

He charged off his fidgets to unaccustomed exercise; he had walked too far for a child of the pavements and on top of that he'd been seen coming from a mausoleum. If that story got back to the boys in New York he'd be a marked man. He'd be more than a marked man if they ever found out he was playing secretary to a crackpot archæologist who'd hired him out of the telephone book.

Then, while he was enjoying his own discomfiture he remembered something Mrs. Lacey had said. About evil. Something about this being good soil for evil. That didn't make good sense coming from a woman who was born and raised on the soil in question; not to mention the pleasant things it had provided in the way of little income and lifelong job. Hadn't the woman lived in and out of this very house ever since she was sixteen? There he was, back at the house again. . . . He literally kicked himself on the shin as a punishment for daring to think of looking over his shoulder. . . .

Mrs. Lacey's trouble was peeve. The more he thought of that, the better he liked it. She was peeved because she was spoiled. She'd probably run the place in the old days and now she was outclassed by a butler. One of these old girls who wanted to be patted on the shoulder every morning and tucked up at night. No patting and tucking, no cook. . . . And she might even be a little queer. You found people like that in mountain villages. Inbred.

He felt much better now. This was a good house and a good atmosphere. Look at those kids, sound as apples; and their strapping father. As for Laura—his eyes went to the Ducroix portrait—well, some women did have trouble after childbirth; but they usually got over it.

He left the portrait and gazed lovingly on the Renoir:
a woman at a sidewalk table under a plane tree, with leaves
and sunlight dropping on the cloth. It made the misty
little Corot on the other wall look dated and forlorn. If
the Corot were his, he reflected, he'd hang it where it
belonged, in the faded little salon with the cupids and the
roses and the harp. Davenport's wife probably played
the harp.

What had Mrs. Lacey said about Davenport's wife?
Oh—she was dead, that's all. She was dead. . . . He
wondered what she had died of.

He stiffened in his chair. Someone was coming slowly
down the dim hall, slowly and with difficulty. He held his
breath, watching the portières swing gently and fall still.
There was no sound. In a bound he was across the room,
wrenching the curtains apart.

Florrie gave him a startled look. She was standing at
the foot of the stairs, a covered tray in her hands. She
put the tray on the bottom step.

"Did you want something, sir?" she asked primly.

"No." Mark felt his face redden. "I—I thought you
were Mr. Stoneman."

She shook her head reprovingly. "I haven't seen Mr.
Stoneman. You gave me a start, sir, jumping out like
that. I'm just taking Mrs. Morey's dinner up."

He gestured back toward the door. "I saw the curtains
move and I thought Mr. Stoneman had—had come along and
—felt faint." He felt like a fool himself.

"Probably a draught," she explained in a kind manner.
"Well, if you don't want anything——" She collected
her tray and started up the stairs.

He went back to the fire, none too pleased with himself.

Perhaps two minutes had gone by when he heard someone clatter down the stairs in a great hurry and turn into
the dining room. It was Morey, shouting for Perrin.

Perrin answered from his pantry, and apparently Morey joined him there. Their voices faded, but Mark could distinguish Perrin's noncommittal tones from Morey's subdued roar. It was the roar of an outraged householder confronted with frozen plumbing.

He was happy to note that whatever it was they were making no secret about it. He lit a cigarette and contemplated the Renoir through the smoke, such a pleasant little woman in a flowered hat, her fingers curled around the stem of a wineglass, a yellowing leaf across her wrist. If he had Morey's money, that's the kind of thing he'd spend it for.

When Stoneman came in rubbing his hands together and smiling Mark was glad to see him. Stoneman looked refreshed and, for him, happy. He declined a drink with an air of virtue and launched himself on the dry seas of Egypt. He was deep in the iniquities of a colleague's greed when a gong sounded for dinner.

Mark offered his arm to Stoneman with exaggerated courtesy and they crossed to the dining room.

Morey turned an exasperated face as they entered. "Sit down and eat while you can, both of you. This is the end of the world."

Perrin came forward and calmly served the soup.

"Lacey is leaving. No reason, no notice—just leaving. God knows what we'll do now in this forsaken hole. . . . East, you saw her this afternoon; what did she talk about? Did she sound sore about anything?"

"We talked about a book," Mark said carefully. "However, she did say she was leaving and I thought — maybe I'm wrong—but I thought she'd been crying."

"Oh, dear," murmured Stoneman. "The poor woman."

"What's she got to cry about, I'd like to know! Why, she simply sent up a written resignation, as smooth as you please. My wife's the one who ought to be crying, and she probably is."

" May I see the note ? " Mark asked.

Morey looked astonished. " See it ? I didn't see it myself My wife tore it up. I was working in my room when she got it and she didn't want to disturb me. Maybe if I'd known earlier——"

Stoneman complained gently. " A very unreliable woman, poor soul. No stamina. But I wouldn't make too much of it, Jim."

" But I don't like things like this," Morey fumed. " Perrin, do you know anything about it ? Have the girls been teasing her again ? " To Mark, " They used to tease her about her size, but I soon put a stop to that. Come on, Perrin, what's been going on downstairs ? "

" I've heard nothing, sir," Perrin said. Mark thought he caught a faint note of condescension. " Mrs. Lacey is accustomed to a smaller household, sir ; Colonel Davenport lived alone, I understand. Perhaps she found the additional work a strain upon her health."

" That's crazy," scoffed Morey. " She's as strong as a horse. I'll bet you've done something yourself to make her angry."

" No, sir. I've always had the greatest admiration and respect for the lady."

" Well, this is what you get when you try to play fair with native labour. I've had enough. You call up the agency you came from and ask them to ship us a cook to-morrow."

Perrin hesitated. " If I may suggest——? "

" What ? "

" Mrs. Lacey recommends Violet. She trained the girl herself as a supplementary cook when Colonel Davenport had guests."

" That's much better," Stoneman agreed. " Violet knows our little habits, Jim."

Morey finished his cup of soup with relish. " Maybe

she does," he said ruefully, " but we'll never get another bouillon like that. Joe, this is all your fault. You and your precious papers and locked doors. They'll all be walking out next."

" No," said Stoneman. " No, Jim. I had nothing to do with this."

" But it's going to hit you where it hurts, Joe," Morey grinned. " No more trays in your room and you'll have to make your own bed. Oh, well, look for the silver lining. We'll have one less mouth to feed ! "

Penny pincher, thought Mark. I never would have guessed it.

Perrin removed the soup cups and brought in the next course : a pair of ducks with wild rice and the green peas Mrs. Lacey had been shelling into her blue bowl. Morey called for claret and Perrin left the room.

" Lacey and Perrin didn't hit it off," Morey confided, " I think she resented his manners. To tell the truth, I resent them myself ; he uses bigger words than I do. . . . We've got to think of something to keep Violet and Florrie happy now. If they leave, we're sunk."

" A little cheque is always efficacious," Stoneman said ; " or you might suggest the possibility of a Christmas bonus."

" Um-m-m," said Morey.

Perrin returned with the claret and a bowl of salad. Morey dismissed him with instructions to serve coffee in the library. " And bring Florrie and Violet in with the coffee," he added. " I want to talk to them. You might try for Lacey too, but I don't think you'll have any luck."

They finished dinner quietly. Stoneman ate very little, and Morey was preoccupied with his own thoughts. " I wanted to have the kids down to-night," he said, apropos of nothing. " But Laura said no."

After dinner Mark tried to go to his room ; he suspected

Florrie and Violet were in for a grilling and he didn't want to hear it. But Morey called him back. He was trying to finish his coffee quickly when the two girls came to the library door. They looked anxious and ill at ease. Morey started right in, but to Mark's relief he was surprisingly gentle.

He gave them a little talk on duty, praised their work, and even had a few kind words for Mrs. Lacey. " I wanted to talk to her," he said. " I hoped she'd come up here with you, but I suppose she's busy with her packing."

Violet agreed that such was the case. She had an awful lot of packing. A big woman like that needs an awful lot of clothes. It's the sweating that does it. And she never threw anything away. Kept everything. She had boxes full.

" Well, I can't very well go down there and beg her on my knees, can I? It wouldn't be dignified."

Violet was convulsed at this and Mark began to enjoy himself. Only Florrie showed no emotion whatever.

" I wish you'd tell me where the trouble lies," Morey begged. " Do you think she'd stay if I offered her more money? You see, you know her much better than I do."

Florrie came to life at this. " No, sir," she said, " it isn't money. She told me to tell you it was just like she said in her note to Madam. It's too much for her."

" I'm sorry. I guess that finishes it. . . . But what about you girls? Do you want me to get a new cook from New York or do you think you can manage between you? . . . There'll be a little extra money, of course."

Violet glowed. " We can manage," she insisted stoutly. " Can't we, Florrie? If you could close off some of the rooms we don't use it would make things easier-like. Say something, Florrie! " She prodded her friend.

Miss Beulah would have been proud of her pet's com

posure. " Yes, sir," Florrie said politely. " We'll do very well. And thank you, sir."

Morey leaned back with a sigh. " What are you doing to-night ? " He winked.

Violet met this with a paroxysm. She rolled her eyes upwards and outwards in an effort not to wink back. She strangled happily and leaned on Florrie for support.

" Nothing, sir," Florrie said. " We have our evenings on Thursday and will continue to do so unless inconvenient." But Violet was made of harder stuff.

" I'm not afraid to tell even if you are," she declared. " It's like this, Mr. Morey. We are going to slip out for a little bit. Mrs. Lacey gave us permission. My cousin Edgar has a truck and he and his friend was going to drive over to Crestwood. Only for a little talk, you know. Not more than half an hour. We done it before, with permission, and no harm come of it."

" Do you mean to say you'd sit in a truck and talk on a night like this ? You'd freeze."

" We don't get cold," said Violet.

" Well, I won't have it," Morey said. He dug down into a pocket. " Here's ten dollars. Take Edgar and friend to the second show over in Bear River and get something to eat afterward. But be sure you get Mrs. Lacey's O.K."

They stared at him. " Go on," he said. " Take it. Have a good time." He reached out and tucked the bill in Florrie's apron pocket. Florrie coloured to the roots of her hair and thanked him.

Mark watched their exit with a broad smile. Violet moved like a rudderless boat, barging into chairs and tables and missing the door by a good yard ; and all because she persisted in bowing herself out backward by way of showing an extra degree of respect. A nice kid ; no rouge, just health.

"That'll keep them happy for a while," Morey said. "Movies, chicken chow mein, and a box of chocolates. Even beer. My stomach's turning over."

Mark turned to Stoneman. "Don't you wish you——" he began, and stopped short. At the same instant Morey reached for a bottle and glass and hurried over to the old man. Stoneman had slipped down in his chair, his head resting on his chest. He was breathing heavily.

"Mr. Stoneman!" Mark rubbed the cold, limp hands. "What is it?"

"No, no," he said thickly. "Go away."

"Let me—I know what to do." Morey held the glass to the old man's lips. "Drink it, Joe. It'll do you good. I mean it."

"He won't take it," Mark said. "What happened to him?"

"God knows," Morey said. "But you can count on it happening several times a year. Listen, Joe, will you take a sleeping pill if I get it for you? You ought to be in bed. I'll get you one of Laura's."

At the mention of Laura, Stoneman made a visible effort to collect himself. "I'll get it myself," he mumbled. "Mr.—Mr. East——"

"Yes?" Mark said. "I'm here."

"If you'll lend me your arm——" He dragged himself to his feet. "If you'll just come with me—and see me through the preliminaries— —"

"Of course. And I'll stay with you."

"No, no! . . . I won't have you spoil your first real evening with us on my account. You must come back here and talk to Jim." He still spoke thickly but he was fighting for control. Mark watched his struggle to stand alone, his pathetic attempts to hold himself erect.

"Come along now," he said gently. They were half-way to the door when Stoneman turned back.

" Who —who'll look after the children now that those girls have gone off ? "

" That's all right, Joe. Stop worrying. They went to bed at seven o'clock and you know they sleep like bears. And Laura's in the next room, don't forget."

" What about that sedative ? " Mark said to Morey.

" You heard him say he'd get it himself. . . . Maybe he will. . . . I think I'll turn in shortly myself."

Once out of the room, Stoneman sagged. He seemed to have reached the end of his endurance. Mark put an arm about his shoulders and half led, half dragged him up the stairs. When they reached the little hall that led to their rooms, he stopped.

" Isn't Mrs. Morey's room off this main hall ? " he asked. " I mean —what about those pills, or whatever they are ? "

" I think I shall try to manage without them. I can always—always get them later."

The house was dim and quiet when Mark took a last look at Stoneman, safe in his bed. The door from the old man's room into the hall was locked. He'd locked it himself, fumbling with the key and dropping it several times. In spite of pleas and persuasions Mark had refused to do the same to his.

" I don't walk in my sleep," he said.

" Did—did Jim——? "

" Now, never mind. You go to sleep, or try to. I'll keep one ear open."

" Aren't you going downstairs again ? But that's so foolish, my boy. These little attacks are nothing, nothing ; I'm quite comfortable already. Won't you go, as a favour to me ? I'm sure Jim——"

" Never mind about Jim. I heard him come up a few minutes ago. Now remember," he patted the old man's shrunken shoulder, " if you get the jitters or want anything, shout. I'll leave the doors to the bath-room open."

He expected a frenzied protest, but to his surprise Stoneman turned docilely on his pillow and closed his eyes. "As you wish," he murmured. " Good night."

Mark left the night light burning in the bathroom and undressed in his own room. It was only nine-thirty but it felt like midnight. He raised one window a few inches, recoiled, and closed it hastily. The wind was like a knife. He stood for a moment staring down into the darkness, trying to see the narrow path and three-foot wall that edged the precipice. But it was too black. He couldn't have seen a face a foot away.

He put out his light and crawled into bed. After a few seconds he saw the door leading from the bath to Stoneman's room slowly close and heard the bolt slip into its socket. The old fox, he thought; he meant to do that all the time. He was grinning as he went to sleep.

Later, when he found himself struggling to wake, he thought he was fighting off a nightmare. But almost too soon he knew he was wrong. The room was in darkness, thick and suffocating. Down by the foot of the bed something was creeping along the floor, dragging at the covers mouthing strange words. It came nearer; he heard its rattling breath and felt it blowing on his face. It was real; it was trying to talk to him. There was no light in the bathroom, no light anywhere.

He struggled upright and felt for the lamp on his bed table, twisting and turning to get out of reach of those groping fingers. The lamp was dead.

He was suddenly aware of another sound far off, insistent, measured, warning. The sound of someone beating on iron. His own heart was hammering when he finally got his flashlight on.

Beside the bed, on the floor, Stoneman was gibbering like an idiot. He was past speech; his head rolled alarmingly and his palsied hand pointed to the door leading into the hall. Mark dragged him to his feet and propped him in a chair. In the light of his flash he saw with relief that there was no blood on his pyjamas. The distant clamour beat its even measure.

" Mr. Stoneman ! " he shouted, terror catching him in the throat. " What is it ? What's wrong ? " Again, the finger pointed to the hall door.

" What's out there, Mr. Stoneman ? What's happened to the lights ? What's that noise ? Try to tell me ! " His own voice was shaking.

The old man turned his rolling head toward the door and stared fixedly. Mark's flashlight followed. He saw the knob turn and the door swing slowly open. A young woman in trailing white stood there.

" I think someone is dead," she said calmly. " Why don't you go and see ? "

Mark stared, speechless.

" I'm Laura Morey," she said. " That is the yard bell ringing. It always means fire, but this time I think it means death too."

Stoneman whimpered in his chair.

" That's Mr. Stoneman, isn't it ? " She came forward quietly. " You can safely leave him with me. And take your flashlight when you go. You'll need it, and Mr. Stoneman and I don't mind waiting in the dark. Do we, Mr. Stoneman ? "

" But what——? "

" I know no more than you do, Mr. East," she said slowly, " but I'm sure you will be quite safe. I beg you to hurry. Someone is in difficulties and you may be too late. Go downstairs, and on your way please stop at the coat closet in the main hall. The fuse box is in there. You'll know what to do."

He still stared without moving. She put a cold hand on his shoulder and pushed him gently toward the door.

Outside, beneath the windows, someone shouted his
name. He hesitated, then ran from the room and down
the stairs. He could feel that cold hand urging him on.
The whole house was in darkness and a faint smell of smoke
drifted through the lower hall. In the coat closet he saw
that someone had thrown the main switch. He changed
that and in a second the night lights all along the wall
softly glowed. He had no dressing gown, so he took a coat
from its hook and started towards the baize door leading
to the kitchen. The smell was stronger now.

The kitchen was dark and filled with smoke, and around
the door that led to the cellar and the servants' rooms he
saw an ominous line of light. He was halfway across the
room when someone called his name again.

"East! Outside! Come outside!" He stumbled forward.

In the kitchen yard he found Morey in his pyjamas
beating an iron ring that hung from a tree. He was
dripping with sweat.

"You can't do anything back in there," he gasped.
"It's a furnace. I thought you'd never get here!"

"Where is it?" Mark shouted above the din. "Cellar?"

"No. Servants' rooms. Perrin saw the glare and
called me. You can't see any of it from our end of the
house."

"Perrin? Where—— ?"

"He tried to go in but his clothes caught fire. He's
down the road now, waiting to direct the volunteers—if
they ever get here. There's a sharp curve that some of
them may not know about. Here—take a turn at this,
will you? I'm done in. We have to keep it up until
we're sure somebody has heard."

"Mark swung at the ring. "Can't we do anything?
Chemicals?"

"No chemicals. We tried the garden hose, but the

water froze. It won't spread if we can get enough people to carry buckets. Thank God the walls and floors in that part are all stone. Luckily those kids went to the movies."

Mark had raised his arms to strike again; he was only half listening, but the words—" went to the movies "—rang like a gong. The mallet fell soundlessly to the ground. He turned to Morey. His tongue was stiff as he dragged out the question he was afraid to have answered.

" Mrs. Lacey ? " he whispered. Morey stared blankly. then his mouth began to work.

" My God," he said, " I'd forgotten her already ! " They ran to the kitchen door and wrenched it open. Black smoke rolled out and through it Mark saw again the lines of orange light. Morey slammed the door and leaned against it. They stood side by side in the smoking darkness.

Mark went forward again, but Morey dragged him back. " Don't be a fool," he warned. " Perrin tried that and he's sorry. It doesn't spread because the place is built like an oven. All we can do is soak these walls. Where's the light ? Damn, I threw the switch because I thought it was safer."

Mark found the button. " The switch is all right," he said. The lights came on.

He saw Morey clearly for the first time. He was on his knees before a cupboard, fumbling frantically with pails, throwing them on to the kitchen floor.

" Fill them at the tap," he ordered. " Keep the walls wet and see what you can do with that door. Why the hell don't they hurry ! "

" How long," Mark panted, " how long since Perrin?—"

" I don't know—years, minutes." They worked in unison, filling and emptying like automatons. " I keep thinking there's something I could have done. But it —it was like a furnace when I got here. . . . Does it look better now ? "

There were shouts in the yard. Perrin came in with two men. His hair was scorched, his face black; a freezing overcoat covered his stained pyjamas.

"Some of the men brought extinguishers," he said. "They're working through the windows from the outside. We'll try from this end."

Mark watched hopelessly as the two volunteers filled their milk pails and went stolidly to work. "Isn't there a fire apparatus?" he asked Morey.

"In Bear River, five miles away. They'll never make it. These fellows are near-by farmers. They know what to do."

Perrin stood by the kitchen table, mixing baking soda and water into a bowl. Treatment for burns, Mark noted. Perrin was as calm as the farmers. When he drew his next pail of water he spoke to him.

"I think the worst is over," he said. "It's queer, it doesn't seem to spread. It seems—locked up."

Perrin gave a noncommittal nod. All he said was, "Yes, the worst is over."

A man came in from the yard; a raw youngster with a red face and red hair. He touched his forehead awkwardly and spoke to Morey.

"Seems like it's all in the one room," he said. "The little one on the end. It's a funny thing. A fellow boosted me up to the sills and I got a good look. The other room ain't hardly touched. Seems like that bathroom in betwixt saved it. That and them walls."

"Do what you can," Morey said. The orange light beneath the door was fading. He watched it soberly.

Mark turned to Perrin in desperation. "Mrs. Lacey was in there," he said. "You knew that, didn't you?"

"I knew," Perrin said.

"Couldn't you have—I'm sorry, I know you tried, but ——" He was too miserable to go on.

" It wouldn't have done any good," Perrin said, and turned away.

In three short hours it was all over. The doctor and the sheriff had come and gone ; and what was left of Mrs. Lacey had gone too.

Florrie and Violet, after an agonizing return, were sleeping in a guest room. Perrin, his burns treated, was settled on a cot hastily set up in the kitchen. He was not badly hurt. Anne and Ivy had slept through the whole thing, thanks to a soundproof night nursery that had been Colonel Davenport's study. Even Stoneman was asleep. Of Mrs. Morey, Mark had heard nothing.

He and Morey sat in the library with a bottle between them, both reluctant to go upstairs. He was thinking of Wilcox, the fatherly—but, he feared, bewildered—sheriff who had taken the two terrified girls in hand and comforted them. They had been sure it was all their fault. If they'd only stayed at home. . . . Wilcox had also handled Amos Partridge, something no one else had been able to do. Amos had worked steadily with the volunteers outside the house and when everything was over had suddenly run amok with a crowbar from the stable. It had taken two men to hold him. He'd burst into the house and tried to go upstairs ; nobody knew why until Wilcox explained.

" Used to court Ruthie Brown when they were children. Lost her to Billy Lacey. . . . He'd sort of begun his courting again."

Mark emptied his glass. " Welcome to Crestwood," he said. " Beautiful, parklike, peaceful. The score to date—one dead and one heartbroken."

" You need another drink," Morey said.

" No I don't. . . . Three-thirty. . . . I've lost track of time."

" If you're going to ask me when the thing started, I don't know," Morey said. " Perrin says between 11.30

and 11.45, but it might have been later. Or sooner. He sleeps over the garage, and that's a quarter of a mile from the house. High wall around it, and plenty of trees. It was pure luck that he heard the horse in the stable kicking up a row and saw the wrong kind of light in Mrs. Lacey's window."

" Did she have any family ? "

" I don't know. I suppose so. I think she's lived here all her life. I'll look into it. I'll—I'll take care of everything of course. . . . I had a hell of a time with old Joe."

" I'd forgotten him," Mark admitted. " He was in a bad way when he heard that alarm, but your wife took over. She told me where to find the light switch too. She "— he was going to say she was sure even then that somebody was dead but he stopped in time—" she was very calm," he finished lamely.

" She can be, when she wants to. She made Joe take some of her pills, rammed them down his throat, he says. Then Dr. Cummings came along and gave him a hypo for good measure. He tried to bite Cummings. But he'll be quiet now for about fifteen hours."

" How did it happen ? " Mark finally asked. " Do you know ? "

" I can guess." Morey looked worn. " The insurance people will be along before breakfast, if I know them. Whatever they say is all right with me. But the real culprit, if you want to know, is Davenport."

Mark stared. " Davenport ? But I thought he was in Europe ? I don't get you."

" Nothing to get. I'm talking through my hat. . . . Well, I'm off to bed. You can sit up all night if you want to, but I've got to be as fresh as a daisy in the morning. So long." He tried to make a jaunty exit, but his shoulders sagged.

Mark felt a tug of pity. Blaming himself, he thought

but it wasn't his fault. Nobody could have done more. But what was that crack about Davenport being the culprit? How could he be if he was in Europe? Crazy. Funny-paper stuff. Davenport crossing the ocean on a friendly bolt of lightning and striking down the faithful cook.

He tapped his forehead significantly and looked up at Laura Morey's portrait. "I've got smoke in my cerebrum," he said to that smiling face.

His jaw dropped when he heard her say: "Mr. East, may I talk to you?"

She was standing in the doorway, wrapped in a soft, dark crêpe. He got to his feet somehow, and bowed, painfully conscious of his bedraggled clothing and sooty face. He tried to repair the latter with a soggy handkerchief; at the same time he watched her, warily. Only a few hours before she had come to his room with a tragic and astounding piece of news. He wondered what this second visit meant.

"Sit down, please," she said, taking the chair next to his. "Do you mind if I ask you a few questions? Mr. Morey has a remarkable streak of old-fashioned gallantry. He tells women exactly what he thinks they should know, and no more. So I came to you because—because I want to know what happened down there to-night."

He told her, trying to make it sound as if it had happened years before, to someone nobody had ever heard of. It was hard to do, with that dead white face bending forward and the wide dark eyes looking blindly into his. For one dreadful moment he thought she was sightless; her eyes were like rounds of black velvet pasted on a marble face. Involuntarily he looked up at the portrait, and he saw her do the same. No—she could see as well as he could. He grinned with relief. She smiled in return, but it was no more than a muscular action that revealed her perfect teeth.

" Dead," she repeated. " Burned to death. . . . What do you suppose people will say ? "

" People ? I hadn't thought about that angle. I don't see that it matters, Mrs. Morey." It wasn't the kind of question he expected from her.

" I mean —the doctor. What does he say ? "

" Just what I've told you. Dead—of burns. Why ? Aren't you satisfied with that ? "

" Oh, yes—yes ! But Mrs. Lacey—it seems so wrong ! "

" It is wrong. But there's nothing we can do to right it. When you get the official report you'll see that it couldn't be helped."

" Official ? "

" The insurance people go into these things very thoroughly. They'll be here in the morning. And the sheriff was here to-night."

" Oh. . . . Does the sheriff investigate—fires ? "

" He does when they're fatal."

" I—I hope he wasn't troublesome. You said yourself that it was unavoidable. Didn't he see that too ? "

" He saw all there was to see, you can bet on that." He thought it was time to ask a few questions himself. He spoke casually. " What do you think about it, Mrs. Morey ? "

" But I wasn't there ! You know that. I don't know —anything. I stayed in my room."

" Not all the time. Remember ? When you came to my room and spoke to me you were already convinced that someone was dead. Is that why you're so interested in the official report ? . . . Did you know it was Mrs. Lacey ? "

" Know ? Mr. East, how could I ! How could I ! "

" I don't know, but that's what you said. You said you thought someone was dead."

" I must have been out of my mind. I was terrified.

It was the noise, that dreadful noise. It frightened you too, and Mr. Stoneman. It was enough to wake the dead. That's it! I must have been telling myself that it was enough to wake the dead, and said it—said it out loud! You see? You misunderstood me. I didn't know anything, anything, until now."

He was sure she was lying and he told himself a kid could do a better job. Perhaps she hadn't actually known anything, but he thought she suspected something. What? Did she suspect suicide? He started to ask, but stopped when she raised her hand in a childish gesture. He thought she was going to speak and to give her a chance to collect herself he reached for a cigarette. When he turned back, the hand was over her eyes; but he saw, in time, that they were filled with tears.

Then he remembered the little he knew about her personal history. She was ill, with a strange and tragic illness that sometimes comes to women after childbirth. Morey had told him that much.

"Forget it," he said easily. "Of course you didn't know anything. I was only making conversation and it was lousy. I'm as rattled about the whole business as you are. We're both tired and we don't know what we're talking about, that's all. But we mustn't let this get us down. Things like this happen all the time, but you never hear about them. Sure, they happen all the time!" In his eagerness to be gentle, he was babbling. "Sure. Too bad, of course, but what can you do? Now if you want some sound advice you'll do what I tell you and trot back to bed like a good girl!" He heard himself with horror. Trot! Good girl! He might have been talking to Violet.

She stood up and smiled at him. It was a better smile this time. "Thank you, Mr. East," she said. "How long are you —staying here?"

He looked startled. "How long? Why—I don't know."

She smiled again. "Good night, Mr. East."

CHAPTER FOUR

SOFT beds and linen sheets had failed to hold Violet and Florrie. The Dresden clock on the guest-room bed table said seven as firmly as its poor relation in the kitchen. So did habit. They washed and dressed silently in the dark because there was no candle; they didn't use the electric light because never in their lives had they had such a thing in their bedrooms. Downstairs in the stone cubicle it was candles or lamps; at home, too. They crept down the hall, shivering and red-eyed, and made their way to the kitchen.

Here was plenty of light, a fire in the coal range and coffee on the gas stove. Perrin was mopping up with rags and buckets. He had already made a pile of half-burned wood and twisted metal in the yard. Florrie, the reader, looked at this dubiously.

"You oughtn't to do that, Mr. Perrin," she said. "There may be something in that débris that the police want. To sift through, like."

"I don't know what you're talking about," he said coldly. "Mr. Wilcox made a thorough examination last night."

"Well, the insurance man, then. Mr. Scott. He's coming this morning. Won't he have to—to——" She faltered.

"Get yourself some coffee and go up to the children," he advised calmly. "I'll prepare their breakfast and send it up with Violet. Mrs. Morey is not to be disturbed

. . ." He softened a little at the sight of her trembling lips. " I'm sorry, Florence. We're all upset to-day. Just try to be cheerful, and keep the children happy. Will you ? "

Florrie smiled tearfully. After coffee, she left.

An hour later Mark woke. He took a look at Stoneman deep in a drugged sleep and happily unaware of unlocked doors, dressed and went downstairs. The fire had been a nightmare that stayed with him. He wanted to see if it was better or worse than he remembered. Once in the kitchen, he stopped short.

Perrin was nowhere to be seen, but Violet was there, struggling with a heavy basket and the yard door.

" What have you got there ? " he asked sharply. " Who's been cleaning up ? "

" It's from her—her room," Violet said timidly. " Mr. Perrin said it was all right. He said we'd got to clean it out sometime."

" Put it down," he said. He prodded among the wet rags and bits of wood. " What is it—do you know ? "

" Her trunk." She looked at him dumbly, full of grief. " Did I do wrong ? "

He patted her arm. " No, Violet. Just leave those things where they are, that's all. We mustn't touch anything, you know. People might think we had something to hide."

She gave him a long look, and turned to the stove. "You want coffee, don't you ? Mr. Morey already had his."

" Has he been down here ? "

" Yes, sir. He's gone down the drive a way to meet Mr. Scott. I can get you some eggs if you don't mind waiting."

" No thanks." He sat at the table and drank coffee. Violet, after much urging, joined him.

" Did you and Florrie lose much ? "

"No, sir. Hardly nothing. We don't keep much here except uniforms, going home every week like we do. It's lucky I was wearing my good silk——" She broke off and frankly cried, hanging her head like a child. "Talking about my silk with her burned to death." She refused to be comforted. "And us just through saying we could get along without her!"

He shivered. A cold wind was blowing over his shoulders, coming from behind the screen that stood where the swinging door had been. All the doors out there were gone, the windows too. In spite of the warm fire in the kitchen range he could smell the desolation at his back. He wanted to walk around that screen, past the cellar stairs, across the square stone hall, into those three little rooms, but he couldn't. He was a secretary, and his boss was asleep upstairs. That's where he ought to be himself, upstairs. He leaned across the table and touched Violet's arm.

"Violet," he said gently, "did Mrs. Lacey ever say anything to you about——"

The yard door slammed and Morey came tramping in followed by a fat man with a face like a boy. They were covered with snow.

"Mr. Scott, Mr. East," Morey said. "Want to get in on this, East? Mr. Scott is Davenport's insurance man. He's going to look things over."

They went behind the screen.

There was nothing left in Mrs. Lacey's room. Perrin and Violet had done a good job. The walls were black with smoke; water stood on the floor. You could see where the bed had been because the wall was blacker there. In spite of the broken window, clumsily covered with boards, the smell of kerosene was still strong.

Violet explained that Perrin had wanted the place cleaned up. Scott nodded his head.

"It's exactly as I thought," he said. "I told Davenport this would happen some day." He turned to Morey "Davenport was a crackpot about this house. He rebuilt, remodelled, and restored—everything but these rooms. Said they were like monastery cells. Refused to wire them. No heat, no light; used candles, lamps, and oil stoves. I told him that if he ever had a fire it would stay within the four walls all right but God help anybody who tried to go in or out before the thing was over. Kicked like a steer about the plumbing in the bath, but he couldn't get around that. Had to do it—servants wouldn't stay if he didn't. Look at this——" He led them to the room the girls used.

Mark saw an iron bedstead, the bedding soaked; two metal chairs, and a pair of water-logged slippers with run-over heels.

"His concession to safety," Scott went on. "It seems to have worked at that. Barring the chance of suffocation—well, never mind that. But the point is, he couldn't control Mrs. Lacey. She put up curtains, laid down a rug, had fripperies all over the place. Paper fans, a fishnet full of photographs. Funny thing, her own house is charming. She used this room here as a dump for all the trash she couldn't bear to throw away. Well, you put all that trash in a rectangle of solid stone, the only exit a nail-studded oak door, and then upset a lamp or a stove—! She was like a trussed fowl in an oven. You found her— well, found her in bed, I understand. Went to sleep with the lamp on. Too heavy to help herself. I'll take care of everything. Nothing to worry about." He turned to leave.

"Hey!" he cried, his eyes on Violet. "I almost forgot about you. You and Florence must put in a claim for damages. Water, chemical stains. Where do you keep your clothes. Lockers?"

Violet nodded.

" Well, open them up ! Give me an estimate. You can figure it roughly, can't you ? "

" I'll take care of that," Morey said quickly.

Violet fumbled at the locks. Then she turned to face them. " There's nothing here," she said. " Only uniforms and—things. We had on our good silks. We—we don't want damages. Damages don't—help."

Morey turned his head. When they filed out of the room he stood back and let Violet go first.

Mark went back to his own room and sat at the desk. Stoneman would sleep until late afternoon and until then he had nothing to do. Morey had gone off with Scott.

Mrs. Lacey's library book, with the sealed envelope inside it, lay before him. He would return it, he didn't feel like reading, and that would give him an excuse for calling on those two women. Maybe they could make him laugh. Petty and Pond, wasn't it ? Bessy Petty, who looked like a child's attempt at paddling a butter ball, and Beulah Pond, who told tall tales and looked like a hatchet. But a nice hatchet, for domestic and benevolent purposes only. He began to grin.

Halfway down the mountain he had another idea. He would stop and talk to Amos. Amos, who had begun to court Ruthie Lacey again and who had tried to go upstairs with a crowbar.

When he came in sight of the station the ten-o'clock train for Bear River, persistently trailed by the ten-o'clock bus, was slowly pulling out. He waited a few minutes before going in. He needn't have worried about the best way to introduce himself or the subject that weighed heavily on his mind ; Amos did that for him.

He turned from the grimy window where he had been watching the departing train, and held out a gnarled hand. " I'm glad you come," he said.   " I'd like to thank you for

all you done last night. You worked as good as one of us."
He sat down with his back to the tracks, facing the little
lane of houses. " I'm sorry if I gave you any trouble,
Mr. East. I lost my head."

" Forget it," Mark said. " I lost mine too. You
know," he added carelessly, " when you came charging
in with that crowbar I thought you were after me."

" No," said Amos. " No."

Mark took the library book from his pocket. " I just
stopped in to rest my legs," he said. " I'm on my way to
Miss Pond's—to return this. . . . Mrs. Lacey asked me to."

Amos averted his eyes from the book ; his face was grim,
but he managed a solemn wink. " You can return it
right now. She's coming down the lane like a bat outa
hell and the fat one trailing behind. Quick work, I call it."

Mark saw them through the window, leaping over and
plunging into drifts as size and figure allowed, veils flying,
arms flaying, eyes avidly front.

" Do you suppose they know I'm here ? "

Amos spat. " Listen. The minute you set foot on this
platform old man Bittner told Ella May. Ella May run to
the 'phone and told Bessy and Beulah. Bessy and Beulah
grabbed some clothes and here they are. . . . I bet they
ain't half buttoned up."

They came in like bombazine cyclones.

" I'm sick," Beulah declared as she unwound Bessy and
began on herself. " We both are. Ella May telephoned
us last night, and we tried to get up the mountain like good
neighbours, but those wretched volunteers sent us back.
Give one of these louts a little authority and he goes crazy.
I want to hear everything. You were there of course,
Amos ? I feel for you. Well, what do we do now ?
Plan the funeral and put up the house for sale ? "

Amos clumped over to the window and said nothing.

" We were all so fond of Ruthie Lacey, Ruthie Brown

she was," Bessy mourned gently. " She came here with her parents when she was a little thing. They worked hard and saved. Colonel Davenport is going to feel this too."

" Do you know anything that I don't ? " Beulah asked Mark. " Ella May says Scott has come and gone already. What did he say ? "

Mark told her. He began with Morey calling him in·the night and ended with Scott's departure. He mercifully left out Amos and the crowbar. He also left out Laura Morey.

Beulah handed Bessy a clean handkerchief and mopped her own eyes with another. " I don't understand it," she said. " Ruthie was so careful. Country people don't upset lamps." She saw the library book and pounced on it. " You haven't read it so soon, have you ? "

" No. I'm returning it. And this envelope." He explained about the six cents.

Beulah shook the pennies into her lap. " That's funny. She didn't have to pay me this way. She could have brought it herself, any day. I mean, she could have if——"

Amos spoke harshly from the window. " She didn't expect to see you for some time. She was planning on taking the ten o'clock this morning and catching the New York train at Bear River."

They stared at him.

" Come over here," Mark said. " How do you know that ? "

Amos came over. " She was going away to-day. She called me up yesterday morning and asked me to say nothing. She wanted me to borrow a truck and come up for her things after she'd gone. I was to store them in her cellar. I got a key. I always have had a key ever since she went to work for Davenport. Even when her husband was alive. . . . She trusted me."

"I knew she was leaving," Mark said. "But she didn't tell me she was going away. She said she was—tired."

"I used to air the place for her when she couldn't get down to do it herself," Amos droned on. "And she told me to have her ticket ready. She never did much travelling and thought you had to order in advance, like Europe."

"New York," breathed Bessy. "I can't believe it."

"No?" said Amos sharply. "Well, you can ask somebody else then. Somebody else knew just what I know. That she was going to New York, and why."

Mark gave him a shrewd look. "Who?"

Amos shrugged. "Dunno," he said. "Wish I did."

Mark lit a cigarette and waited a few seconds. Then, "I liked Mrs. Lacey. I only saw her once in my life but I'll never forget her. But—I don't feel right about this business. Of course it has nothing to do with me; I'm employed by Mr. Stoneman just as Perrin is employed by Mr. Morey and I have no right to meddle in Mr. Morey's household affairs. But when I talked to Mrs. Lacey she'd been crying. And she said some odd things about evil. I wondered then if she was frightened. Or if she was simply being silly about some trifle."

Amos bristled. "She wasn't silly about anything! She was frightened!"

"Ah. . . . Of what?"

"I don't know. Never heard her so upset. Wanted to leave right away. Even said the girls could pack for her. But it was Sunday and the trains ain't so good. First one she could get leaves here at six in the evening. The New York train leaves Bear River at eight. Put her in New York around midnight—too late for a lady, I told her." He turned his head. "I wish I'd let her go," he said softly.

Beulah cleared her throat. "But New York? Why did she want to go to New York?"

"Going to see her niece. I asked her what for because the niece is going to have a baby and Ruthie always believed in leaving women alone at times like that. Better for them, she always said. So then she said it was the niece's husband she wanted to see."

"Why did she want to see the niece's husband?" Mark asked patiently.

"Didn't tell me, except to say she had some business for him."

"What is his business?"

"He's a police captain."

"That's funny," Beulah said slowly.

Mark lit another cigarette. "Could be anything," he said carefully. "Could be advice about her property. She may have wanted to make some provision for the baby. . . . Amos, what did you mean when you said somebody else knew about her plans?"

"I was waiting for you to get around to that," snorted Beulah.

"She was telephoning me from the garage," Amos said. "Told me she didn't want the girls to hear. She said the garage was safe because there wasn't anybody there. But Ruthie wasn't smart about telephones. That garage 'phone is connected to the house 'phones. Anybody that saw her go out there could have listened if they'd wanted to."

"Did anybody?"

"I thought there was somebody on the line besides her but I wasn't sure. So when she hung up I waited. Sure enough, I heard someone else hang up too."

Beulah broke the silence that followed. "Scott says it was an accident," she said thoughtfully. "What did Dr. Cummings say, and that good-for-nothing Perley Wilcox?"

"They all agree. Accidental death. But they seem

to think it wouldn't have happened if Davenport had put in proper light and heating. I think we'd better agree with them."

Bessy, who had been rooting around in Beulah's lap looking for another handkerchief, suddenly held up the white envelope.

"There's something else in it!" she shrilled. "A lot of money and a letter!"

Beulah snatched it quickly. "Ridiculous," she scoffed. But there was. She drew out a folded paper and a five-dollar bill. She read aloud : "*Miss Pond, the six cents is my fine. The book was lovely. I am going away and will see you on my return. The five dollars is something for you to do for me if you will be so kind. When you go over to Bear River next Sunday please drop it in the poor box at St. Michael's. I will appreciate. Yours, R Lacey.*"

Bessy looked stunned. "Why does she want to put money in the poor box ? She has her regular collection envelope like everybody else."

Mark didn't have the answer. He said good-bye as soon as he could and left them poring over the note. On his way up the mountain he was overtaken by a crew of workmen. They gave him a lift and talked about the fire. They were carpenters, come to replace the burned doors and windows.

There was a tray on the desk in his room and a note from Florrie asking him to drink the soup in the thermos jug and eat the sandwiches and bring the tray down to the pantry when he was. through, please.

Stoneman was still asleep. He ate his lunch slowly and carried the tray downstairs according to instructions. Florrie was cleaning silver in Perrin's pantry and showing clearly that while she knew it wasn't her job she'd do it anyway, because she was that kind of girl.

"Just put them down anywhere," she told Mark.

" And thank you. In times like this everybody has to pull more than their weight."

" Where's Perrin ? "

" Out somewhere. An easy job if you ask me. Not that he's the only one around here with an easy job. Are you working this afternoon or taking another walk ? "

Mark got the point. Equals now, he said to himself, and no more sirs. " Neither," he answered. " I'm going to help you, if I may. Mr. Stoneman is still asleep."

" Well." Florrie softened. " You can do that urn if you want. It's really too much for me. So Mr. S. is asleep, is he ? I wish I could say the same for Mrs. M. We're a pair, you and me. Tied down to a couple of notional people."

" What's Mrs. M.'s trouble ? " he asked as he rubbed.

" Nerves. I've seen nerves before and I know. Lots of ladies come to the summer hotel with nerves. Looks to me like it comes from having too much money. Now, if I had too much money I'd enjoy it, I would. Plenty of time to rest when you're old."

" Maybe your Mrs. M. is really ill," he ventured.

" Ill ! Her ! With all those evening gowns ? Dozens, I tell you, and this year's style. And fur coats. And jewellery. Just like in a magazine. She didn't buy all those things to wear in bed, which is where she spends most of her time now."

Florrie was a different girl when she forgot her refinement and enjoyed herself as she was doing now. Mark was delighted, and showed it—carefully.

" I guess her husband gave them to her to cheer her up," he said.

" Him ! " Florrie collapsed against the table with joy. " That one ! Why, he has to ask her for every penny ! She's the one with the money around here. I think he married her for it. Not that she's close with it, I'll say that for her. Very liberal. She pays double wages to what you'd get anywhere else. That's why I stay. That and the children." She gave him a side glance. "No girl with a heart could help but love children, don't you think?"

Mark returned the glance but decided to circulate a rumour that he was married.

"But he's good to her, for all her tantrums. I think he's handsome, don't you? And between you and I, not a bit fresh. When you work out, you appreciate that. The things I could tell you!"

"I can believe it," Mark said admiringly. "And I wouldn't blame any man who——" He stopped and let the suggestion take root and flower into a blush. "But," he went on easily, "if the wages are so good I don't see why Mrs. Lacey, poor thing, wanted to leave."

Florrie's eyes clouded. "Oh, she was well-to-do in her own right," she explained. "She only came to help the Moreys because they were the Colonel's friends. And she wasn't so young any more, you know. All this nervous business, and people not coming to meals, and wanting trays ; and that Mr. S. of yours being really worse than my Mrs. M. Fed up was what she got."

"But my Mr. S. had nothing to do with Mrs. Lacey."

"He had enough to nearly drive her crazy. Locking himself in his room and only opening the door to take in food. And making her swear nobody had touched it but herself. He used to say he had a creese. Perrin says that's French for fidgets. Personally, I think he suffers from a mania."

"I believe you're right," Mark said admiringly. "Did Perrin work for the Colonel too?"

"My," said Florrie. "You don't know a thing about us, do you? Perrin came from one of those agencies that deals with only the highest type. Mrs. Morey got him. His references would give you a thrill. Dukes and so on, titles on the other side. I never saw them myself, but Mrs. Lacey did. He had a bad cold one day and Mrs. Morey asked her to go out to the garage with some medicine and things. She's real thoughtful that way. She told Mrs. Lacey she knew it wasn't her work and it was a long walk for a heavy woman, but she thought it would look better than sending a young girl. He was in his bathroom when she got there and the papers were lying on his table. She couldn't help but read them."

" Um," said Mark.

" He's high-toned, Perrin is." Florrie took satisfaction in this. " So is Mr. Stoneman high-toned. It comes from their foreign contacts. I understand Mr. Stoneman dug up things in Europe. Some digger, too, if you ask me. I bet he could get things out of you that you wouldn't breathe to a soul. You should have heard him with Mrs. Lacey ! "

" Florrie ! " cried Mark, enslaved. " You're wonderful ! The things you know ! . . . Don't tell me Mrs. Lacey had a past ? "

" If you mean what I think you mean," sparkled Florrie, " no. But about two weeks ago he came down to the kitchen and gave her five dollars and——"

" Florrie ! "

" And gave her five dollars," went on Florrie with a look, " if she would tell him exactly what she was doing and where she was the night before. She hadn't been any-where and hadn't done anything, so she told him so. And gave him back his five dollars and ran him out of the kitchen. He'd die if he knew I knew."

" Um," said Mark again.

" After he left she cried and cried. She thought she was alone, see, and nobody would know."

" Apparently they both thought they were alone. How did you ever find out, Florrie ? Did she tell you ? "

" Tell me ? Not her ! Close-mouthed. But I was

right in here hanging down the dumbwaiter shaft. The voices came up clear as a bell."

Mark put down his cleaning rag. "You don't know anything else, do you?" he asked respectfully.

"No. Except he kept after her. The last time was yesterday morning—imagine that—only yesterday. When you went out for a walk he had her up in the library, asking her all over again. She said all she knew about that night was that there were broken bottles all over the cellar next morning, and somebody had swiped the light bulb on the stairs. She said did he think she broke the bottles. He said no, he only wanted to know if she was in her room all the time and if she saw or heard anything."

"Did you and Violet hear anything?"

"Not us. That was one of the times we slipped down the mountain, with permission. Well, you can say what you will, but it looks like fate. That was only yesterday and when she came back to the kitchen she was crying like anything and saying, 'God help me.'"

"And," prompted Mark.

"He didn't," Florrie said simply. "She wrote out her resignation and had me take it up to Mrs. Morey. But she died just the same."

Mark regarded her thoughtfully. "Sure nobody knows you were hanging down that shaft, Florrie?"

"Who could? That's the kind of thing a person keeps to herself."

"When is the funeral?"

"I don't know, but I'm going. Perrin is the head here and he'll let us off, I'm sure."

"I'll go with you."

They both jumped as Perrin entered quietly.

"Speaking of the devil," said Florrie brightly. "I was just saying how obliging you were. And Mr. East "—

she was a great lady distributing largess—" Mr. East is very nice and friendly too."

Mark felt himself flushing. " Well, if that's all——"

" I've got to run up to Mrs. Morey and give her hair a good brush. Then I'll pick up the library a bit. And then it'll be time to take the children out for a run. They're pestering."

Mark plunged. " I'd like to do that, if I may. Take the children out." He found himself addressing Perrin. " I have nieces of my own," he lied sadly, " and I miss them now and then. Especially—now."

Florrie looked eagerly at Perrin. She was thinking of the nice long letter she wanted to write to her boy friend, telling him all. " Honestly," she murmured, " Violet and I are that rushed. And if Mr. Stoneman could spare Mr. East——"

In less than ten minutes Mark found himself prancing through the snow with two small girls.

Young Anne was sturdy and poised, almost grave. Ivy was a dumpling who rolled into drifts and rolled out again under her own steam. They liked Mark and he liked them. It was good to feel their icy little mittens tucked in his hand.

They led him directly to a small clearing a few yards from the terrace. It faced the house and was backed by a semicircle of trees and rocks. It was their den ; they told him so, proudly. It was degrees colder than the terrace, but they didn't seem to mind.

There were old brooms and shovels littering the ground and several wrecks of snowmen standing about ; headless dwarfs, no taller than their waddling creator. Mark made derisive comments and offered to build another. When he produced straws from one of the brooms and told Ivy they were eyelashes, he reached the stature of a god. Anne left her snowballing and joined them.

He had been watching her for the last five minutes.

She aimed at impossible targets and never missed. Her grave little face was twisted into a scowl and there was something studied and patterned in the way she handled her right hand and wrist. He thought he knew what it was, and when she came over to help Ivy he laid a small trap. He tossed a snowball himself, holding his hand as she had held hers.

" Pelotari ? " he grinned.

She threw him a look of dismay but recovered herself like a woman. " Lots of people over here play pelota now," she said carelessly. " They have teams."

" Yes, I know." He gave her a smile, and felt like a heel because he was setting traps for a baby. " I like the Basque country, don't you ? "

" I love it," she said quickly, and then again the painful flush and look of dismay. " I mean, I think I would. I've seen pictures, in books." She turned swiftly to avoid his eyes, and kicked at the snow. " I'm going to find some bits of coal for buttons. We saw one in Bear River with buttons."

" Wait." He put his hands on her shoulders and bent down so that his face was level with hers. He said : " For some reason, and I don't know what it is, I've made you uncomfortable. It was that question, I think. Well, you forget all about it and I will too. I was only trying to be friendly but I guess I'm clumsy." Then he waited.

Anne waited too, weighing and appraising. Her eyes searched his and he felt as if he'd taken a bottle from an infant. But he stared straight back. Suddenly, to his intense relief, she relaxed, but there was no eight-year-old smile on her face, only a look of thoughtful surrender.

" You were quite all right," she said. " I am the one who was wrong. I shouldn't have answered that question but you asked it so naturally I forgot to be careful. You must forget what I said, Mr. East, because I promised my mother I would forget. I promised not to speak of places to anyone ; not to anyone at all."

"But I'm not just anyone," Mark said quietly. "I'm nobody. I don't count."

"You mustn't say that," she frowned. "Everybody counts. But you understand what I mean, don't you, about forgetting ? . . . It upsets my mother to remember Europe. But we were very happy there and she isn't happy here."

"It upsets lots of people, Anne. Don't worry about it. You'll go back again some day."

Then she said a curious thing. "If I'm obedient."

He wasn't sorry to see Morey coming toward them. There were other questions he wanted to ask, but she had him licked. It was that obedient clause. And now her blue eyes were watching him closely.

"Friends ? " he whispered.

"Friends," she whispered back.

Morey came up with his usual bounce ; there were circles under his eyes, but he grinned happily at the children. "Don't fall in love with this guy," he warned. "He's not half as nice as I am." He tossed Ivy into a drift and watched her scramble out again. "I'll take over now, East. Joe's up and raring to go." Ivy went into the drift once more, but this time she complained loudly.

"Don't give her any sympathy," Morey said to Mark. "She needs toughening up. Her mother spoils her." They both watched as Ivy staggered off with an injured air.

"How is Mrs. Morey ? " Mark asked casually.

"Not too well. Last night did her up."

"Me too," Mark said. "There I was in the pitch-dark with Stoneman howling on the floor and you whamming that iron. A nice way to wake up. Give me a sunbeam across the eyelids."

Anne ran over, followed by Ivy. "Here comes Mother,"

she said. "She's—she's in a hurry." She rested one hand on Ivy's shoulder and waited.

Laura Morey was running toward them, hatless and without a coat. Her dull red dress was like a stain on the winter landscape. She must have fallen, for it was caked with snow.

Morey hurried forward. "Laura! Do you want to kill yourself!" He took her arm, but she wrenched it away and dropped to her knees before Ivy.

"Are you cold, darling?" she begged. "Tell me, are you all right?"

Morey looked at Mark and shrugged. "Of course she's all right," he said quietly to Laura. "Tell your mother, Ivy. We were just having some fun, weren't we?"

Ivy complied. "Fun," she agreed.

Laura ignored Mark. He wasn't even sure she had seen him.

"You know Mr. East," Morey prodded her gently. "I think you called him last night when the—excitement started."

"Yes." She turned to Mark with blank eyes. "Of course I know him. Good afternoon, Mr. East." She gathered Ivy in her arms. "I'm sure it's too cold. It is too cold, isn't it?"

Anne touched her mother's arm. "I'm here," she said softly.

Laura's hand went out to the child's head and rested there, as if in apology.

"I know you are. I forgot. Forgive me. Don't you want to come in now?"

Anne hesitated. "Here comes Perrin," she said. "He'll stay with us a little while. And he'll bring us in. We'd like to play, if you'll promise not to worry. It—isn't too cold, really."

Mark watched Laura's face. The scene was incredible.

She had been frantic a few minutes ago and now she was calm and diffident. She put Ivy down as if she neither wanted nor needed her.

"Oh, play as long as you like," she said lightly. "I'm selfish. But do keep in sight of the house, Anne." She turned to Morey. "Come back with me. You don't want to stay here, do you? Come back with me. We can —have a nice talk."

"In that case I'll come," he said gravely. "You go on ahead. I'll follow with East."

She looked at Mark. He was at once reminded of Anne; there was that same look of doubt and restraint, of holding something back. She's afraid to be alone, he said to himself. Out loud he said, "We'll both go back with you."

She left them without another word, not running this time but walking slowly with her head down. Several times she looked over her shoulder, furtively. When Perrin passed her with a slight bow she stood still and waited until he joined the others.

Perrin spoke to Morey. "I saw Mrs. Morey leave the house," he said.

"Take over," Morey said briefly.

Mark and Morey moved off together. Once they looked back to see Perrin retying hoods and brushing off shoulders.

"That fellow acts like a woman," Morey complained. "I don't see how my wife stands him."

Mark accepted this as a change of subject. "Any more news about the Lacey business?" he asked.

"All settled. Funeral the day after to-morrow. I didn't see her. Nobody will. The undertaker's going to seal the casket. I tried to arrange things the way I thought Davenport would like them, but her old friends here in Crestwood want to run the thing themselves."

"This is the time for old friends," Mark commented briefly.

They crossed the terrace and Morey opened the door. "This is kept locked at night, you know. Has anyone given you a key?"

"No. I hadn't thought of needing one."

"I'll give you one, anyway. Hey, look!" He picked up a note from the hall table. "Addressed to you. Lady's writing. Delivered by hand. Maybe I'd better give you a key now!"

Mark put the note in his pocket. "I'll go up to Stoneman," he said. He waited until he was in his room before he opened it. It was from Violet. Amos had telephoned and asked that Mark be informed of an insured package waiting for him at the station. Anytime this evening or to-morrow. She was his, Violet. He knew there was no package because he'd left no address. Amos was being cautious and elaborate about something. He'd find out.

Stoneman came in from his room, rubbing his hands and beaming.

"Why, you've quite a colour, my boy," he said heartily. "This is doing you a world of good already."

This sudden exhibition of health and high spirits gave Mark a slight feeling of distaste. "You're looking almost buxom yourself," he said dryly. "Quite a change from the last twenty-four hours and a complete transformation from last night."

"Dear fellow, I've been ill for several days. And frankly, I was petrified last night. I thought the world had come to an end and I couldn't find my teeth." He laughed soundlessly. "But now I've had a good rest. And you, you've been pleasantly occupied, I hope?"

"No. I've been worried."

Stoneman sobered instantly. "I know," he said. "It's a frightful thing. And your feeling does you credit. It shows you have a heart and know how to use your head.

But you did all that was possible, all those brave fellows did. It's over now and you must forget it."

" Can you forget it—so soon ? "

" Yes. I have a disciplined mind ; nothing is allowed to come between me and my work."

" Me and my work are like that too," Mark said. " That's why I get upset when a secretarial job comes between me and it. I feel an uncontrollable urge to act like a detective."

" Please! I thought we agreed not to mention that—that lapse of mine ! Really, Mr. East, you force me to an unwilling conclusion. If you are not happy here perhaps you'd better return to your proper niche. I refer to New York."

Stopped again. First by an eight-year-old and now by a septuagenarian. And leaving Crestwood was the last thing he wanted to do. Stoneman was no longer afraid. He was almost gay. Apparently the thing he feared had been removed. Could that have been Mrs. Lacey ? . . .

" I'm sorry," he said meekly. " I do want the job. I— I need it."

" Now, now," beamed Stoneman, " just forget the whole thing ! Of course you'll stay. And we'll ignore that other life of yours—such an ugly way to earn one's bread ! But I'll be fair with you, my boy. If I should be burned to death in my bed you may be as inquisitive as you like ! "

Mark laughed agreeably. " I will be," he promised. " It's a little after four, Mr. Stoneman. Do you want to start some work now ? "

" No, no. To-morrow. To-morrow will be excellent."

" Then if you don't mind——" He handed him the note. " It's my laundry. I asked my landlady to send it on."

" Execrable writing. Not even the rudiments of composition. Yes, you may go."

Mark left the room slowly, as if he were loath to exchange his present company for a clean shirt ; but once round the bend in the drive, he ran.

CHAPTER FIVE

AMOS was waiting on the platform when Mark came up. " Saw you coming," he said. " I've locked up so we can start right off."

" Right off what ? "

Amos hobbled down the steps and turned into a neatly shovelled path that wound off behind the station. " Come along," he said impatiently. " You knowed there wasn't any package, didn't you ? "

" Sure I knew. But what's this we're starting ? I'm a working man and I've got to get back."

" I'm a working man myself. There's a train coming through in four minutes."

" Then why——"

" It don't stop. Now, listen. I was over at Ruthie's a little while ago getting out the clothes she put away to be buried in. Told you I had a key. And I knew just where she kept the stuff because she showed me last time she had her neuralgia. Anyway, I didn't want them two old buzzards rooting in her things."

" Quite."

" If she willed them anything they'll get it, legal. But no more. Well—when I was getting out her white stockings I found a little bottle in the bottom of the drawer. It was some pills Cummings gave her to take when the pain kept her awake. Sleeping pills. She only took a couple, I know. Well, sir, that bottle's almost empty now ! So—wait. This is Ruthie's house, here."

They'd reached a small white cottage set back from the path in a thicket of bare bushes. " Lilacs," offered Amos fitting a key into the lock. " There's prize chickens in them coops back there. Mine now." He coughed. " Go on in."

They went from a tiny entrance hall into a room that was grey in the winter twilight. Amos struck a match and lighted a lamp. Mark caught his breath.

Someone's living hands had made a picture out of Ruthie Lacey's best room. Fresh white curtains ruffled at the windows, red geraniums and potted ivy trailed along the white sills ; the old cherrywood gleamed, the brass and irons shone, and the chintz roses on the chair covers bloomed as if it were June.

" Did it last night when I got back," Amos said. " Want things nice when folks come to sit up with her." From a drawer in the fine old highboy he took a medicine bottle, half filled. " See what I mean ? "

" I'm not sure," Mark said carefully. " You'd better tell me."

" Well, this here clears things up to my mind. I think she carried the rest of these pills up to the big house, in case the pain came back again. Then last night when she was feeling low in spirit she took a couple, to make her sleep. So, being under the influence, as you might say, she couldn't wake up in time to save herself." He looked appealingly at Mark.

" That's a good theory, Amos." He saw some of the shadows fall away from the old man's face. " Yes, it's a good theory."

" You don't know how much better I feel now, Mr.— Mark. I couldn't of slept nights for thinking—maybe—it wasn't natural."

" Then you don't think there was anything behind that anxiety to get to New York ? You didn't like that, you know. And you thought someone listened in on her conversation, too. Remember?" He didn't mention the crowbar episode.

"I know. But I changed my mind since I found this bottle. Sure she was upset. She had too much work to do and she didn't like all the drinking. Maybe one of the men up there said something to her—kind of fresh—and she got scared. Remember you said she was scared and talked about evil? That's it, sure's you born. Pinching out of wedlock is evil. Ruthie was very religious."

Mark struggled to meet that earnest gaze. "All right so far," he said. "But what about that listening in? And why did she have to see the police captain—on business?"

"The listening in was nothing, I figure. I was just imagining things. Somebody wanted to use the 'phone and was waiting for her to get off the line. And the police captain is her only male relation. She wanted to ask him if she should write the Colonel and give him her reasons for leaving. Don't that all tie up?"

"Why didn't she ask you, Amos?"

"Ashamed to, I guess. Very modest woman. Figured it was more refined to keep such talk in the family."

Mark looked at his watch. "I've got to run. Uphill, too. But I'm glad you called me. This makes things all right, doesn't it?"

"Not all right," Amos said softly, "but better." They went out into the little hall, after carefully extinguishing the lamp, and then to the porch. Amos locked the door. "What you going to do about having no package?"

"I'll sneak in. Nobody'll see me." He held up the bottle. "Do you mind if I keep this awhile?"

"Not going to take any, are you?" Amos asked anxiously.

"Not now. I thought I'd just hang on to them—in case. O.K. ?"

Amos nodded gravely. They parted at the station and Mark turned slowly homeward. The snow began again.

He sifted over all that Amos had said. Amos had the kind of theory a man works out for himself when he is hurt and confused. It took care of everything, the evil, the fear, the policeman. It even explained the crowbar, for Amos had probably been jealous of the urban Stoneman; it might also explain the five-dollar bill so properly destined for the poor box. It was a satisfactory solution, but not for him.

He might believe it, he thought, if he had been in love with a little girl named Ruthie Brown. But the woman he had known was middle-aged and weighed over two hundred pounds ; he had been in her presence for less than half an hour. She was nothing to him and he would never miss her ; but because he could remember her frightened face her death was something he could not brush aside with talk of sleeping pills and a surreptitious kiss.

He let himself in the house with the key Morey had given him and went upstairs quietly. Stoneman's room was dark and empty. After a few minutes he went down to the library. That too was empty. He stretched out on a sofa and closed his eyes. If Stoneman didn't give him some work to do to-morrow he'd know the whole thing was a set-up. But a set-up for what ? He dozed off. The next thing he knew Violet was shaking him gently. He struggled to his feet.

"I'm sorry, sir, but we rung the gong and you didn't hear. It's dinner."

Perrin watched correctly from the doorway. "Dinner is served," he said, and moved quietly off.

"Everybody else down ?" he asked.

"Not yet, but Perrin said to wake you up. Dead to the

world, you was. You ought to go to bed right after dinner."

"Thanks for the sympathy. Maybe I will. Say "— he took the bottle from his pocket—" did you ever see these before ? "

Violet was horrified. " Now, Mr. East, you're not going to take any of that stuff ! You don't need it !" She came closer and lowered her voice. " Mrs. Lacey had a bottle just like that. I seen it often. Put her to sleep, she said. It was in her stocking drawer."

" Don't leer at me like that. I haven't done anything I shouldn't. These were given to me and the whole thing's proper, but a secret. A secret. Understand ? " She did. as exemplified by crossed fingers and eyes turned to heaven " Look me up after dinner," he said hastily as steps sounded in the hall. " I want to ask you something."

He left her in a useless and becoming trance and went over to the dining room. Stoneman and Morey joined him at the door.

The dinner was excellent. Violet, it seemed, could really cook. Morey still looked tired, but Stoneman had retained his new bounce and freshness and gained an appetite as well. Mrs. Morey was dining in her room, as usual, for which Mark was grateful. His three encounters had left him cold. He turned a devout look on Violet's sole Mornay, bubbling fragrantly in a ring of little potatoes.

" Did you have a good afternoon, my boy ? " asked Stoneman.

Morey laughed. " What did you hire him for, Joe ? He spends all his time running around the village with quaint characters and playing with the kids. He ought to be on my payroll."

" So much has happened," Stoneman sighed. " But," he wagged a playful finger, " from now on there will be no more interruptions. To-morrow, or perhaps this evening, we shall begin to do great things. Great things, eh, Mr. East ? "

Perrin approached Morey and spoke quietly. " Two ladies have called, sir, asking to see Violet or Florence."

" Two ladies ? You mean actually calling at the front door ? "

Perrin produced two cards and handed them over. " Miss Petty and Miss Pond, from the village, sir. They apologize for the hour, but as they were just passing by——" Perrin stopped tactfully.

" Passing by ! " Morey repeated with awe. " Passing by a mountain in a snowstorm so they climb up and drop in. On the level, what do they want ? "

" Mrs. Lacey's things. They are prepared to examine the personal effects and take charge of those items which might be profaned by prying eyes." Perrin had it straight from Beulah's mouth.

" I think it's a case of friendly snooping and ganging up on Amos Partridge," Mark explained. " He has a key to Mrs. Lacey's house but he won't let the old girls in. So they're going to work this end if they can. You know, read her letters, count her handkerchiefs, swipe her perfume if she had any."

" But there's nothing here ! " Morey was exasperated. " Not a rag. Perrin and I went through the lot. Take them down to the kitchen and let them grub through the stuff themselves. . . . No—wait. What's for dessert ? "

" Chocolate soufflé, sir."

" Then the kitchen is out. Take them up to the day nursery and give them some port. They can talk to Florrie and do their grave robbing later. . . . I wouldn't put it past that Pond woman to open the oven door."

Stoneman smiled happily to himself and hummed a little. Morey and Mark said nothing ; each was busy with his own thoughts. The meal progressed silently through roast lamb with artichokes, salad, and down to the soufflé. Mark could hardly wait until it was over. The nursery drew him like a magnet.

Bessy and Beulah drank their port in water goblets filled by themselves. They turned back their skirts and put their wet feet on the nursery fender. They missed nothing, from the bright German prints that made a border around the walls and the white fur rug on the hearth to the adjoining juvenile bath and the firelit bedroom beyond. Bessy ran a plump hand over the woollen nightgear that hung on a chair not too near the blaze.

"Nice and warm to get into," she murmured. "And hot water to wash in when they get up."

"You mumble like an idiot," Beulah said agreeably. "What's the matter now?"

"I slept in the attic at home," Bessy explained, "and I really did break the ice on my water pitcher in the mornings. Papa believed in making little folks hardy, though I must say I've never found it useful."

"You're enjoying now what he saved on fires then," reminded her friend. "Florrie? Oh, there you are!"

Florrie came in from the bedroom and gathered up small garments. Her mouth drooped at the corners even when she smiled.

"Sit down," said Beulah. "Have a drink. I won't tell anybody."

"I can't," Florrie explained. "Not yet, anyway. Ivy ought to be in bed at seven and here it is eight and I'm not half done. And she gets wild when she stays up. I can't be in two places at once and I haven't stopped all day. If it wasn't for Mr. East——"

"Troublemaker?" Beulah asked richly, pouring herself another glass.

"Not him," protested Florrie. "Made his own bed this

morning and Mr. Stoneman's too. Helped me with the silver. No, if they were all like him——" She turned at the sound of a scuffle in the bathroom. Fat Ivy, clad in a loose bathrobe and nothing else, came through the door in a lurching run, followed by her sister.

"Well, what's this, what's this!" cried the delighted Bessy. "Don't tell me you've come to say good night again!"

"She wants to kiss you," Anne said. "She won't go to bed until she does. Will you let her kiss you just once, Miss Petty? It will make things easier for the rest of us."

Bessy glowed, Beulah tapped her foot, and Florrie stood by helplessly while vows of love were exchanged and the talcum flew.

Perrin, with Mark at his shoulder, stood in the doorway and watched.

"No more kids for me," Florrie said fondly, "unless they're my own." She saw Perrin and Mark and flushed with embarrassment. "They take it out of one," she said primly. "Did you wish for something, Mr. Perrin?"

"If you've come to take us to the lower premises," boomed Beulah, "we have decided not to go." There was still a drink in the decanter. "Later, perhaps, later."

"There's nothing left," Mark told her. He gave her an edited version of Morey's description.

Perrin watched the love scene being played by the fire. "Do you need any help?" he asked Florrie, while the little girls eyed him warily. "Sometimes they come to heel more quickly for a man." Florrie nodded. He disentangled Ivy and carried her off, followed by Anne. Florrie wound up the procession with a backward grimace indicating her eventual return.

Bessy tipped the decanter sadly. "That man has rubber soles on his shoes," she said.

"So have I," Mark said. "Listen, when you ladies are

ready to leave I'll be happy to escort you down the mountain."

"Foosh," jeered Beulah. "We got up alone and we'll go down the same way. That man has his eye on Florrie. I don't like it. I see her married to a nice farmer. She's a very superior girl and I think it would occur to her to send me a ham every Easter."

"Do you know what that little Ivy has?" Bessy looked boastful. "A little gold cross with diamonds all over it. Real diamonds. She wears it next to her skin."

"Here's Florrie," cried Beulah. "Now what's the matter? You've been crying. Where's that man?"

Florrie sat down without permission. "He went out the other way. Honest, it isn't worth the extra money. Now it's my night's rest they want."

"Take it easy, Florrie," Mark said. "What do you mean?"

"Mrs. Morey. She's having another creese. She wants me to sleep on the chess lung in her room. You can't really sleep on those chess lungs. They're a kind of French sofa. And I was looking forward to a good bed to-night." She managed a wan but proud smile. "You know, Mr. Morey won't let us use the old rooms any more. He gave us the morning-glory room for ourselves, from now on. You ought to see it! Morning glories on the paper and the drapes, and blue silk covers on the beds. None of your rayons. Real silk. I was that doped last night I couldn't take it in. Now it looks like I won't take it in to-night either."

"Stand up for your rights," advised Beulah. "You're entitled to a bed. What's wrong with that woman?"

"Nerves again. She's been terrible to-day. Mrs. Lacey's trouble started her off. Standing at the window all afternoon, crying, and looking like she saw things. There's nothing to see but snow, and that's her trouble if you ask me."

" What's the matter with Morey ? " Mark asked. " Let him take the chaise—chess lung."

Florrie hitched her chair forward and lowered her voice. " Had a fight. I don't know what about, but she was screaming at him. Other noises, too. I would have heard something good, I bet, but Perrin come along and I had to step down the hall."

" What kind of noises ? " Mark asked.

" Banging. Opening and shutting drawers, banging things about. But I guess they heard Perrin and it must have scared them off. They shut up."

" Nobody can hear Perrin," Bessy insisted. " He wears rubber soles."

" Then they must have heard me. Oh, well, there's other places." She gathered up an assortment of dolls and put them in the toy cupboard. She didn't look happy.

Neither did Mark look happy. " Sure you didn't hear anything, Florrie ? " he persisted. " Or better yet, can you be absolutely sure they didn't hear you ? "

" Of course I'm not sure," she said crossly. " But I don't care if they did. And all I heard in there was shouting and banging. You can't make anything out of that."

" If you lose your place, you come straight to me," Beulah said. " I can keep you busy until the hotels open."

Florrie cheered up and collapsed again in one breath. " But I couldn't leave Violet. She leans on me. And she isn't what you'd call trained. I ought to be helping with the dishes this minute."

" Violet too," Beulah said recklessly. " Five hundred books to clean and two hundred bulbs to put out. I don't approve of anything in this house. Diamond crosses. Caviare. And I know where that morning-glory room is, too. Next door to that old man. Come, Bessy."

" But I'm next door to the old man myself." Mark

was still frowning. "On the other side. I'll look after the girls."

Beulah threw him a pitying look and rose grandly to her feet. She fell promptly back. "Well !" she said.

Bessy rose more slowly and smiled cordially at the ceiling. "One of our dizzy spells," she murmured.

Mark calculated the distance to the door and charted the furniture. With Beulah on one arm and Bessy on the other he started down the stairs ; Florrie, in the innocent roll of bumper, preceded. He propped them against the hall table and went for his hat and coat. Morey called him from the library and he went in, grinning.

"What's so funny ? " Morey asked.

"Was that a full decanter you sent up to the ladies ? "

"Full of the best. Why ? "

"A-w-w gone."

Morey jumped up. "Then they're cockeyed and you've got to take them home ! I'm going too. It's just what I need. Reeling down the mountain with a couple of old—"

"Jim !" Stoneman spoke sharply from the table, where he was turning over a folio of prints. "You stay here. Those poor women are sufficiently embarrassed."

Mark said, "As a matter of fact, they aren't at all. They're being so elegant they look at least two inches taller."

Morey gave Stoneman a sulky look, but he didn't insist. "Take the car if you want to, East, but I don't think it's safe in this storm."

"Air is what we need. I'll see you when I come back, Mr. Stoneman."

Mark tried to keep to the middle of the drive. The wind was howling, the temperature was down to zero. He had all he could do to stay on his own feet. His clinging companions tramped firmly from one side of the road to the other ; sometimes they went backward. They admonished each other to breathe deep ; they made frequent halts for the rebuckling of goloshes and retying of veils ; they pitied the poor on nights like this. When they pulled up in front of Beulah's house he was more dead than alive. But he was strong enough to resist their invitation to a little drop of something to warm him up.

"And we can tell you all about the will," cajoled Beulah. "Ella May was a witness and she told us."

"Save it until later," Mark said. "Honestly I've got to get back and work."

"Amos gets the house and the chickens and the niece gets the money, about a thousand a year. Now Amos can move out of that rat-trap over the station and live like a Christian. If he knows how."

"That's fine. Good night."

"You're coming back to the house after the funeral, aren't you ? We're serving coffee and cake to those who care to drop in. As a mark of respect."

"I'll try. Good night."

"Bring Mr. Stoneman," urged Bessy. "I think we have a lot in common. I've been to Pompeii and we could talk about the frescoes."

He had been moving steadily off and the last word reached him on a high note as he closed the gate. He waved an arm and started down the lane on a run. There was a light in the Bittners' parlour window and he saw the curtains twitch. Three more reputations ruined. And what was that about Bessy and the frescoes ? How did she work that, he wondered. Probably by giving ten dollars to the guide and the slip to Beulah.

Stoneman's voice was the first he heard when he entered the house. He was whining like a baby, and Morey was laughing at him.

"Joe's trying to make me back an expedition," Morey said. "I tell him he'll have to wait until after the war, but he won't believe me. You go to work on him."

Stoneman broke in eagerly. "I can get into Mexico," he said. "I know I can. I can go anywhere in South America. Aztecs. Indians. It will be quite inexpensive, too. Greece can wait. After the war, I can get to Greece."

Morey looked at Mark. "I promised I'd help him, but I can't make him see that it isn't practical now. In another year or two——"

Mark shrugged and said nothing. Stoneman glared and went back to his folio. He was mumbling under his breath. The wind cried outside and the snow tapped softly at the windows.

Morey got up and wandered aimlessly about. "How do they dig a grave in weather like this?" he asked. "The ground must be solid."

"The men around here are used to that," Mark said. "Been doing it all their lives."

Morey shivered. "Are you thinking about Mrs. Lacey?" Mark went on. "I've been thinking about her too."

Stoneman looked up with a show of interest. There was no sight of his recent temper. "That burial is Wednesday, isn't it? Too bad. Much simpler in the spring. The early spring with its first fine thaw. Still, if you think these good people will not misunderstand my motive, I should be most happy to assist."

Morey stopped pacing. "Professional tricks, eh?"

"In a small way," Stoneman said mildly. "There are tricks to every trade, you know, and I have had a varied experience. Getting a body into the frozen earth is much the same as getting one out. I remember one old fellow in Mesopotamia ; he was in a shocking state, literally crumbling. I understand Mrs. Lacey also—but then, she has the advantage of a stout coffin. And this is a question of entrance, not exit. Much simpler."

"Skip it, Joe!"

"He has no science," Stoneman observed to Mark. "I was about to speak of dynamite. Efficacious in some cases, but I think not here. It is apt to destroy bones. While bones do not enter into the case of Mrs. Lacey, we must show some consideration for the relatives and good neighbours who have gone before and will now share the earth with their old friend. No, no dynamite. I suggest a nice fire, if they haven't thought of it themselves."

Morey tramped out of the room. Stoneman watched his exit with twinkling eyes. "That's the only way I can tease him," he confided. "He doesn't like graves. When he is rude to me, as he was to-night, I always bring the talk around to graves. But I do not mean that—about the fire. . . . Now, my boy, look at this!" He held out a photograph of a pile of stones and rubble. "Beautiful?"

Mark looked closer. It was still a pile of rubble to him and a poor likeness at that. "What is it?"

"Troy! Literally Troy! That crumbling wall, that heap of barren stone! That's Troy, the greatest city of romance the world has ever known. Schliemann found that, against opposition and in spite of limited funds. Everybody thought he was crazy, but he believed in himself. He believed. A German, but a sound fellow." His eyes actually filled as he worshipped the dim little print. "I could find something too," he murmured, "I could find something too."

"Sure you could," Mark said. "Sure you will. But you've got to be patient for a bit. By the time you finish your book the war may be over and you can take the first boat out for Greece!"

"Yes, yes. We'll occupy ourselves with the book. We'll begin to-morrow. Do you know my subject for the first chapter? Walls! Not graves or warriors' weapons, which were necessities instead of gestures, but walls! The first man who dragged a clumsy stone from its earthy cradle and stood it in a new place may have thought he was building a wall but he was beginning an avalanche. Perhaps he wanted privacy for his people, a sheltered spot where his women could walk in safety. But. . . . ! Have you ever wanted to climb a wall, my boy, simply because it was there ? Of course you have. Even when you knew what lay behind it ; a field, a bit of garden, perhaps a fruit tree. If the place had been open you'd have passed it by without a thought. But walled—ah ! You scramble over, wasting your energy and ruining your trousers, and help yourself to the fruit although you neither want or need it. You see what I mean, my boy ? That first little stone, so rudely disturbed, has spawned our Maginot Lines."

Mark felt a surge of affection for the old man.

"You've got something there, Professor," he said. "From now on I'll never put a wall around anything. I'll even make a bet about your city of romance. I bet Helen was beautiful only because they had to climb a wall to get her back."

Stoneman chuckled. He dragged out more photographs and prints and kept Mark talking until mid-night. He walked the floor and pounded the table. He confessed to a belief that he could find a lost island off the French coast. He could do anything. He was perfectly happy, but when they went upstairs to bed he asked Mark to lock him in as usual.

There was a note from Violet pinned hopefully on Mark's pillow. If he still wanted to see her she was waiting in the small sitting room near the back stairs. He found her upright in a chair, trying to keep awake.

"You a good girl," he said, "and I won't keep you long. Now tell me, did you ever see any of these pills in this house ? " He held up the bottle.

"Not the bottle, but the pills I did. Mrs. Laccy sent

me down to her place once to get some for her. I put them in a little box she gave me and brought them back. She kept them on her bed table."

" Anybody else know she had them here ? "

" Well, I guess everybody. I mean it wasn't any secret. She used to talk about not sleeping right and taking stuff to help her."

" Fine. Now try to remember something else for me. What was Mrs. Lacey doing when you girls left for the movies ? "

" Packing. That's all she was doing. Packing."

" Did she plan to pack all evening or not ? I mean, was there anything in her plans that would cause her to leave the kitchen or her room, even for a few minutes ? "

" Well—lemme—yes ! There was a big wooden box that had her photographs and pictures in it. It was too heavy to lift easy and no way to get a grip on it without knocking it around and maybe breaking the glass on the pictures. Is that what you mean ? "

" How in the world do I know ! Go on, Violet, before I choke it out of you ! "

" Well, she looked for a piece of rope to bind it with, but there wasn't any down cellar. So she said she'd have to go out to the garage and get some from Perrin if he had any."

" And did she go ? "

" I wouldn't really know. Florrie and me left before then." She'd been watching him nervously, and now when his face cleared she began to smile. " I know it's a terrible secret, but if I've helped you any I wish you'd tell me."

He was tall enough to pat her on the head, which he did. " You've helped a lot. Now keep your nice little mouth shut tight and say nothing. Not to anybody. Not even to Florrie. Someday I may ask you to tell it all over again, but until then, play dumb. Do you think you can play dumb ? "

" You ! " she giggled happily.

He waited while she tiptoed down the hall, and when she was out of sight he followed ; but on the way he stopped at the linen closet and verified the contents of the chest. His big case was still there, undisturbed.

The snow was banked high against the windows when he woke the next morning. In the bathroom, where he'd left one window open for ventilation, there was a fine drift on the floor and an even finer puddle. Stoneman minced about in velvet slippers, full of benovelent complaints and clucking like a happy hen. They went down to breakfast together.

A change had come over the whole house. It felt alive and warmly human. The children could be heard stamping around in the nursery and Violet's high heels clicked cheerfully as she flounced from table to sideboard.

"What makes everybody so gay?" Mark asked Morey.

"Everybody isn't," Morey answered. "Florrie's getting the children ready for a drive and to look at her you'd think they were going in a tumbrel. Perrin's down in the kitchen, fighting with a stonemason." He snatched a boiled egg from the bowl Violet was handing to Mark. "Violet would like to be in the kitchen too, but I dragged her away. The stonemason is young and I am cruel." Violet tossed her head.

"The kids are going Christmas shopping," he went on. "In an old sleigh we found in the stables. They've been singing ' Jingle Bells.' Want to go along ? "

" No thanks. I'm working."

" I'll believe that when I see it," Morey grinned. " But though absent you'll not be forgotten. I examined the lists and you're down for a tube of shaving cream, ten-cent size. You'll be here for Christmas, won't you ? "

Mark looked at Stoneman.

" He'll be here as long as I am," Stoneman said. " He believes in me."

Morey looked impish. "I've been thinking about last night, Joe. I'm going to give you some money. Not as much as you want, because that's bad for you, but enough to keep you happy. Say half the cost of an expedition now, and the other half when the war's over ?"

"Thank you," Stoneman said quietly. He signalled to Violet, who dragged back his heavy chair. "I'll be upstairs when you're ready, my boy. Don't hurry."

"The old fellow gets a bang out of having you around. I get a bang out of it myself."

"Thanks," Mark said. He hesitated, then, "Look. You and your wife are my hosts. If there's anything I can do for her—cheer her up—why, I'll try."

"I appreciate that, but there's nothing anybody can do. It's up to Laura herself. She can pull out of it if she wants to. I think she will; she's a sensible woman at heart."

They left the table and went upstairs. In the upper hall they met Florrie coming out of the broom closet with a dustpan and brush. When she saw them she ducked inside again and made a great pretence of looking for something else. Mark's cheerful hail brought a mumbled response. For a moment he caught a glimpse of her averted face ; it was pinched and hollow-eyed.

"Poor old Florrie," Morey whispered. "The chess lung must have been a dud. I wonder if we ought to raise her wages again ? She's doing too much."

"They're all doing too much. Why don't you get another woman in ?"

"I will. I'll speak to Perrin." He went on down the hall to his wife's room, and Mark turned into his own.

He thought there was more than fatigue bothering Florrie. She'd been afraid to meet them, afraid even to look at them. That averted face was meant to hide something, but what was it ? In another kind of girl it might mean guilt or shame. But in Florrie ? Ridiculous.

Florrie was a prim little mouse.

Stoneman was sitting by the window, scratching happily away with a bad pen. He didn't even know it was bad. They worked steadily until lunch. Mark roughed out two chapters and Stoneman contentedly rewrote and polished his opening paragraph. They were both startled when Violet came in with a tray holding their lunch.

"You'll have to eat up here again," she said stiffly. "I hate to ask you, but it's easier for us that way. Not that anybody cares how much you do around here.' Her mouth was set in a grim line.

Mark looked thoughtful. "What's happened to you since breakfast ? You look venomous."

"I don't know what that means," she said. "I'm mad, that's all. Plain mad."

Stoneman shook a reproving head. "Dogs go mad, people become annoyed," he said.

"Well, I'm mad and I can bark to prove it. I didn't do a thing out of the way and neither did Florrie. But he won't get me crying ! He's no better than I am."

"Came the revolution," murmured Mark. "What's eating you, Violet ? And what's the matter with Florrie ? Are you kids getting nerves too ? "

"Nerves ! He's the one with the nerve ! All a girl does is her duty and someone who isn't a bit better than she is tries to make me look like I did wrong."

Stoneman closed his eyes and winced. " Settle this," he said to Mark.

"Who tried to make you look like you did wrong ? " Mark asked.

"Perrin. Day in and day out Florrie takes the waste-baskets from all the rooms and stands them in the hall. And I come along with a big bag that I empty them in and carry it down to the back yard and burn it in the incinerator, day in and day out. But to-day it's wrong."

" Why ? "

" Don't ask me. He just looks at Florrie and me and says where is the wastepaper and we tell him we're burning it up like always. And he rolls his eyes and says—I wouldn't repeat the word—and walks out talking to himself. Florrie is upset worse than I."

" Yes. Mark looked thoughtful. " Did Perrin tell you what was wrong ? "

" Not him. He walks out in the yard and puts the fire out and grubs around in the mess. Dirtied himself all up too, and I'm glad."

" Well ? " urged Mark.

" Well, I'm sort of curious, so I go out and ask him if anything is lost. He don't answer that. He says was the trash from Mrs. Morey's room burned with that lot, and I say certainly but if he thinks there was anything valuable in it he's crazy. Because Florrie went over every bit herself like she always does because once Mrs. Morey dropped her chequebook in by mistake. I told him there wasn't anything in this lot but facial tissues and newspapers and a cigarette package with one cigarette in it. I told him I took the cigarette but I'd buy her a whole carton if that's the way she felt about it. He calmed down after that. But then he went after Florrie all over again and she cried."

Stoneman opened his eyes. " Didn't he ever tell you what was missing ? "

" No. And if you want to know what I think, I think it was a piece of jewellery and she's afraid to tell her."

" If it's jewellery," Stoneman said, " then there's nothing to worry about. It's all insured. I shouldn't worry in any case."

Violet was slowly, if reluctantly, thawing. " Then you don't think I ought to complain to Mr. Morey himself ? "

" No, I wouldn't do that." Stoneman smiled at her. " He has enough on his mind. And when to-morrow comes you'll have forgotten all about this—upset. . . .

Now, what have we here ? " He dipped a soup spoon into the bowl before him. " Violet, but this is delicious ! What do you call it ? "

" Pot aw few," said Violet. " More in the kitchen." She made a beaming exit.

" You handled that very well," Mark approved. " Next thing you know you'll have her singing again. But what's behind this tragic burning of the trash ? "

" I don't know." Stoneman sighed. " Probably nothing. One servant bullying another."

After lunch they worked for another hour and Mark carried the tray down to the pantry. Apparently Florrie was still nursing her wounds in seclusion, but Violet was much in evidence, checking over a shopping list with Perrin. She was being very hoity-toity ; still mad, like a dog.

" Two trips in one day is plain ridiculous," she told Perrin. " You could just as well have bought these things when you took the children. And don't say breast of veal to me again. I want a hen turkey. Anybody'd think you were paying the bills yourself. Breast of veal ! "

At last Perrin closed his book and took up his hat. " Will that be all ? " he asked quietly.

" No." Violet pulled a crumpled ten-dollar bill from her pocket. " This is a little errand that Florrie and I hoped to do ourselves, but we're both too upset "—she gave him a black look—" we're both too upset, naturally. You will please go to the florist and order a nice wreath for Mrs. Lacey. Nothing's too good. And here's the card to go with it." She handed over bill and card. " Something pink, if they got it," she called after him.

" I feel kind of sorry for that guy, Violet," Mark said.

" I fixed him good, didn't I ? " she glowed. " Did you want something, Mr. East ? "

" No. My boss is taking a nap. Can't I help you ? "

" No, sir, you can't. You go take a nap yourself or read a

book. Go in the library. Nobody won't bother you and I'll call if you're wanted."

He did both. He read a book and fell asleep.

CHAPTER SIX

HE woke in the dim, firelit room when the clock struck six. The comparative peace of the morning was gone and that old, wary feeling had returned ; he felt someone watching him. He lay quiet for a minute, without moving, and listened for a sound of breathing other than his own. Little by little his eyes adjusted themselves to the dark and then the dull ring of a glass set down on a table told him where to look. He made out Stoneman's figure in an armchair on the far side of the fire. He sat up.

Stoneman laughed softly. " Tell me, is it youth or a good conscience that lets you sleep like that ?"

"Neither." He sauntered over, turning on lamps as he went. "I was probably drugged." Stoneman blinked and said nothing. "What's that you're drinking ? " he went on. " Sherry ? "

"The glass is designed for sherry. I'm using it for Scotch. Help yourself."

He did, and noticed an extra glass, partly filled. "Company ? "

"Jim's. Laura sent for him." Stoneman took out a handkerchief and patted his forehead. "Warm in here."

It wasn't warm ; if anything it was cooler than it should have been. Mark watched closely. "When I woke up I felt as if—I mean, is anything wrong ? "

"Nothing unusual. When it grows dark, she—sends for him."

"Can't anything be done about that ? She'll ruin her husband's life and her children's too."

"That's what we tell her." Stoneman closed the subject with a shrug and deliberately turned in his chair. His mood had changed abruptly with the mention of Laura's name, and he met all further attempts at conversation with a grunt.

Mark gave up, and until dinner was announced they sat without speaking. Stoneman looking into the fire and re-filling his glass too often and Mark turning the pages of a book he didn't want to read.

Stoneman's lapse into gloom had apparently spread to Perrin. Even Morey noticed it. "Are you warming up to be a pallbearer?" he asked. Perrin twisted his mouth into a smile.

"I question the taste that prompted that remark," observed Stoneman. He looked as if he would like to throw the knife he held in his hand, and Morey, his handsome face suddenly flushing, looked as if he would return it, accurately.

"The girls have chipped in for a wreath," Mark said hastily, "and now they're wondering if they can both go to the funeral. I more or less promised to ask."

"Everybody's going," Morey said. "It's a gala. More bad taste. So they bought a wreath, huh?"

"Perrin got it for them. Are they pleased, Perrin?"

The smile that had been no more than a fixture softened into the real thing. "They are, sir. The florist informed me that Violet telephoned shortly before my arrival there, to make sure that none of her money was diverted into beer. He described his stock over the phone and she made her own selection. All I did was pay for it and get a receipt."

"What did she get?"

"A small cross composed of pink carnations, with a ribbon streamer lettered in purple plush." He deftly served Stoneman with a piece of turkey breast. "The plush

says, WE WILL MEET AGAIN. It will, I understand, knock
the living daylights out of Miss Pond's chrysanthemums."

"And out of the Moreys' chaste lilies, I fear. Like-
wise out of Joe's modest violets. Frankly, I thought Joe
would run to more than violets. You and Mrs. Lacey had
an understanding, didn't you, Joe?"

Stoneman shook with suppressed fury.

"I mean she used to fuss with your food and fight your
battles with the laundry," Morey soothed. "That's all
I meant, Joe. Just a little joke."

"A poor time for a joke—on the eve of that unfortunate
woman's funeral," Stoneman snapped.

Mark intervened again. "You said everybody was
going. You don't mean the children too? I thought they
—didn't know anything about it."

"They don't. We're leaving them with Mrs. Wilcox
in Bear River. Sheriff's wife. Laura insists on joining
the mourners, nobody knows why, so we have to park them
somewhere."

When they reached the coffee, he asked Perrin to serve
it in the library. "And no brandy," he added, with a
calculating look at Stoneman.

After quantities of black coffee had worked a soothing effect, Morey engaged Stoneman in a complicated game
of double solitaire; in a short time the two were bickering
amiably. Mark collected a few novels and excused himself. He was afraid Stoneman would object, but to his surprise and pleasure the old man insisted on finishing his game.

"You run along, my boy," he said. "Enjoy yourself in
your own way. As for me—I may even play another game.
Two games. I feel so much better. Do you know, I
remind myself of a barometer. Up and down, up and
down. We'll send you a nice toddy, won't we, Jim?"

Drunk as a fool, thought Mark. But good-natured.
He'd be out cold in another hour. True to instructions,

Perrin had omitted the brandy, but Stoneman had provided himself with a bottle of Scotch and Morey wasn't doing anything about it.

Mark gathered up his books and departed. Although it was only nine o'clock there was complete silence on the second floor. The hall lights had not been turned on and, what was more unusual, his bed had not been turned down. Evidently Florrie was still sulking. He had meant to ask Perrin about the wastepaper episode, but had forgotten. Just as well, he figured. It was Perrin's job to keep the girls in line and he might resent interference. Florrie had probably made off with a pair of misplaced nylons.

He bathed and settled in bed, his books piled on the table beside him. He guessed that a half-hour had passed when Perrin knocked discreetly and entered with his toddy. The fragrant, steaming mug must have held a pint.

" How's the game ? " he asked idly.

" They are—fairly well matched, sir, though I believe Mr. Stoneman is slightly ahead. Mr. Morey is encouraging him to win."

" Does that mean a long session ? "

" Oh, no, sir. Mr. Morey has instructed me to lock up at ten-thirty."

Whether it was the book or the toddy he didn't know, but soon he was overwhelmingly sleepy. When he found himself re-reading the same page for the third time he decided he had had enough and turned off his light. Let Morey lock Stoneman in to-night. The bathroom was dark, as he had left it. If Stoneman wanted the night light on he'd have to take care of it himself. He burrowed into the pillows and went to sleep.

Outside the snow fell softly and silently, covering the tracks of nocturnal animals and deadening the fall of feet.

He slept on. . . . Something travelled lightly over his chest and came to rest on his shoulder. He moved uneasily. It came again, faint but insistent, and this time it stopped on his forehead. He opened his eyes to darkness.

There was a black shape beside his bed, between him and the open window, cutting off the air, blotting out the faint grey of the snow-filled night.

For an eternity he counted his heartbeats and then, slowly, he became aware of a soft, rhythmic sound, coming with painful regularity. At first he thought it was his own laboured breathing, but it was too fast for that. Then he knew it came from that shapeless mass. He knew it wasn't Stoneman. It was too big. He was afraid to reach for his lamp.

Suddenly the room took form again in the grey darkness. The thing had moved. He could see the window and the footboard. It moved awkwardly and silently, around the footboard to the side of the bed nearest the door. It bent over him. He could see an arm. This time his breath came in a rattling gasp. He gathered strength to shout. Fingers touched his throat. They were wet.

"Don't," he managed to whisper.

They withdrew. Then close to his ear a voice whispered his name. He recognized Violet.

"Don't make any noise," she said, "and don't turn on the light. Florrie's gone."

He sat up. "Sit on the edge of the bed," he whispered. "Here." He put out his hand, found hers, and drew her down beside him. He knew that she wore a coat over her nightdress and that her hands were clammy. He felt the bed give under her weight. He put his face close to hers. "Tell me again. You say Florrie's gone? Where?"

A hot tear fell on his hand. "I don't know. I don't know what to do and I don't know who to tell. Mr. East, it's three o'clock and her coat's gone too!"

He got out of bed. "Stay where you are. I'll be right back." He groped quietly through the bathroom to Stoneman's door, feeling his way carefully. But Stoneman's door was locked. He put his ear against the crack and listened. The old man was asleep ; at least he could hear the rasping snore he had come to associate with him. He closed the bathroom door as he came back and turned on his bed lamp, carefully draping a scarf over the shade. He drew the blinds.

" Nobody will see us," he said. " Not that I give a damn ; and we won't be heard if we keep our voices down. Now what's this—about Florrie ? "

Violet, shuddering, told all she knew, which was very little. She and Florrie had gone to bed at ten. Florrie had been very quiet—" not a bit like herself, but you know she was upset all day." Violet had tried to cheer her up, but it wasn't any use. Even the morning glories on the wallpaper, that Florrie never failed to smell when she came into the room, had lost their charm.

" I turned down her bed for her," whimpered Violet, " and showed her how there was a little bunch of glories hand-embroidered on the blanket cover, but she didn't even look. I asked her what the matter was and told her if she was worrying about that trash-basket business she was crazy. She said maybe she was crazy. She didn't feel sick anywhere because I asked her. I read a magazine for a little while and then I put my light out. She never turned hers on at all. I guess I went to sleep right off, Mr. East, but I never would of if I'd known she was in any real trouble. I just thought she was blue. About Mrs. Lacey. Then I woke up. Don't ask me why—I just woke up sudden. Her bed is closest to the window and I saw it was empty. Sick after all, I said to myself, and I went into our private bathroom. But she wasn't there. I even went down the hall to Mrs. Morey's room and listened, but it was all dark and quiet. And she wasn't in the night nursery. I didn't know what else to do, so I went back. She might of been in Mrs. Morey's room, sleeping there, I said to myself, so I looked in her closet for her dressing gown. Florrie "—Violet stroked her shabby cotton tweed —" Florrie has a regular dressing gown of a hundred per cent. pure all wool. It was hanging on the hook, but her coat and hat was gone. And a dress. She was all dressed, shoes and all, when she—went."

Mark patted her hand and held it. It was a long speech for Violet, and it left a chill around his heart.

" Should we get Mr. Perrin ? "

" No. Not right away. Let me think. How long ago was this ? "

" You mean when I found out she was gone ? About ten minutes. It's a little after three now and I came right here when I saw her coat—her coat——"

" Violet, nobody gets all dressed up in the middle of the night to go out and meet trouble," he lied. " She may have been so fed up with the job that she simply walked off."

" Without telling me ? "

" Why not, if she was overtired ? People do funny things then. Or, how's this ? Maybe she went out to meet a boy, and lost track of the time. That's happened before, too. She'll probably come back as gay as a lark. Why, she may even be back now ! "

" I'll go look ! " Violet slipped out of the room like a little ghost, her bare feet making no sound, her cheap little nightdress gleaming pinkly around her ankles.

Mark forced himself not to think as he pulled a pair of trousers over his pyjamas and got into a heavy sweater and shoes. He slid a flashlight into his pocket. He was taking a coat from the closet when Violet returned.

" Not there ? " He didn't have to ask. He saw it on her trembling mouth.

" N-no. . . . Are you going somewhere, Mr. East ? "

" Only downstairs, to have a look around. Did Florrie have a key ? "

" There's one hanging on a nail in the kitchen that we take if we're going to be late.   I could show you."

" Get something on, then.   Shoes, and a sweater if you have one handy.   I'll wait for you outside."

He turned off the lamp and stood in the dimly lit hall. Violet's pitiful and immaculate nightdress touched him as few things had.   He thought he would never forget the worn hand stroking the shoddy coat and the pride in her voice as she described Florrie's hundred per cent. pure all wool.

She came up silently to join him, wearing battered sneakers and an old skirt under the coat.

" We'll use those back stairs you told me about," he whispered.

" We can, but we'd have to go by Perrin's room—he's sleeping in the house since the fire.   You said we didn't want him."

" Not yet we don't.   Well, we'll go the front way. . As quiet as two mice.   We don't want to do anything to embarrass Florrie in case this turns out to be girl meets boy."

They reached the first landing without a sound when Mark stopped suddenly and looked back.   A light flashed down into their faces and a voice thick with sleep and rage said, " What the hell ! "

Mark put a protecting hand on Violet's shoulder. " Come on down, Mr. Morey," he called softly.   " No noise, please."

Morey joined them, flash-lamp in hand, clutching a bath-robe over his shoulders.   "What the hell goes on here!" he glared.   " Violet, you're fired. 'As for you, East——"

" Wait.   Come on down to the library.   I've got something to tell you."

Morey followed stiffly.   " It had better be good," he commented.   When they reached the library Mark turned on one light.   " We don't want to rouse the house," he

said coldly. " You'll understand when you hear what I
have to say. Florrie has disappeared."

" What do you mean ? "

" I mean she's not in her room or anywhere else in the
house, as far as we know. And her outdoor clothes are
missing. It may be a harmless jaunt with a boy friend and
it may not. Violet came to me for help and we were about
to check on the kitchen key. We didn't want to disturb
you unless it was necessary, but now that you're here you
can take over. After apologies, of course."

Morey's face lost its angry look ; annoyance took its
place. " Sorry," he muttered, " but you can't blame me.
It looked funny. . . . Disappeared ! In my eye ! She
was too tired to sleep in my wife's room. Upset my wife
by refusing point-blank. But she's not too tired to go off
with some man. Who is it, Violet ? Don't stall—you know."

Violet drew herself up. " My cousin Edgar is Florrie's
friend and she didn't go off to meet him. He wouldn't
ask her to do such a thing. She was blue, and she looked
terrible, and if she off on her own accord it was because
she had to. Or else somebody made her go."

" Well." Morey looked uncertain. " Well, what do
you suggest ? That key you were talking about. Let's
look for that."

They found the key hanging on its nail beside the kitchen
door. Morey took it down, looked at it as if he expected
it to tell him something, and put it back.

" Could she get in without it ? " Mark asked.

" No," wept Violet. " No. You could get out all right,
but you couldn't get in. She's down in the cellar with her
throat cut."

" Wearing hat, coat, and goloshes ? " Mark snorted con-
vincingly. " Don't be silly." But Morey was already
on his way and he followed him. The cellar, open, orderly,
and well lit, was empty. Morey went into the wine

room and came back with a dusty bottle of brandy.

" You probably won't like the taste of this," he said to Violet, " but you're going to have a swig just the same. Take her back to the library, East, and get some down her throat. I'm going to wake Perrin."

" Any ideas ? " Mark asked in an undertone.

" I'm beginning to think it wasn't a harmless jaunt. She'd have taken the key with her. I don't think she meant to come back."

" But why ? "

Morey looked at Violet, sitting disconsolately on the bottom step. " She was in a lousy mood all day. I noticed it, but I don't know why. Maybe the boy friend jilted her. She'd consider herself disgraced. These kids haven't much stability—or sense. And then again, she may have been in what is quaintly known as ' trouble.' There are lots of places around here when she could jump." He went on upstairs to wake Perrin.

Mark took Violet to the library and settled her in a chair. He gave her brandy and she took it without protest. She was too frightened to notice anything. He built up the fire and waited.

When Morey came back with Perrin they were both fully dressed.

" I've told Perrin," he said. " He doesn't know anything about it. Now, listen. Somebody's got to go out with the car and look around. And somebody's got to stay here. Who'll it be ? "

Mark said he would do whatever the others decided. He wanted to stay, but he was afraid to show his hand. They might guess what he had in mind. With Morey and Perrin out of the way and Violet as his guide and ally he could comb the house from top to bottom, something he had wanted to do ever since that first morning when Stoneman sat in front of a fire and shivered with fear.

It was Perrin who settled that. "I think we should all go, Mr. Morey," he said calmly. "I'm sure Violet can manage here alone. I know she can if she tries."

Violet gave a faint scream. "I couldn't! I'd die! Oh, Mr. East, don't leave me!"

"If Mrs. Morey should wake," Perrin went on, "which is extremely unlikely, Violet need only say that we have gone to Bear River with Florence, who is ill."

"That's it! Back to your own room, Violet. Sleep or sit up, I don't care. We'll be back before you know it."

"I'm afraid."

"Of what? A sick woman, two children, and an old man?"

"But somebody—somebody else might be—here."

Perrin spoke sharply. "There's nobody else here, Violet! I locked this house myself to-night. Nobody got in. Somebody got out, that's all."

She looked at Mark, dumbly.

"I think you'll be all right," he said. "Why don't you lie down on that sofa in our hall? Mr. Stoneman is the only one likely to wake. You can kid him along."

"He won't wake," Morey said. "Half a bottle of Scotch."

She finally agreed, with her eyes on Mark's, like a lamb pleading with the butcher. She went to the front door and watched them depart. Then she fastened the chain and went to her room and dressed, weeping silently.

Perrin drove slowly down the mountain. The snow had stopped, but the road was deep in drifts. It was dangerous, but not one of them thought of that then. They left the car a dozen times en route and turned their flashlights where the trees and underbrush were thickest. Once, Morey stood before a soft white mount and gently prodded with his stick while the wind cried and Mark held his breath. It was only snow. Someone gave a shuddering sigh. Mark didn't know who it was; it might have been himself.

At the bend in the drive they looked back. Ivy's snowman stood like a leering ghost against a cyclorama of dark pines. They walked slowly back to the car and drove on.

"No footprints except the ones we're making now," Morey said. "Florrie must have left some sort of trail—unless she flew. Does anybody know when the snow stopped? It was a regular blizzard when I went to bed."

"It stopped shortly after twelve," Perrin said.

"How do you know?" Morey asked sharply. "You locked up and went to your room when Mr. Stoneman and I did. That was ten-thirty."

"I had some letters to write, sir."

Mark spoke thoughtfully. "Not a single footprint other than our own, no car tracks, no broken branches. That means Florrie was out of the house and off the grounds well before twelve, if Perrin has the time right."

"I'm not sure she is off the grounds," Morey said. "But I don't see how we can do much more to-night. We need daylight and more men."

They came out into the road before the station and Perrin stopped the car. Mark looked at his watch; it was nearly five. The little lane of silent houses stretched up the hill to the lonely lamp that marked the end of the way.

"Look!" Morey's voice cracked out suddenly. Startled, they turned and followed the direction of his pointing finger. It had been dark before, but now a warm yellow light glimmered behind a thicket of bushes beyond the station. "What's that?"

Mark knew. He could visualize the room the light came from. "They've heard us and someone's carried a lamp to the window. It's Mrs. Lacey's."

"But she—isn't she——"

"They brought her home for this last night. Her friends are sitting up."

"Oh." Morey smiled wanly. "This is beginning to

get me too. . . . Say, do you suppose we could go over there and ask them if they saw or heard—no, I guess that wouldn't do. But how about the girl's family? Do you think we might drive over to Bear River? She may be with them."

"If she is," Mark said, "she's all right. If she isn't, they'll need their sleep to help them face what's coming. Anyway, how could she get there? Trains and buses don't run that late."

"Somebody may have picked her up. All arranged beforehand." They trudged back to the car. "What in the name of this and that am I going to tell Violet?" Morey went on. "Hysterics all over the house, nobody to cook and clean. Blast the day I ever came here!"

Mark made no comment.

Perrin had a suggestion. "I'll take care of Violet, sir. At least for the present. Then in the morning, if Florence's family has had no word, we might inquire among her friends. Discreetly."

"Discreetly! In this hole?"

"If we don't report her absence ourselves, sir, her family will. And if I may say so, it will look better if we make the first move."

They drove home slowly, under the arched and snow-bound trees. When Violet opened the door, Perrin took her by the arm and led her away, talking quietly. She made no sound.

Morey and Mark had a drink and went back to bed. Later they both confessed it was not to sleep. Morey sat by his window, staring at the night. Mark lay on his back, staring at the ceiling. Only when the sky turned light did they close their eyes.

Violet blurted out the story of Florrie's disappearance to Stoneman when he came down to breakfast. He was her first audience and she looked for horrified attention and emotional response. What she got was a look of sudden surprise which quickly passed. He made it clear that the prospect of poor service was infinitely more upsetting. He had to wait while she plugged in the percolator for coffee and made toast, and when she told him she hadn't had time to boil eggs he was openly hostile.

" Gone off with some man," he said crossly. " Exactly the sort of thing she'd do. But why should that effect my eggs ? I'm old—I must be properly nourished."

" Gone off with some man ! " Violet snatched his empty orange-juice glass. " That's what everybody says. Well, let me tell you something, when a girl goes off with a fellow she takes her clothes with her. Here's your toast."

" Probably married by now," continued Stoneman, " and forgotten your existence. . . . Aren't you going to butter it ? "

She did, but with a scant hand. " You haven't any heart, Mr. Stoneman. She'd never get married without me. We've had it planned ever since we were kids. I'm to stand up with her in dusty pink. Something's happened to her. You know yourself that she was all upset yesterday. I told you so, and you even said you'd do something about it. Short memory you've got. You was sympathetic enough then.

" I'd be more sympathetic now if I had a few soft-boiled eggs," he suggested.

" And everybody was out all last night looking for her. Everybody but you. You slept through it all. Poor Mr. East——"

Stoneman twisted in his chair. " Here's poor Mr. East now." Mark came in wearily.

" If you don't mind waiting, Mr. East, I'll cook some eggs for you," Violet said pointedly.

" Never mind." He sank into a chair. " Mr. Morey's been talking to Florrie's family on the 'phone. They don't know where she is." To Stoneman. " Violet tell you the latest ? "

"She did. I don't pretend to understand the excitement. What's this about searching all night?"

"Morey's afraid she may have done something—foolish. He—well?"

Morey joined them. "Her brother and some of her friends are coming up here to search the woods. I've notified the police. Her family asked me to. Coffee, Violet, then you go up and help Mrs. Morey with the children. And no talking, understand?"

Violet gave him the coffee and left reluctantly. Grief and fear had left her limp and red-eyed, but she could still enjoy her troubles.

"You're making a mistake, Jim," Stoneman said. "You're letting Violet and all these other people think this may be a tragedy. That's bad."

"Well, what would you do?"

"What I've already done. Pretend a lack of interest or concern. You must keep up the household morale. Actually, I'm as anxious as you are, but in spite of my fears I still hope for a happy ending."

Mark drew another cup of coffee. "Happy or not," he said evenly, "what are you going to do with Violet?"

"Huh?" Morey looked startled.

"Violet. Is she going to be another casualty? How can she handle this place without help? Perrin is all right, but he's not enough. Who's going to make the beds, clean the baths, plan and cook three meals a day, take care of the kids? And I seem to remember that your wife requires a lot of special attention."

Morey answered stiffly, "I've already asked Perrin to wire his agency for help, but he seems to think it's useless."

"It probably is. No woman in her right mind would spend a night in this house after she knew what happened to Lacey and Florrie."

"And exactly what did happen to Florrie?"

" I don't know. But I'm not as optimistic as Mr. Stoneman. I don't look for a happy ending."

Morey's voice was like ice when he answered. " Don't you think you're stepping out of line a little, Mr. East ? You're Stoneman's secretary, not mine. When I want your opinion, I'll ask for it."

" I may be only Stoneman's secretary but I notice I'm the one your servants come to when they're in trouble. If you want me out of the way, say so."

" Mr. East ! Jim ! " Stoneman fluttered his hands and looked horrified. " You don't know what you're talking about, either of you ! These dreadful days ! But you must control yourselves. Jim, apologize to Mr. East at once. He has been a great help to all of us. We need him."

" Sorry," muttered Morey. " But what the hell am I expected to do ? "

" Ask Mr. East what he thinks. He knows more about the house than you do. Ask his advice, and follow it. Believe me, you won't go wrong."

Morey was still ruffled, but he managed a conciliatory shrug. " I ask you, East. Stay here and see us through this, and then we'll all get out."

" All right. Now—you know as well as I do that you'll never get a servant from this neighbourhood. Or from outside, for that matter. You might persuade somebody in New York to come up and take the job, but she'd walk out on you within twenty-four hours. Somebody in Crestwood would see to it that she heard about the others."

"You seem pretty sure that Florrie is sunk without a trace."

" Not without a trace. I think we'll find more of Florrie than we did of Mrs. Lacey. You've got to admit it looks ugly."

" It does. But why heckle me ? Lacey upset a lamp or a stove. That's Davenport's fault. Even his pal Scott said so. And we don't know about Florrie yet. I still think she got herself into a delicate situation and has done something about it. She looked like the devil yesterday."

"I—" Mark started to say something about the waste-paper episode and then thought better of it. "I noticed," he said. "But what I'm building up to is this. If Violet isn't going to crack up, she needs help. And I think I know where to get it. But I want your wife's permission first."

"You can't get it. She can't see anyone. She's—indisposed."

"I'll give you another piece of advice that you haven't asked for. She belongs in a hospital."

"No," said Morey, surprisingly calm. "She doesn't. She'll be all right if we leave her alone. Why do you need her permission? Why won't mine do?"

"Maybe it will. I'll think it over. In the meantime, we'd better join this searching party. Make talk if we don't."

Stoneman coughed nervously. "What about Mrs. Lacey's funeral? Won't it 'make talk' if we aren't represented there? Oh, my poor book! All this is too distracting."

"I'll call Miss Pond and explain about the funeral," Mark said. "If Violet still wants to go we'll get her there."

Perrin came in quietly. "They've found her hat," he said. "On the footpath that comes out of Miss Petty's house."

"Was she going up or down?" Morey asked.

"They can't tell, sir. No footprints."

"I'm going to make that 'phone call," Mark said. "May I talk to you later, Mr. Stoneman?"

"Certainly," said Stoneman. He looked faintly uneasy. "But whatever you do is satisfactory to me, my boy. Don't ask my permission for anything. Just do as you think best."

"I'll see you in your room in five minutes then," Mark said. He walked briskly out.

Morey gave a low admiring whistle. "Who's boss?" he murmured.

Stoneman smiled. "I am. And don't forget that for an instant, my friend. I am. There was something else, too—ah, I remember now. Did you, by any chance, send those violets to Mrs. Lacey with my card? You did? Thoughtful of you, Jim, very thoughtful. I will do the same for you one day." Still smiling, he trotted out of the room.

The Bear River operator, who also handled the Crestwood calls, told Mark that Miss Pond was not at home and that her messages were being cared for by Mr. Partridge at the station. She put him through to Amos.

Bessy and Beulah had spent the night at Mrs. Lacey's, in company with other friends, Amos told him. They were still there. Could he do anything?

Mark told him to tell Beulah he would call on her in the late afternoon or evening. He tried to tell him about Florrie, but Amos knew all about that. The ubiquitous Ella May had a second cousin in Bear River who had seen the posse leave, and she had spread the news. Amos had persuaded Ella May to keep her lip buttoned, he said. He didn't want Bessy and Beulah to know anything about it until Ruthie had been put to rest in a seemly manner with full prayers and eulogy. He felt that Bessy and Beulah, if they heard about Florrie at the wrong time, might desert the grave and join the posse.

Mark asked him to explain the Moreys' absence to Mrs. Lacey's friends and relatives, and hung up.

When he reached Stoneman's room, Stoneman was already there, smiling, and pacing the floor. "Now what's this interview all about?" he asked jovially. "One would think really, that our positions were reversed. Even Jim was amused."

"Anything for a laugh," Mark said wearily. "Now, listen. You can pay me a week's salary and my fare to

New York, or you can answer some questions. Straight answers this time. Which is it to be ? ''

" Don't go." Stoneman meant what he said.

" Then tell me this. Do you still say Mrs. Lacey's death was accidental ? ''

" Two professional men, the coroner and the insurance adjuster, say it was. Absurd, don't you think, for a man like myself to disagree ? ''

" Evading. What do you think about Florrie ? ''

" A dreadful little girl, but I don't think she went off with a man. I suggested as much to Violet because with females of that class a shady little excursion is normal behaviour. I believe it is called living and is accompanied by giggles. I thought it would please Violet, and actually it did. She stopped crying. But I don't think that's what happened. I think Florrie's sins found her out, but what they were, I don't know."

" Florrie has neither the manners nor the morals for sinning. Or enough blood. . . . Look, Mr. Stoneman, this thing smells, and you know it. Roll your memory back to our first interview, to your letter to me. I'm a private detective and you hired me for a secretary. You tried to make me believe it was all a mistake but you didn't send me back to town ; you clung like a leech. Now do you want to know what I think ? I think you knew what you were doing all the time. You knew I was a detective and you knew I could do secretarial work in a pinch. So you hired me—for a bodyguard."

Stoneman licked his lips. " Ridiculous. I'm disappointed in you, my boy."

" No you're not. I'm doing just what you hoped I'd do. One person in this house is suddenly and violently dead, and one is missing. But you are alive and kicking. That's the way you wanted it, isn't it ? ''

" No. No. I wanted you for my book. You've seen

my notes, we've done some work. It's quite legitimate. These other things are—accidents."

"Fatal ones. And all of a sudden. Mr. Stoneman, if you're withholding information that would prove these accidents were premeditated crimes, things are going to be tough for you. And for me too, because in a way I am the law. I'm on thin ice and I don't feel so good. I think you hired me because you fear personal violence and you expect me to sit back and say nothing when violence strikes the person next to you. The Lacey business is all sewed up, thanks to a couple of good, clean-thinking guys, but if Florrie turns into a tragedy we'll all be on the spot. We'll be interviewed, and our pasts will be the well-known open book. You'll have to answer questions then and the boys who ask them won't be in your pay. They'll hound you, brother, and me. What kind of a story can I tell?"

Stoneman stood with his hands in his pockets and his lips pursed. His thoughtful gaze never moved above Mark's tie.

"Tell them you are my secretary. We have pages of notes to prove it. That is your story and it is also mine."

"They'll check my background. What story will I tell them?"

Stoneman shifted his gaze to the window and the leaden sky. A new storm was gathering; slowly and evenly it dropped its thick white curtain. "More snow," he said. "I think we shall move on shortly. . . . You will tell them I am an eccentric. You may even call me a crackpot, if that will help your position. This whole conversation is absurd, of course, because there will be no questions of any sort. Your imagination is much too healthy, my boy, but I suppose you can't help that. Still, it's a bore."

"Sorry. It's not imagination. It's—conscience."

"Dear me. Well, if your conscience tells you to play watchdog, please confine your watching to me. I pay you, and I am your first and only consideration."

"In other words, mind my own business."

"Well—yes."

Mark drew a long breath and spoke slowly and carefully. "Mr. Stoneman, you were a frightened man when I came here. You still are—I can see it in your eyes. If the thing you fear is behind these other things, I mean Lacey and Florrie, don't you see how wrong your attitude is ? "

"Do I really seem frightened ? " He smiled and patted Mark's shoulder with affection. "I'm not, really. I'm probably mad, like all men who dig in the past. And my attitude is undoubtedly wrong. It always has been. But that is my affair, not yours. Now I want you to promise me one thing, a very easy promise. Stay with me for at least another week. We can do wonders in a week. Then, if your conscience still gives you trouble, you may go back to your—legalized snooping. Will you do that ? " He laughed gaily. "I'm really not being fair with you because in another week we may all leave."

"All right," Mark agreed.

"Done ! " Stoneman clapped his hands like a child. "Now go back to the others and do what you can to help. And stop worrying. I shall stay here and work on the book. We're coming on splendidly, aren't we ? "

CHAPTER SEVEN

MARK went downstairs with the feeling that he had been neatly gagged and bound. One more week, he reflected, and he'd know where he stood. Or, one more week and he might be lying in Beulah's dream mausoleum with footprints going away from the door and none of them his. In the meantime, he had his own secret weapon, the other suitcase, hidden under the blankets. He might have to use it after all. If he did, somebody was going to get a surprise. But who ?

He went out with Morey and Perrin and joined the men who were combing the mountain. They found nothing. Once he looked back and saw Laura Morey standing at her bedroom window. He wondered what she made of all this. Would they tell her the truth, if the truth were ugly ? Or would they spin a pretty story ? Probably the latter. She looked as if another tragedy would crack her up for good. He wondered, uncomfortably, if she'd had a premonition about this one. Would she come trailing into his room again and tell him someone was dead ?

He was cold and miserable when they all went back to the house for lunch. It was a casual meal of canned soup and bread and cheese, with a tuna salad. Violet asked permission to feed assorted male relatives in the kitchen and was told to go ahead. She was also given permission to attend Mrs. Lacey's funeral, in Mrs. Morey's limousine, but her heart wasn't in it, she said. She thanked them just the same but she didn't even want to see her own pink cross.

According to Morey, his wife had stirred from her lethargy and was talking about trains and trunks. " I'm sick of the place myself," he said. " I think she'll go south with the kids. I don't care where I go just so it's far, far from here."

" Does Mrs. Morey know about Florrie ? " Mark asked.

" Certainly not. There's nothing to know. Why ? "

" Just wondering. Mr. Stoneman said something about leaving too." Stoneman had already left the table. " I didn't know it was a general idea."

" It wasn't, until this morning. He must have been talking to Laura. When she gets an idea everybody works. She probably told him to start packing this afternoon."

But nobody packed that afternoon and nobody went anywhere for some time. Mark was finishing his coffee and Morey was lighting a cigarette when the sheriff from

Bear River, who hadn't stopped for lunch, telephoned from the Crestwood station. He wanted to see Mr. Morey at once.

Amos, on one of his trips to the tool shed behind Mrs. Lacey's house, had found Florrie. She was lying behind the door, on the concrete floor. She was frozen. But that wasn't why she was dead. She'd been strangled.

Mark and Morey went down to Crestwood at once, leaving Perrin in charge of the house, with instructions to keep the news from everybody.

" We'll handle that when we come back," Morey said. " And I don't look forward to it.

There were closed cars parked at the station, their curtains drawn. A small boy in a red stocking cap, with signs of recent tears on his face, stood on the station steps and directed them to the shed. They walked up the path between heavy drifts and skirted the bare lilac bushes. Mark stopped short before Mrs. Lacey's little house.

" Not here," Morey said irritably ; " it's the shed, around at the back." Then he saw Mark's horrified face and followed his look. An icy streamer of lilies hung on Mrs. Lacey's door.

" Good God, is she still there ? " he gasped.

Mark shivered. " Yes," he whispered. " The funeral's at two. We'd better get off the path. . . . This is—this is laying it on thick."

They crowded back into the bushes and stood bareheaded while the coffin was carried out.

" It looks too small," Morey said mechanically. " Too small. She was so—so——"

" Not any more," Mark said.

A straggling little group, dressed in black, followed the flower-covered box. Amos detached himself from the end of the line.

" Come on," he said, " I can't do no more here." He led the way around to the shed.

" Bessy and Beulah ? " Mark asked.

" They went over to the church early, to get things ready. Orphans going to sing." He cleared his throat. " This other—this other happened after they left."

A handful of heavily garbed men hung around the open door to the shed. They stood aside when Morey and Mark entered.

It was an ugly picture they had to view. Florrie was lying on her back, with her small mittened hands pressed over her eyes as if she couldn't bear her last look at the world. Mark thought he knew why. Death had entered the shed in a familiar form, and like a child she had tried to blot it out. Those hands stayed stubbornly in place when the coroner's men moved her. The weather had fixed them there. He winced at the sight of that little figure, perpetually rigid with horror, eternally refusing a second glance.

" How long ? " asked Morey. " I mean, can you tell when ? "

Dr. Cummings turned from the wicker basket and wiped his hands. " Not exactly. It's too cold. I've talked to the men who were searching and we figure it must have been before twelve. You know yourself—prints. No marks around here except the ones Amos made."

" You're not thinking about Amos, for heaven's sake ! " Morey looked aghast. " That's impossible ! "

" No. Not Amos. Anyway, he's alibied up to the neck. He sat up all night with Mrs. Lacey's body. Got witnesses to prove it, too."

" Which is more than the rest of you got," Amos said quietly. " Don't waste your time worrying about me."

" What about marks on her throat ? " Mark asked.

" None. That is, no fingermarks. He must have used a cloth, a scarf, or something."

" Sheriff ? " Morey turned to the lean little man who was

whispering to Amos. " Have there been any strangers around here lately ? Tramps, or transients coming in on the train ? Partridge might know."

" Nobody comes in here that I don't know or know all about," said Amos.

" Why do you think it was a stranger ? " the sheriff asked.

Morey hesitated. " East, you remember Mr. Wilcox ? Sheriff, Mr. East. Well, I can't think of anyone else in such a connection. If she was killed in Crestwood it has to be a stranger. The only men in the place are the ones in my own household, and Partridge here. We can't consider old man Bittner. He lives in a wheel chair."

" He can get around in it, too," Amos said sourly. " Ever see that ramp he's got built from his sitting-room window to the side yard ? Sails up and down it easier than I can walk." Amos knew Bittner was innocent but he had to accuse somebody. He pointed the finger at Bittner because for the last half-hour he had seen that worthy wielding his binoculars in the kitchen window ; and because he hated the buses. " If Bittner didn't do something he seen something," he concluded.

The others ignored him. " She might have been picked up by a car, driven off somewhere, killed, and brought back here," Morey said. " There would have been time."

" No," said Wilcox. " Dr. Cummings says she was killed right here. He can tell from the position and condition of the body. He had a suicide once when he was a young fellow and the weather was like this. So he can tell. As for strangers—you're a stranger around here yourself, Mr. Morey." He turned and walked off.

Morey's jaw dropped and he stared after Wilcox. " I don't like that little man," he whispered to Mark. " He was fine about Lacey, but he's sore about this."

" Maybe he thinks two is too much. Wait here—I'll go over and see what's going on."

He spoke to Wilcox and Cummings and was back in a minute. " We're to go home," he said, " and wait for the law. Wilcox and his deputy, who, God be thanked, is Amos, are coming to give us a going-over. I'm to tell you this—we're to say nothing about how Florrie died. Just say she's dead, that's all. He's emphatic about it."

" Right. I suppose he wants to break the news and watch for guilty reactions. I wouldn't mind watching Joe's face myself. He's going to have a fit. As for Laura, if this thing starts her off again, or makes her change her mind about leaving, I'm going to go crazy. I don't see why we can't say Florrie went to the hospital with acute something or other. . . . I was afraid this might happen. I hoped to get her away before it broke."

" You wouldn't get as far as the corner. Wilcox is no dummy. Besides, I think Mrs. Morey knows—something. She was watching us from her window this morning."

" Look." Morey held back. " They're taking the body away. What are they going to do with it."

Mark took him by the arm and started of. " Buck up. It's out of our hands now. Florrie will eventually come to rest in her father's parlour and Violet can chip in again."

The unpleasant task of informing Mrs. Morey of the sheriff's interview fell to her husband. Mark wanted to do it himself ; he didn't know why, but he wanted to. He was ashamed of the eagerness he suddenly felt. He wanted to watch her hands. He offered his services to Morey, casually, and got a lifted eyebrow for an answer.

Stoneman was coming down the stairs as they entered the house. When Morey brushed by him he looked startled.

" East wants to see you," Morey said shortly.

" Now what ? " complained Stoneman. " Why did you all go off and leave me without a word ? More man hunts, I suppose. Well, you won't find anything and I think it's extremely inconsiderate——"

"Quiet," Mark said sharply. "Wait for me in the library. I want to talk to you."

He went on down to the kitchen and broke the news to Violet. When he came up ten minutes later he was feeling more dead than alive himself. There was one thing clear and certain in his mind. If this business was not satisfactorily solved by the end of the week he would stay on in the village and see it through himself. He wouldn't take another job until he knew why Florrie had refused to look at her murderer.

Stoneman, pale and curious, was waiting for him in the hall. "Laura's been screaming," he said. "At times it's quite audible."

"Yes," Mark said. "I can hear it, thank you." He led Stoneman to the library. "I think I'll give you a drink."

Stoneman glowed. "Good of you, my boy, but I was going to help myself in any case. Yes, Laura is upset again. Jim is with her."

Mark stared up at the ceiling. The screams had subsided into faint wailing. "Nice for the kids," he said. "Where are they?"

"Perrin took them out some time ago. Come now, you're trying to break something to me, aren't you? What is it?"

"They've found her body," Mark said briefly.

"Body?" Stoneman closed his eyes for a minute. "Dead?"

"Frozen," Mark said truthfully. "There's to be the usual inquest sort of thing, here, in a few minutes. You're to be ready for questioning. I told you it might happen that way," he added.

"Poor girl." Stoneman made no move to touch the drink Mark had poured. "Do they have any idea what she was doing out in that storm? And at such an unseemly hour?"

" If they have, they didn't tell me." He noted gratefully that the wailing had stopped. " She'll have to come down, you know. She'll have to face this."

" Yes. This time she'll have to face it. . . . Wait. Do you hear anything ? "

" Only a car on the drive. I suspect the inquisition is about to begin."

Mark opened the door to Wilcox. Amos trailed along behind the sheriff, representing the law of Crestwood, and in that capacity he gave Mark a cold stare. It said plainly that friendship was in abeyance and everybody was guilty until proved innocent.

Wilcox took over the library with an outward appearance of calm. He was awed by the gilt frames on the paintings, and the thick rugs felt like quagmire to feet accustomed to braided rag and straw matting. He stole a look at himself in a mirror and was delighted with his frowning reflection. If this was murder, and it certainly was, he didn't aim to let folks know it was his first. He barked at Amos ; that is to say, he worked up the feeling of a bark in his throat. It wasn't his fault that he sounded as if he were calling children from play.

Amos trotted off to round up Violet and Perrin, and Mark went upstairs to tell Morey that he and his wife would be needed shortly.

Stoneman watched these activities from his chair by the fire, a cynical smile on his face. Then, when the room was emptied, Wilcox began to question him.

Upstairs, Mark found Morey in the hall outside his wife's room. He looked as if he'd been having a bad time.

" She sent me away," he said. " And now she's locked the door. I can't make her see that she's got to come down. Wilcox won't understand it."

" No, he won't," Mark said. " I came up to tell you he'll be ready for you both shortly."

"What am I going to do? I've told her she'll be all right. I've even told her what to say but she won't—she won't——"

"You've no business telling her what to say. You ought to know that. And you'd better get her out of there before Wilcox gets sore and sends for the state's attorney. He'll do that if he thinks he's getting a run-around." He raised his voice when he said that.

"My God. . . . East—look here. You try. You offered to before. Give me a break and take this over, will you?"

"Go on down to the dining room and wait," Mark said briefly.

He watched until Morey was out of sight and then he rapped softly. "Mrs. Morey? This is Mark East. I don't want to come in. I only want to speak to you a minute, out here. I'm alone, and I won't ask you to do anything that will hurt you."

He waited. The door opened and she faced him calmly. There wasn't a sign of grief on her face. It was as beautiful and empty as a Florentine marble. He felt cheated and a little angry. Maybe she'd been screaming for a new bracelet.

She closed the door behind her.

"Yes, Mr. East? If you've come about Florrie, I've already been told."

He couldn't believe she was the same woman who had run frantically through the snow because she thought her child was cold. But she was. And now when another woman's child—a girl who had performed a hundred intimate services in her behalf—was cold in death, she had taken time to rouge her mouth. She leaned against the panelled door, half smiling, as if he had brought her flowers.

Suddenly he knew she was more powerful than he was, but he didn't know where the power lay.

"I'm sorry," he said coolly. "I thought perhaps I

could help you. You probably don't need help, but just the same I'm going to tell you what I came up to say. You've got to see Wilcox."

"I intend to. I decided that a few minutes before you knocked on my door. Mr. Morey—finally convinced me."

"If that's the case, I'll go. Sorry I intruded."

"Wait," she said. He turned back. Her face had altered in that brief moment. The alabaster skin was grey. "Do you know exactly what happened to Florrie ? "

"That's the same question you asked me once before. . . . I know as much as you do," he said carefully.

"He said she was dead. There can't be a mistake about that ? "

"No. She's quite dead. I saw her. There's no mistake. She's as dead as—Mrs. Lacey."

She closed her eyes at that and leaned more heavily against the door.

He watched her without emotion. It was a good act, but he'd seen others do it better. They did that when they were stalling for time. He waited for her to give him a lead, but she didn't speak or move.

"Did you have a premonition of Florrie's death too ? " he asked. "No ? Too bad. We might have been able to do something. Ring the alarm, maybe ; get the farmers out of bed again. We might even have found her in time."

He saw two tears roll slowly down from under her closed eyelids. . . . The old compunction hit him again. Pity began to soften him, and he fought it off.

"Well," he said lamely, " you can't blame me for being sore. I'm all mixed up. I don't understand any of this business. I don't understand anything in this house. You can have me fired if you like, but—I don't understand you either. They tell me you're ill. I'm sorry. I heard you screaming a while ago and I thought it was, well, hysterics. About Florrie. I was prepared to be as nice as

I knew how. But when you came to the door you were as cool as—ice. Not a single tear or sign of one. Until now. Now you're crying. Why ? "

" I'm crying about Florrie." She lifted her hands to her eyes, both of them together.

He'd thought all along that she was holding a handkerchief. Now he saw that he was wrong. The handkerchief was tied around her hands, both of them. They were tied together.

She saw his eyes narrow.

" I bite my nails," she said quietly. " When I'm— thinking—I bite my nails. That's why I tied them. That's true." She held her hands out like a child. " You can see for yourself. Anne does it too. I'm trying to set her a good example."

He'd meant to notice those hands He did now. The finger tips were raw and bleeding. He didn't say anything because there was nothing to say.

" I did scream," she said. " I'm sorry you heard. But Florrie was—too much."

" Forget it," he said, and remembered he'd said it to her before. " I mean, don't worry. Everything will be— fine. Wilcox won't bother you. Just—just come down when he sends for you." He left her standing there, leaning heavily against the door.

What had he got out of that ? Nothing. She was obviously ill. He'd known that before. She had strong hands, strong enough to choke the life out of a frail girl. But had she done it ? He didn't think so. That grief looked genuine.

Halfway down the stairs he wondered if she stood against the door because she was afraid of falling. He told himself he was crazy.

When he re-entered the dining room Morey was there, with Violet and Perrin.

"Mrs. Morey will come when she's wanted," he said.

"Can't you tell them to go easy on her?" Morey asked.

"Tell them yourself," Mark advised. "I'm a stranger here, therefore a suspect."

Morey turned to Violet. "Can you pull yourself to-gether long enough to get us some very hot coffee? I'm sunk, and if I take a drink they'll smell my breath and say I'm drowning my conscience."

Violet went off at a creeping pace, with several backward looks.

Morey watched her departure with a wan smile. "I'm waiting for her to remember that the ribbon on her pink cross said WE WILL MEET AGAIN. Then we'll be treated to some plain and fancy yowling."

"Where are the children?" Mark asked.

"Perrin parked them in the kitchen with one of Wilcox's men. He cuts things out of paper and they love it."

After a few minutes Stoneman came across the hall and joined them. "They're not at all bad," he said. "Ex-tremely simple, in fact."

Amos stood in the doorway behind him, beckoning. He didn't like being called simple and showed it. "You next, Mr. Morey," he said with dignity.

Violet came in with a percolator. Morey took a cup and carried it away with him. Violet looked so forlorn that Mark stood beside her with his hand on her shoulder. "Don't worry," he said. "I'm Sherlock Holmes." They drank their coffee in silence.

Morey came out of the library and went directly up-stairs. Perrin went in next; then Violet. None of them stayed longer than three minutes.

Then Laura Morey came slowly down the stairs alone and entered the library. Mark had a brief glimpse of her white face.

"Saving me for the last," Mark said to Violet. She

hadn't said a word since returning from her interview and now she nodded dumbly.

"Go get the children, Violet," Perrin said. "Take them back to the nursery. If they want to be noisy, don't stop them. And no tears, please?"

She ducked out of the room. Morey came back and leaned against the door, watching the hall. When his wife came out of the library he took her arm and led her away. Then Amos beckoned to Mark.

He found Wilcox sitting behind a small table with a box of Morey's best cigars in front of him. He wasn't smoking. He smiled at Mark and fingered a cheap note-book.

"I won't keep you long," he said. "Just want to check your opinion of yourself with what the others say about you. Partridge seems to think you're all right, but he's been wrong before."

"But only at election time," said Amos. He and Wilcox exchanged wintry smiles.

"You're a secretary to Mr. Stoneman and you've been here since Sunday night." Wilcox didn't refer to his book for that. "Correct?"

"Yes."

"Tell me something." Wilcox leaned forward confidentially. "How did you get off that train without Amos seeing you?"

"I was riding the rods and I rolled off," Mark said.

"None of my business, is it? Well, maybe not. Now, Mr. East, everybody here tells the same story. Last night they all went to bed early and read themselves to sleep. That's a nice, safe way to spend your time while a young girl is being murdered. I guess you were so deep in your book that you didn't hear the front door open and shut."

"I couldn't hear that from my room, anyway. Besides, I was asleep before ten-thirty and Florrie was still in her room then, according to Violet."

" I see you've been checking on the time too. I wonder if you know anything about a fuss over a wastebasket ? "

" Not a thing. That was a domestic fracas and out of my line."

" Now, Mr. East, this next question sounds kind of foolish, but I've got to ask it. It's what you might call routine. Do you know of any person who harboured a grudge against this girl or who would benefit in any way from her death ? "

"No. She was a nice kid." Mark felt, rather than saw, Amos give Wilcox a long look. The next question told him why.

Wilcox coughed gently. " I can't help wondering," he said, " if you think there's anything funny in two violent deaths in four days."

" Why should I think it's funny ? Your own office listed Mrs. Lacey's death as accidental."

" Maybe I didn't put that right ; we'll try it this way. Take a group of people living peacefully together and then add a stranger. Result, two ladies die very sudden, one by fire and one by strangling. If you were me, wouldn't you wonder about that ? "

" I certainly would. But I have a correction. They didn't live peacefully. Also I didn't burn or strangle anybody. What are you getting at, Mr. Wilcox ? "

" Nothing." Wilcox looked uncomfortable. " I had to ask that. . . . Mr. East, did you tell Mr. Stoneman that Florence Simmons was strangled ? "

Simmons. Florence Simmons. He hadn't even known her last name. That seemed crude and shocking now. He didn't know Violet's either. Simmons. Suddenly he jumped. " What did you say ? " He stared at Wilcox. " What did you say about Stoneman ? "

Wilcox repeated the question.

" I did not ! " Mark declared. " And I warned Mr. Morey. We told nobody."

" Maybe you didn't, but how can you be sure of Mr. Morey ? "

" He didn't have a chance. He and Stoneman passed each other on the stairs when we came in, but Florrie wasn't mentioned. I told Stoneman she was dead, that's all. He could have gone upstairs again while I was with Violet, but Morey was with his wife then. In that case, Mrs. Morey would know too."

" She didn't. I tried her out. . . . Stoneman let it slip. That's why I wanted it kept dark. I was hoping somebody would show he knew more than he ought to."

" Did you ask Stoneman how he knew ? "

" Ask him ? I threatened him with jail. He says he doesn't know where he picked it up, and he swore it wasn't from you or Morey. He couldn't make up his mind if it was second sight or Perrin."

" If he has any sense he'll stick to the second sight. Perrin wasn't even in the house when we came back. He didn't come in until you people arrived and he didn't see Stoneman until you'd finished with him. He was outside with the kids and he certainly didn't get it from them."

Wilcox closed his little book without having written a word in it. " Well, that's that. Interesting, isn't it ? You got any ideas ? "

" No."

" That lady, now. Mrs. Morey. Is she all there ? She talks all right, very quiet and polite, but she looks funny around the eyes."

" I don't know. She's an invalid."

" Hum. That's all. Don't leave the neighbourhood. The verdict will be person or persons unknown, but that won't bother me."

" Going to knock the anonymity into a cocked hat ? "

" I'm going to have a try. Nobody'll sleep around here if I don't." Halfway to the door he turned. " Say, if I call you up before long will you meet me some place and have a talk ? "

" Delighted," Mark said. If Amos hadn't given him a doleful wink on the way out he would have been worried.

Morey was waiting for him in the hall. He wore a look of combined surprise and worry. His wife wanted to see Mr. East. Immediately. She had a favour to ask. He shifted from one foot to the other and watched Mark anxiously. " I don't know what it's all about but I don't dare not send you. Agree to anything she says, will you ? I think she—likes you."

" Are you coming along ? " Mark asked.

" No. She wants to see you alone. I'll wait for you down here. If she says anything—queer—just take it with a grain of salt, will you ? "

Mark went up the stairs slowly. He didn't want to talk to her again. He didn't even want to see her. She was getting under his skin. He took a deep breath before he knocked softly on the door and went in.

She was sitting by a window in the cold north light. She had changed to a grey dress, and a bowl of white hyacinths stood at her elbow. At that minute she was the most beautiful woman he had ever seen, and she looked dead. The smile she gave him was so perfect that he winced.

" Sit down, Mr. East," she said. There were no tears now. There was no handkerchief on her hands, either. She wore diamonds. " I won't keep you long. You haven't had a very pleasant time here, have you ? "

He mumbled something. Her wide black eyes were so searching he had to drop his own.

" Never mind. I don't expect you to be cordial. Are you self-supporting, Mr. East ? "

" I am," he managed to answer.

" I'm afraid these tragedies have spoiled your opportunity for work. I'm sorry and I'll try to make amends.

If we leave here shortly, as I think we will, you will be reimbursed. However, that's not what I wanted to ask you. We need replacements here. Whether we leave or not, Violet must have assistance at once."

Replacements, Mark repeated to himself. As if Lacey and Florrie were two broken cups. "I think so too," he said stiffly.

"I'm glad you agree. Obviously we won't find anyone in Crestwood or Bear River. Anyone in the domestic class. But Perrin, and Violet too, have unwittingly given me an idea. There are two elderly women in the village who——" She broke off suddenly. "Mr. East, you look as if you were reading my mind."

"I am, if you're talking about Miss Petty and Miss Pond."

"You're quite right. I've heard about their visit here ; Anne and Ivy speak of little else. Miss Petty, I believe, is particularly loved. Mr. East, do you think they can be approached ? "

Mark examined the tips of his shoes before answering. It looked as if somebody had been reading his mind also.

She talked on. " No housework, only the supervision of my little girls. I know they are considered women of position, but I feel—I feel——" A new note crept into her voice and he watched her closely, waiting for the trick.

" Yes ? " he prodded.

" Do you think they would come as—friends ? I need them. I mean—will they come simply as good neighbours ? I know they sit up with the dead. Will they watch over my children ? "

He braced himself against an urge to shiver. " As a matter of fact, Mrs. Morey," he said carefully, " I had the same idea myself. I don't know whether they'll come or not, but I'd already planned to ask them. Subject to your approval, of course," he added hastily.

" Then that's settled."

"Not at all," he corrected. "These ladies are not young and they don't need jobs. They're pretty important people around here. They might—they might just possibly feel insulted."

He didn't believe that for a minute. He knew exactly what Beulah would say. Something slightly profane and thoroughly agreeable, with Bessy squealing and concurring in her wake.

"But you'll do what you can?" Her voice pleaded and almost broke. "They're friends of yours—you can ask them in a way that will be hard to refuse. Please try, Mr. East. As for salary, I'll pay them both at the regular governess rate. They can give it to charity if they like."

"I'll see." He stood up. She was twisting her hands in her lap; he tried not to look at the raw finger tips. "Would you like to interview them yourself, providing they agree?"

"Oh, no. I have no demands to make. I doubt if I shall see them at all. I only ask that they come as quickly as possible. There'll be no housework—just the children. Can you—how soon will you know?"

He said he would go at once.

Then, when she turned in her chair to watch him leave he saw that one pane in the window behind her was cracked. Someone had covered it clumsily with transparent tape. It didn't seem important, but he told himself he'd better remember it.

It was beginning to grow dark when he telephoned Beulah. She screamed with relief at the sound of his voice and told him to run all the way. Bessy had moved in with her, bag, baggage, hot-water bottle, and grandmother's pearls. She was afraid to sleep alone. They didn't know anything. Nobody knew anything. Not even Ella May. And they'd called up Florrie's mother but she wouldn't come to the 'phone. He was to stay for supper. Baked ham, creamed potatoes, hot biscuit, and that pear conserve everybody tried to copy but couldn't. And he was to run fast, all the way.

He took his things from the hall closet and stopped to talk to Violet. She wanted to go with him and cried bitterly when he told her she must stay. He promised to bring someone back to spend the night with her, but she didn't believe him. She thought he was going away himself and clung to his arm. He felt like a traitor when he finally closed the door and left her only partly convinced. He looked back once and saw her face pressed against the glass of the French window.

The ladies welcomed him with lamplight streaming out across the snow and with the smell of superior cooking. They had been crying too, but they crackled and chirped in unison and made jokes about the gargantuan highball they set before him. They gave him the softest chair in front of the fire and pulled and pushed a small table into place under his elbow.

"We'll have our supper on that later," Beulah said. She settled herself with a highball as large as Mark's and handed one to Bessy. "Mostly ginger ale," she winked. She tossed her grizzled head gaily, but he knew she was whistling in the dark.

"We've had the police," Bessy announced.

"Police!" scorned Beulah. "Amos Partridge and that little Perley Wilcox who used to be a thief second to none. His weakness was Concord grapes."

"I had him in the fourth. He was bright."

"He stole grapes," said Beulah. "Now you tell us everything you know and we'll tell you what we know. Begin at the beginning and don't skip."

He complied, up to a certain point. The real reason for his visit he kept until later. They listened soberly.

" Doesn't anybody in that house have even the slightest idea about this ? " Beulah asked. " Do you mean to say you haven't any suspicions yourself ? "

" I don't know who killed Florrie and I don't know why it was done. I don't get the point at all but I'm sure there was one. I'm more or less counting on you two for help. You've known her from childhood, you knew her friends, her hopes, her possibilities." He looked at Bessy. " She was one of your pupils, wasn't she? What was she really like?"

Bessy said she was a good girl. " Her friends were just the boys and girls she grew up with. The person who killed Florrie must have done it by mistake."

Mark took a long drink. " Somehow, I don't think it was a mistake. She had that same look Mrs. Lacey had the day before she died. I'm almost willing to say they both knew it was coming."

" That's crazy," Beulah said. " Or maybe it isn't. You see, I'm so upset I don't know my own mind. But I'll tell you what I told Amos and Perley Wilcox. It was somebody in that house. Everybody else around here is above reproach. People like us don't kill, except in wars."

Bessy nodded sagely. " Of course in wars."

" That's nonsense, Miss Beulah——"

" No more Miss. Beulah and Bessy, please. It saves time."

" All right, but you've got to be fresh with me too. The name is Mark and I'm pleased to meet you. Now, as I started to say, you were talking nonsense. People like you, and me, do kill. Lots of impeccable ladies have brewed arsenic and wielded the axe with great success. Also a few gentlemen, who got tired of their wives, but they usually got caught. There have been some nasty but well-bred little girls, too, with death in their chubby hands. Everybody kills."

" Not me," said Beulah firmly.

" You know what I mean. Now, answer me this.

You can keep it anonymous, but is there anybody in this neighbourhood who is—a little cracked ? "

Bessy blinked rapidly and looked at Beulah.

" No," Beulah said. " I know what you mean ; I've read books. But I say no. Mark, do you think Florrie's murder and Lacey's death are—the same thing ? "

" I do."

Bessy gave a little cry. " Then anybody, anybody at all can be killed too ! "

" Not anybody. Only some unlucky soul who knows what poor Lacey and Florrie knew."

" What they knew ? " shrilled Bessy. " Did they know anything ? "

" They must have. That would supply a motive ; unless our man is that good old standby, the homicidal maniac, who kills whenever he gets the urge. But he doesn't seem to fit in here. Apparently his urge only functions with Morey's servants. Or could it be Davenport's servants ? "

" I won't hear a word against the Colonel," Beulah said flatly.

" Poor Ruthie Lacey murdered ! " Bessy's eyes filled.

" You mustn't say that," Mark cautioned. " After all. it's only my idea. You must openly accept it as an accident. . . . Beulah, is there any connection between Florrie and Lacey in the past ? Are they related, or were they ever involved with Davenport outside of the domestic angle ? "

" No. No to everything you've asked. . . . Why ? "

" I was wondering why Florrie was killed in Lacey's shed. That's over a mile from the house. The weather was frightful. Yet she got out of bed in the dark, dressed, and went all the way down to that shed to meet death. You see why I keep thinking there may be a tie-up."

" I see all right. And there we were, sitting in Lacey's parlour the whole time, and we didn't hear a thing."

" I wondered about that too."

" I say we didn't hear a thing. And don't look at me like that. You know the wind was making an awful racket."

" Of course it was. How lucky. A fine strong wind to drown out a little girl's cries. Who was with you, Beulah?"

She told him, speaking each name with reluctance and trying to read in his face what he was thinking. She looked as if she were slipping a noose around the neck of one of her friends and she counted on his eyes to tell her which one.

" Bessy, of course," she said airily. " And some of the ladies from the Guild at our church. I suppose you want their names. Linder, Pross, Medinger, and Marshall. Two of them left before ten o'clock because of the weather. Their husbands came for them. The other two stayed until six and rode home on the milk train. Amos was there too, all the time, but he was back in the kitchen. I hate to give him an alibi but I could hear him rattling the stove all night. Ella May was there all the time too. She's got ears like an animal. She took the lamp to the window when she heard your car, but of course she didn't tell us the real reason then. Said she was looking to see if the snow had let up. She admitted the truth this morning. Said she thought you were all drunk and she was saving it to tell her cousin first. But she didn't see or hear anything out at the shed. She never could have held that in. And Bittner didn't see or hear anything either. . . . Anyway, we were all in front of the house."

" Beulah. Didn't anybody leave the room for—anything ? "

" Oh, you don't go outside for that any more. It's right at the head of the stairs."

" When did Ella May leave ? "

" At seven o'clock, when Bittner blew an old bus horn out of the window and yelled for breakfast."

" I haven't got a bus horn but I'm hungry," Mark said.

Beulah fled to the kitchen with alacrity. " You poor thing ! Just you wait ! I'll have things ready in a jiffy ! "

That was exactly what he wanted. He turned to Bessy, who was staring into her empty glass. " What did you do all evening, Bessy ? "

" I slept," she confessed. " I cried myself sick, I really did, so I went to sleep in Ruthie's bedroom. Do you know we couldn't have the cake and coffee after the funeral ? None of the ladies felt like it, after Florrie. We sent it to the Orphanage in Bear River."

Beulah came rustling back with a heavy tray and they helped her set the little table.

While they were eating a suspiciously fresh and rich coconut cake, which would never be missed by orphans. Mark led up to the reason for his call. He coloured it up.

" Would you girls like to help catch Florrie's killer ? "

This caught Bessy at a moment when she was not quite ready to exhale and forced her into a premature action. Beulah wiped away the fine spray of coconut. " Say that again," she requested.

He told them about his interview with Mrs. Morey and baited them nicely with a description of the splendours of her room and wardrobe. " I was going to ask you myself, even before she spoke. I'm sure you'll be perfectly safe —I wouldn't let you come otherwise. Aside from the possibility that you may help Florrie and Lacey, you'll be a godsend to those kids."

" I understand about the children," Beulah said slowly, " But Bessy and I could never catch a killer. We simply haven't had the experience."

" Perley, the grape stealer, will do the catching. You will do the looking and listening. Who knows you may see or hear something that will lay a bad old ghost and make this little town a peaceful place again."

" Let's," said Bessy.

Beulah had to do something in the face of such heroism. " Fools rush in," she said grandly, with just enough renunciation. " I don't mind burning to death myself, but I have to think of Bessy."

" I'm thinking of you both. You'll be all right, just as I have been. We three are strangers to that family up there, we've had no previous contact. I think that's important."

" Lacey and Florrie were strangers to them too. They hadn't any previous contact."

" They hadn't any with the Moreys, but they'd worked in that house before."

" House ! Are you crazy ? What's the house got to do with it ? "

" I don't know. But it gives me the creeps, that's all."

" But Violet ! She's alive, and she's worked there before. Not often, but a couple of times. To help Mrs. Lacey when the Colonel had a party."

" Violet is a darling little dummy. Neither Lacey nor Florrie was that. They could put two and two together, which Violet could never do, and that was their downfall. I'll bet you on it."

"My church forbids it. If we came, where would we sleep?"

" With Violet, in the wonderful morning-glory room. We'll move in another bed. Is it a deal, Beulah ? "

"Yes. . . . Mark, you're giving a lot of time to this mess. I know you're working for Stoneman, but for who else ? "

" Justice. A lot of people work for justice in their spare time. Not only policemen, but people like you and me and Bessy. We don't want money, we only want to clean up. If we can clean this up, we'll snore happily. If we don't, maybe we won't snore at all. I'm not kidding you, it may be dangerous. But if we keep our eyes open we may find out why Florrie went out to meet a killer and then couldn't bear to look at him."

Beulah stood up and began to collect dishes. "I'll take these out to the kitchen. You go get your bag, Bessy. Thank heaven you were in no condition to unpack. We won't be a minute, Mark. I'll just throw some things together for myself."

He waited by the fire while they tramped firmly over his head.

When they came down, there were bits of pink and white trailing out of Beulah's bag and her hat was worn as its maker never intended. She bulged on one side.

They raked out the fire and took a last long look.

"Ready?" Mark asked.

"Ready," said Beulah. "I stacked the dishes in the sink. They'll draw bugs, but I'll probably never live to know it."

Going up the mountain, Bessy examined the present and the future. "I don't know what the future holds," she said, " but I do hope it doesn't hurt. You know, I can't get that poor woman's face out of my mind."

"What woman?" Mark asked.

"Mrs. Morey. I saw her at the station the day she came. Sables, and sad eyes. My grandmother had a picture in her parlour that looked like that. A female figure, clinging to a rock. A very haunting figure. My heart aches for that woman."

Mark tucked her arm under his. "Look here, Bessy. Don't you go letting your heart ache for anybody in this piece until the curtain comes down on the last act. You may pick the wrong character."

CHAPTER EIGHT

VIOLET had the door open before Mark could get out his key. She was overjoyed to see Bessy and Beulah; and when she heard they were going to help her with the children and even sleep in the same room, she almost smiled.

"I've got a poker under my pillow," she said, "but I won't need it now I've got you, Miss Pond." Beulah looked pleased, though she had never cared for Violet.

Mark wanted to know if everything was under control. Everything was. Nothing had happened at all. The children had gone to bed without any fuss although they had asked for Florrie. Violet told them Florrie had her appendix out, which was what Perrin said to tell them. Nobody had come to call except that Partridge. "Calling himself police," she added gloomily. "And taking all of Florrie's things away. Her uniforms and all. Her diary and even the old market lists she always saved in case the butcher tried to pull something funny. Even her nail polish. Everything. Calling himself police."

Perrin and Morey both helped with the extra bed. It came from the rose room and was very properly covered with rose-patterned chintz. The ensuing horticultural riot gave Violet much pleasure.

"A red cabbage rose, I'd say," she deduced admiringly, with one finger laid thoughtfully against a round cheek. "If it's just the same with you ladies I'd like to sleep in it myself. I haven't got the heart for morning glories."

"Everything in order here? Got everything you need?" Morey stepped around briskly. "Haven't overlooked anything, Violet?"

"No, sir."

"Then I'll get along. I want some chess with Stoneman."

"Where is he?" Mark asked.

"Locked himself in again. He'll come out now that you're home. Perrin, bring some ice to the library. What are you going to do, East?"

"Talk to these people for a bit. Play the genial and grateful host, if you've no objection."

" I get it ! " Morey went up to Bessy and Beulah with outstretched hand. " Forgive me. I haven't said a word about how I appreciate this. You're helping us over a bad time. Mrs. Morey will see you in the morning and tell you herself. Can I send you anything? A sandwich, a drink? "

" No," Mark said quickly and flatly. " I'll see you later perhaps. If I don't, will you send Stoneman up fairly early ? I think he needs rest."

Morey nodded and left.

Violet burst into sudden activity, turning down beds, plumping pillows, opening and shutting closet doors. " I'll help you get settled," she said. " There's that big bureau, nice and empty, with clean paper in the drawers and never been used. Here Miss Pond, give me that bag. Oh, what an awful mess ! You're no packer. My land, have you got something in your coat pocket too ? "

" Leave me alone," Beulah said crossly. " I'm keeping this coat on. I'm cold."

Mark seized his opportunity. " Violet, you help Miss Petty. I want to talk to Miss Pond privately." He led Beulah to the far end of the hall, safely out of earshot. They sat on a window seat and he faced her with some trepidation.

" I've got to confide in you because I've nobody else," he said bluntly. " I hope I'm not making a mistake. . . . Can you keep your mouth shut ? "

She examined him thoughtfully. " That depends. I can keep it shut if you tell me how I can help solve this dreadful business. But if you tell me you did it yourself they're going to hear me up in Canada."

He told her the whole story, as far as it had unrolled. He began with Stoneman's letter to his agency and the old man's insistence that he hadn't known Mark's real work. " So, having nothing else to do at the time, I accepted. Partly curiosity, partly because I needed a change. I knew

I could always back out legitimately. I didn't tell him what day I was coming. I wanted to surprise him. Then at the station I had a hunch about walking in unannounced. Somehow I knew that limousine came from here, so I just watched it leave the station. Then I deliberately walked up the lane, knowing it was the wrong direction. I wanted to meet a resident, someone I could pump later if I had to. I have pumped you a little but from now on I play straight. See ? "

" That was a good hunch," Beulah said enviously.

" Yep. I hadn't talked to Stoneman for one minute before I knew something was wrong. Maybe I'm psychic, like you ! "

" God forbid," Beulah said.   " Go on."

" Stoneman was afraid of something. Mrs. Lacey was frankly terrified.   Florrie was uneasy, Perrin too restrained.   Mrs. Morey in a definite state of collapse. Violet was the only normal person in the outfit.   Morey seemed all right, but under close observation even he wasn't as gay as he looked.   What upset me most, and this came later, was one of the little girls. The baby doesn't count, of course ; I mean the older one. She was holding herself in check, a very unchildish thing. That child, plus Mrs. Lacey's death, decided me. I stayed. And now we have this new terror."

" What do we do first ? " asked Beulah.

" We install a dictograph."

" G-man ? " asked Beulah, blanching slightly.

" No. But thanks just the same. . . . I brought the thing with me—hunch again. But I didn't want to look like a fool in case I was wrong, so I hid it in a closet down the hall. This is the time to drag it out. But where to put it and how to listen is the problem. That's where you come in."

Beulah leaned her forehead against the window and

looked at the black night.   After a bit she said, " If I had any sense, this is where I'd go out. . . . You don't want Bessy to know about this ? "

" No.   This is one of those times when ignorance is bliss.   If Bessy knew, her nice old face would be sure to give us away.   Maybe to the wrong person."

" You—you think it's somebody in this house ? "

" I don't think anything, yet.   First of all, where to put the dictograph.   I want two locations, one for the sender and one for the receiver.   The first must be some room where everyone goes and where two people can talk together, without fear of being overheard.   Where their presence will cause no comment.   Where they will feel safe—to talk.   The second room must adjoin it, or be over or under it.   And that must be a room off the beaten track, a nice lonely room.   Where will we find those ? "

Beulah thought ; she closed her eyes and clenched her hands and her chin quivered.   Mark waited respectfully for the trance to run its course.   He was beginning to be anxious, and wondering if perhaps he'd made a mistake, when she gave a little jump.

" Eureka ? " he asked hopefully.

" Mrs. Morey's room," she said.   " For the first.   Everybody goes there, the children, Violet, Perrin, Mr. Morey and even Stoneman, I suppose.   She runs this house from that room.   And for the second, there's a very small sewing room next to it, opening on the day nursery.   Just that one door, to the nursery, but one wall is part of her wall, too. The nursery door, leading from the hall, is exactly opposite the sewing-room door.   If you left it open you could see whoever went down to her room.   And you'd know when to listen, wouldn't you ? "

" I don't suppose you know what her wall looks like ? " he asked hopefully.   " Or if there're any pictures or things on the sewing-room side of it ? "

"I don't know what the bedroom wall looks like now, but Colonel Davenport had a big tapestry there. French and very fine, he said. So I guess she's left it where it was. The sewing-room wall is full of shelves, to hold materials and such. I saw them myself the other night. You look happy!"

"I'm tickled to death. It's so perfect I'm afraid of it. Now all we have to do is clean up a few details. I take it you won't be shy about listening to things that are none of your business?"

"In peacetime I'd resent that, but this is war. I'll listen."

"And if that set-up is no good we'll switch to the kitchen. Now, can you get Mrs. Morey out of her room to-morrow? Only fire and murder have done that so far. And one slight excess of maternity."

"Out of her room? I'll get her out of the house."

He put his hands under her elbows and lifted her to her feet. "East and Pond would look good on an office door."

"Pond and East. . . . What do I do now?"

"Go back to the roses and the morning glories. After that, you're on your own. I'm going to bed. You might encourage Violet to talk all she wants to. And remember, the second door down the hall is mine. Come to call if you feel jittery."

He left his door ajar and the sound of voices pursued him to bed. Violet didn't need encouragement, only an audience.

Nothing happened during the night; at least nothing that called for hands on his shoulder and frightened whisperings. He slept soundly. Even Stoneman, fumbling with his locks and bolts and falling over furniture, failed to rouse him. He was up at eight and having breakfast at eight-thirty, with Bessy and Beulah sitting across the table. Perrin, scrambling eggs at the sideboard, told him that Morey had finished but Stoneman had not come down. Should he call Mr. Stoneman?

Mark said no, he'd be along presently. This was one time he wasn't worried. He'd left Stoneman engaging and retreating from a cold shower where he was slowly and noisily winning a battle over last night's Scotch.

" We've seen the children and given them their breakfast," Bessy said happily. " After a bit, we're all going for a nice walk in the snow, Beulah says. Mrs. Morey, too."

" Fine," said Mark, avoiding Beulah's eye. " Perrin ? " The man hurried over. " Are you going to Bear River this morning ? "

" No, sir. But if there's anything——"

" There is. I need carbon paper." This time he looked squarely at Beulah. " Didn't you say something about paste and painting books for the nursery ? "

" And crayons," she answered promptly. " I wouldn't give the ones they have now to a cat. Why don't we all drive over ? "

" And Mr. Stoneman, too ! " Bessy insisted. "He needs air. He looks frail."

" Certainly, Mr. Stoneman. You ask him, Bessy. But I'm afraid Mr. East has work to do. Haven't you, Mr. East ? "

Quickly and gratefully, Mr. East admitted this was so. But he was willing to help others have a good time. " How soon do you think they could start, Perrin ? "

Perrin was also helpful. " Mr. Morey is taking the two-seater. He has an appointment with Mr. Wilcox, a legal formality. If he doesn't want me to drive him, I can bring the big car around whenever you like."

" Ten o'clock, then," said Beulah. " I'll run down to Violet and see if she needs any supplies. And I think I'll ask her to bake a nice cake, too." A complicated, engrossing cake, her look said. When she stalked out, followed by Bessy, Mark mentally saluted.

She had cleared the decks for him like a veteran, but there was still Stoneman to consider. He'd probably

refuse, work himself up into a state, and take refuge in
another bottle.   But to his surprise the old man made no
objection.

He was a little languid after his trial by water, and
slightly blue around the mouth, but his manner was gravely
cordial.   He'd been talking to Miss Petty, he said ; a nice,
comfortable woman who wasn't afraid of a good corset.
And a little drive would be a change.   Morey was going too,
he understood, in another car.   And Laura.   Incredible.
Well, well, quite a family outing.   He accepted coffee from
Perrin, shuddered at the first swallow, and smiled vaguely
at nothing.   " I feel that this will be a happy, happy day,"
he murmured.

Mark, to his own surprise, grew suddenly angry.   " Did
you drown Florrie in that Scotch last night ? " he snapped.

Stoneman raised one eyebrow in rebuke.   "My dear boy!"

" A happy, happy day.   That girl looked after your
comfort, carried your damn trays, pressed your pants ;
and now when she's lying on a cold slab you talk about
your happy day."

" I can't bring her back, East.   I wouldn't if I could.
Life has nothing to give the Florries and they have nothing
to give life.   You needn't frown at me ; it makes no impression.   Actually, what did the future hold for her ?
Marriage, too many children, too much sickness, too little
money.   No, Florrie was a pleasant girl, but after a year
even her family will be happy without her.   In another year
the only trace of Florrie in this world will be a small marble
marker.   And inferior marble, I'm afraid. "

Mark bit back an urge to ask him how he knew about
the strangling.   That was Wilcox's job.

He watched them all troop out on the terrace at ten
o'clock.   Anything less like a family outing he had never
seen.   Except for Beulah, Bessy, and the children, they
resembled a group of refugees with only one peck of dia-

monds between them. Morey scowled in a topcoat from
Regent street; Laura Morey was somnambulistic in
Russian sable; Stoneman was furtively shivering in four
English sweaters under an astrakhan coat of dubious clean-
liness and a matching cap with ear muffs.

They herded themselves into the cars like driven cattle.
It was the first time he had seen any one of them conform
to a general idea. It made him vaguely uncomfortable.
Had Beulah's acid tongue been able to bring about this
miracle? Or was it Bessy, that good woman unafraid
of a corset? Or were they all together because they were
afraid to be apart? Just then he would have given anything to confide in Wilcox.

Morey drove off first, by himself, and the big car followed
slowly. He watched until it rounded the first turn in the
drive, then he went into the house. He checked on
Violet, who was beating eggs and humming. He could
hardly believe his ears. She told him it was another
" Indian Love Lyric," called " There is no Breeze to Cool
the Heat of Love." It made him feel normal again, so he
took a handful of the cookies she offered and went more or
less happily about his business, telling her he was not to be
disturbed.

Behind closed doors he went to work with the agility of
long practice. The tapestry was where Beulah said
it would be and the sewing-room shelves were in a
gratifying mess. When he finished, he tested the apparatus with a portable phonograph from the nursery and the
strains of " Little Jack Horner " told him what good boys
they both were. He swept up the bits of wood and plaster
and told himself it was a neat job. Only an expert who knew
what to look for could have spotted it. He was through at
eleven-thirty and went to his room for the sake of appearances. Stoneman found him there busily pecking at the
typewriter when they all came back.

After lunch the children napped and Beulah sat in the day nursery ostentatiously going over a mending basket. Bessy sat by the fire and nodded. When her gentle snoring filled the room like a distant hive of bees, Beulah walked softly to the hall door and opened it wide. Then she went into the sewing room, and stood the door ajar. Her little eyes snapped, and two bright pink spots burned on her cheeks.

The house settled down to a quiet afternoon. Mark and Stoneman worked ; Stoneman's voice droned through page after page and Mark's pencil patiently travelled the lined yellow paper. Laura Morey was in her own room, the door closed as usual. Morey was in the library, adding up columns of figures ; Violet was in the kitchen, sprawled over the table with her head on her arms, sleeping like an exhausted child ; Perrin had gone back to his old job of cleaning silver in the pantry. The only thing that moved from room to room was the little ghost of Florrie, flitting through everybody's mind with her mittened hands over her eyes.

Time passed and darkness fell abruptly, and with it more snow. The orderly clink of silver and china in the pantry told that Perrin was beginning the preliminaries of dinner. Stoneman, in his own room, was hesitating between sack suit and black tie in honour of the ladies. Morey was still in the library, eyeing the liquor cabinet and wondering if someone would join him. Laura Morey was still behind her closed door.

Beulah hadn't stirred from her chair in the sewing room, although her legs were full of pins and needles. No sound had come from the room behind the wall. It had been quiet in there for hours. She would wait another ten minutes, no longer. She eased her aching back into a new position and smiled sourly at the chatter that came in from the nursery.

The occupants of that room had no secrets. She'd heard them wake up, wash their faces, blow bubbles, and argue. She'd even seen them briefly as they passed her partly open door. They hadn't referred to her once or asked about her. She snorted, but quietly.

"But truthfully, Miss Bessy," that was Anne's voice, "truthfully, do you believe in being rescued by knights in armour?"

"In a way, in a way. Maybe not in armour, but knights, certainly."

"On horseback?"

"Well—on bicycles. Or on foot. Horses have sort of gone out, except for farming, and I wouldn't care to be rescued on a horse. An automobile, now, or an airplane, or a nice motorcycle with a sidecar would be lovely."

"Yes." Anne, crouched on the window seat, pressed her face against the glass.

"But who gets rescued these days?" Bessy answered herself. "Nobody. Ladies can take care of themselves, more's the pity."

Beulah, watching the clock in her retreat, leered.

"Whatever are you staring at, Anne?" Bessy rocked happily. "You'll flatten your nose all out of shape and nobody'll want to dance with you when you're sixteen. There's nothing out there but trees and snow. Do you see anybody coming?"

Ivy took it up. "Sister Anne, Sister Anne, do you see anybody coming?" she chanted, leaning against Bessy's knee and looking up into her face.

"Well, if this isn't a smart girl! I used to read that story myself when I was little." Bessy and Ivy beamed at each other.

"We have it in a book." Anne spoke over her shoulder. "I read it to her, but she likes to act it out better. It makes her feel important."

"Sister Anne, Sister Anne, do you see anybody coming?" persisted Ivy.

"We might as well play it," Anne said maternally. "She's very s-t-u-b-b-o-r-n. Come here, baby; climb up." She lifted the little girl into the window seat. "Now wring your hands, Ivy. Remember, this is very sad. We really ought to have the window open, Miss Bessy. I'm supposed to lean out."

"And catch your death. No." Bessy crossed over and stood behind them. She drew the curtains back and raised the shade high. "There, that's as good as leaning out." To a watcher in the snow they were a picture framed in light.

"Go on," encouraged Bessy. "If you act it prettily I'll give you two chocolates for dessert."

Ivy, kneeling beside Anne, wrung her fat hands and wrinkled her brow.

"Sister Anne, Sister Anne, do you see anybody coming?" wailed Ivy.

"Only a cloud of dust," said Anne.

"Sister Anne, Sister Anne, do you see anybody coming?"

"Only a flock of sheep."

Bessie bent over and kissed each shining head.

"Sister Anne, Sister Anne, do you see anybody coming?" Ivy braced herself for the joyful climax.

"I see—I see——" cried Anne, and stopped.

Beulah heard the crash of glass and Bessy's frightened scream. Bessy was crying, "Beulah, Beulah."

She got to her feet, but they were weighted with lead. "I'm coming, I'm coming," she tried to shout, but her hoarse old voice cracked in her throat. Something had struck at Bessy, someone was hurting her. Bessy wouldn't know what to do.

Another sound rose and fell, the thin and frightened wailing of a child. She staggered to the door.

Her mind reeled back, unbidden, to a day she had forgotten long ago. She saw a little girl with round blue eyes standing knee-deep in buttercups, weeping because she was lost. Those sobbing breaths returned across that far-off summer field. She flung the door wide open. "Beulah's coming," she cried. "It's all right, Bessy, Beulah's coming!" And her voice was young again and as staunch as her heart.

The room was like an ugly jigsaw puzzle with each piece in the wrong place. Anne sat on the floor under the window seat with bright red stains on her white frock. That was because Ivy's head was in her lap. Ivy was covered with blood.

Bessy stood with her back against the wall and her hands before her face. A thin red stream trickled through her plump fingers.

"Help!" shouted Beulah above the sudden sound of slamming doors and running feet.

Almost at once, before she could gather strength to scream again, the room was full of people. A strange fury took possession of her soul and began to burn. Even while she was dragging the fingers down from Bessy's face. she carefully counted them all, saw that they all were there. All except Violet.

"Doctor!" shouted Morey. He held a cocktail shaker in one hand and frantically rang the service bell with the other. "Somebody call Cummings!"

Before Mark could move Perrin was at his elbow, speaking rapidly. "Will you make that call, Mr. East? Quick! Use the 'phone in Mrs. Morey's room!"

Mark ran his eyes over the group. Anyone could put in the call. He wanted to stay where he was, and watch. Already he had noted one disturbing fact.

Someone plucked at his sleeve and he turned with relief to find Violet. She was breathing hard, as if she had been running. He pushed her to the door. "Call Dr. Cum-

mings and tell him to rush it.   Then you come back here
to me." She gave him one horrified look and fled.

Laura Morey was bending over Ivy, smoothing back the
dark curls.   Perrin gently drew her hands away.   He
carried Ivy into the bathroom, calling over his shoulder :
" Miss Pond, bring Miss Petty in here."   Then he added,
" It's all right, madam.   I know what to do."

Mark moved slowly over to the window.   Laura Morey
was there, sitting where the children had been, turning
something over and over in her hands.   It was a rock.

Morey sat in a chair with Anne in his lap, clumsily
wiping the blood away with a handkerchief.   She wasn't
crying.   She looked rigid with fright.

" Is she all right, Morey ? " he asked.   He pitied the man for
his awkwardness but he himself could have done no better.

" I hope so, I hope so," Morey mumbled.   " Laura ? "
The woman at the window raised her eyes.

" Take Anne with you," he begged.   " Take her to your
room.   I'll bring Cummings as soon as I can."

She looked steadily over his head without replying.
Mark followed that look and saw Stoneman.

They had run down the hall together at the first scream
and entered the room at the same time.   In the confusion
that followed, he'd forgotten the old man.   Now, somehow,
he didn't look old.

" What the hell is this ? " Stoneman said in a new voice.
He stood with his thin shoulders squared, coatless, the
ends of his black bow tie hanging loose.   His face was
blotched ;   his eyes were blazing.   " What the hell is
this ? " he repeated.   " Are children butchered now ? "

It was Morey who answered.   " We haven't had time
to find out," he said.   He set Anne on her feet and gave
her a gentle push.   " Go with Uncle Joe, honey.   Joe,
take Anne and Laura back to Laura's room.   I've got to
see what that fellow's doing to Ivy."

Stoneman led Anne from the room without a word. Laura Morey followed. At the door she stopped, and placed the rock on a small table. She looked straight ahead, but Mark felt that she was looking at him when she did it.

He went into the bathroom with Morey. Ivy was lying on a bed of thick towels and Perrin was patting the blood away with cotton soaked in water. He had discarded his blue denim apron and rolled up his sleeves. Beulah was swabbing Bessy's face at the washbasin.

" Tell Violet to find me some tweezers and boil them at once," Perrin said to Mark. " I need them for the glass."

"Do you know what you're doing ? " Morey asked harshly.

" I did this in the last war. The routine hasn't changed much." He gave Morey a brief look. " If we leave it until Cummings gets here, it may be bad. Miss Pond, do you find much glass there ? "

" No," said Beulah. " I don't think so ; it's mostly this dreadful gash along her cheek. I think it must have been that rock."

" Keep on with the warm water and then I'll look at it." Perrin straightened up. " I'd like to see Anne too, if I may."

" She's with her mother," Morey answered, staring hard at Perrin. " She's all right. We'll wait for Cummings."

Perrin hesitated. " I'd like to see her," he repeated. " But you must use your own judgment."

Violet came to the door, still breathing hard. " He's coming, the doctor's coming," she said. " As fast as he can. He's bringing Mr. Wilcox with him. He says he's got to bring Mr. Wilcox, no matter what anybody says."

Perrin sent her away once more, this time to find tweezers. He asked Mark to take over the sterilizing.

Morey sat on the edge of the tub. " You give orders almost as well as you take them," he said to Perrin. If Perrin heard, he gave no sign. He bent over Ivy again and talked to her softly while he sponged her face and hands.

Cummings and Wilcox came screaming up the mountain in a police car. Wilcox later apologized for the siren. "Sometimes people stampede when they hear it," he said. "Or so I've been told. It sounds like hell broke loose and the guilty ones are supposed to do something foolish to give themselves away."

But nobody gave anything away that night. They all might have been deaf. In spite of himself Mark thought of Ella May, running from window to window with Bittner's binoculars.

Little by little order was achieved. Bessy's cheek required eight stitches; Anne had escaped with a shallow cut, under her hair. Ivy's face and arms were peppered with glass, and Cummings clucked angrily while he worked. He said he believed in miracles. He had to. Nothing else could have turned the glass away from those eyes.

He worked on the children in their mother's room, while Wilcox faced the household gathered in the nursery.

"I've sent for some men," Wilcox said dryly. "Two for the outside and two for the inside. This place is giving the county a bad name. Miss Petty, are you able to talk?"

"I'd love to," quavered Bessy.

"Well, what happened?"

"I don't know. I was standing by that window and the children were leaning up against it, on the window seat, you know. And then that rock came through. It was just a bang and a crash, and that's all."

"Did you see anyone outside? No, of course you didn't."

"Then why ask?" observed Beulah.

Wilcox went on calmly, "I talked to the older child and she didn't see anyone either. It was pitch-black. I've been out there myself and there's no prints. It's all paved terrace and the wind blows the snow off as fast as it falls. And you've all got alibis, too. I don't know as any sheriff in the world ever came face to face with such plain alibis. You're all dressed up for it, like a lot of actors."

Mark felt his worries slip away. This was no yokel.

"Miss Pond," Wilcox continued, "Miss Pond tells me you all arrived on the scene at the same time, which was as soon as possible. That's fine. And each one of you was interrupted at some innocent private business. I ask you to observe Mr. Morey. Mr. Morey says he was mixing drinks in the library and he brings along his shaker to prove it. Mr. Stoneman was dressing for dinner, and if you don't believe it, look at him. Mr. East was next door to Mr. Stoneman, tying his shoes. One of them is still untied. Mr. Perrin was in the pantry, setting out the plates for dinner. He dropped one when Miss Pond, or it may have been Miss Petty, screamed. A ten-dollar plate, he says. I saw the remains. Mrs. Morey says she was lying down, and that's one of the stories we can't prove. They straightened up the bed when they put the baby on it. We can't prove anything about Violet either. She was a mite late getting on the scene, maybe that's because she had farther to come."

"Mr. Wilcox," wailed Violet, "if you're insinuating that I——"

"I've known you since you were born, Violet. It makes you sick to help your mother kill a chicken. But you'd better tell us what you were doing."

"Nothing I can prove. I was just sitting. I heard that scream, though, and then I heard the plate fall on the floor right after. I ran as fast as I could, but I fell down twice on the stairs."

"That's too bad. Now you've all heard these stories. Does anybody want to call anybody else a liar ? "

"What are you getting at ? " demanded Morey.

"Nothing. I have to ask that."

Nobody spoke. He went on. " I forgot to say that

Miss Pond is clear. She was in that little room, mending and napping. She couldn't get out and back. Miss Petty says so, and so does the little girl." He waited. Still nobody spoke. " Well, do you want to know what I think ? I think it looks too much like an outside job. Much too much. What do you think, Miss Pond ? "

" I haven't decided," said Beulah.

" Miss Petty ? "

" Bad boys," said Bessy. " But I'm sure they didn't mean any harm. Just bad boys, throwing rocks for fun."

" And where would they come from, Miss Petty ? No boys of any kind in Crestwood. Bear River ? Do you think they'd come all the way from Bear River to heave a rock ? Plenty of windows to break and kids to scare closer to home."

" Kids to kill," Beulah corrected fiercely. " You're not going to write this off as a prank, Perley Wilcox ! It's more than that ! Coming on top of the other——" She dabbed angrily at her eyes.

" Now, now," said Wilcox. " Nothing to cry about. Everything's well in hand. You'll be guarded night and day—if Mr. Morey doesn't object."

" Object ! I'm all for it ! " Morey sent a reassuring smile across the room to his wife. She was sitting outside the circle with Stoneman. Following their first brief statements, neither of them had said a word. It was hard to tell if Laura Morey had even been listening.

" And now," said Wilcox, " there's nothing left for me to do but come to the point. Mr. Morey, I want to warn you.   One of your servants has been burned to death ; I'm doubting now that it was an accident. Another was strangled. And to-day someone has made a malicious attack on members of your own family. All in less than a week. Who hates you like that ? "

Laura Morey moaned softly.

"Nobody." Morey looked blank. "I don't know more than six people by sight in the whole neighbourhood."

"Mrs. Morey?" He made his voice gentle for the woman huddled in her chair.

"I don't know. We'll have to go away. This can't go on. We'll go away to-morrow. I can't bear it, I can't bear it, Jim!"

"You can take her back to her room," Wilcox said to Morey. "But explain to her that she can't go away just now. In a few days, maybe. After the Simmons case is closed."

Morey and his wife left together.

"That's all for now," Wilcox said. "You're all free to do as you like, but if you leave the house it's at your own risk. You can make me take the guards off too, but I don't advise it. Mr. Stoneman, will you ask Mr. Morey to meet me in my office to-morrow morning? At his convenience. Thank you." He touched Bessy's cheek with a sympathetic finger, pinched Violet's, and bowed gravely to Beulah. Then he went out, followed by Perrin.

They sat where he left them, each one eyeing the other. Stoneman spoke first, furiously. His rage was directed at Morey, who crept back into the room like a comedy burglar, finger on lips.

"You fool!" he shouted. "You congenital idiot! I wish that man Wilcox could see you now! You've handled this whole thing like an imbecile! . . . Why did you let him talk like that? Ridiculing perfectly innocent people! I refuse to be involved in such an asinine proceeding. Suspecting me—me—of assaulting nurseries! I tell you I was dressing for dinner; I can prove it by East."

"What did you want me to do, Joe?" Morey asked mildly. "Throw him out? I could have, but he'd have thrown me straight back—into the pokey."

"I'm sure nobody suspects Mr. Stoneman," Bessy said. "I don't think he's the criminal type."

" You hear that, Joe ? What are you worrying for ? You're safe."

" I can vouch for him too," Mark said. " I heard him cussing his collar. I hope he can do the same for me." He looked down at his shoe. " Well, I'll be," he said, stooping to tie the lace.

Perrin came to the door and asked about dinner.

" Wait a minute," Morey said. " Perrin, I'm beginning to think I'm in trouble. I don't like the way people are looking at me. Now just suppose I were the kind of guy who would sneak out in the dark and half kill his own kids ; would you say I'd had the opportunity ? "

Perrin flushed.

" That's not fair," Beulah objected. " I'll answer. You're the only one in this house who could have done it. That French window. You could have done it easily."

Morey's jaw dropped. " But I was making an ungodly racket ! Shaking cocktails—I even dropped the shaker. Look." He held it up. " A new dent. In fact, the only dent. And I dropped the fire shovel too. Come on now, Perrin, you know you heard me. Didn't you ? "

" No, sir," Perrin said painfully.

" What a pal you turned out to be," moaned Morey. " But I don't harbour grudges. I heard you in the pantry. I know you didn't do it. . . . By the way, Cummings says that was a first-class job you did on Ivy."

" Thank you, sir."

" Get along now and find us something to eat. Cummings wants broth for the children and something light for Mrs. Morey and Miss Petty. You send it up and I'll feed them."

Violet, who had seen and heard enough to keep her in conversation for the rest of her life, trailed after Perrin. The others went to their rooms. Stoneman, lagging behind, paused at the table by the door.

" What happened to the rock ? " he asked Mark.

" Wilcox palmed it. But he won't get any prints. It's too rough."

Beulah shared a tray upstairs with Bessy. Cummings joined the men in the library for coffee. He left with assurances that all three patients were comfortable and would probably sleep until noon the next day. " Sedatives," he said. " I believe in them." Bessy, he said, would be marked for life, but Ivy had youth on her side. Any scars she bore would be on her mind.

" A nasty idea," observed Mark. " In short, a nasty business."

Cummings shrugged, and departed.

Stoneman went to bed at ten o'clock and before he locked himself in he gave Mark two weeks' salary. " I may go to New York for a few days." he said briefly. " You'll need this to go on with. Christmas, you know."

" What about Wilcox ? "

" I expect no trouble from Wilcox. . . . Don't discuss my plans with anyone, please. I don't want them generally known. It's—private business."

" Sure," agreed Mark. " You'll leave some work for me ? "

" I will," Stoneman said with a wintry smile.

Before Mark went to bed himself he tapped on Beulah's door. She joined him in the hall.

" I expected you," she whispered. " I thought you might want to give me a pat on the back for remembering to turn off that gadget when the trouble started."

He gave it. " I'm sorry, Beulah. I didn't know the fireworks would start so soon or that they would be so bad."

" Somebody wants Bessy and me out of the house, eh ? Trying to scare us off ? "

" I think so. Any guesses ? "

" No. But I noticed something funny. It was the way everybody acted. They acted like the people in London did, when there was a blitz. They all poured into the room and began doing the right things, giving orders, taking charge, calling the doctor. They acted as if they knew all about it, before. Not a single, solitary person asked what had happened."

"That bothered me too," Mark said. "You're smart. Nobody asked anything—except Stoneman. Do you remember what it was Stoneman said? 'What the hell!'"

CHAPTER NINE

WHEN Beulah came down the next morning and found three used plates and scraps of cold toast littering the breakfast table she deduced that three people had already eaten and that Perrin and Violet were taking advantage. She also found a note addressed to herself.

It was from Mark; he said he was glad she was alive, as she must be if her eyes met this, and suggested that she take things easy, preferably in that quiet little sewing room. She folded the note and slipped it into her petticoat pocket, an old-fashioned refinement that made her seamstress weep every spring and fall. There were other things in the pocket and she patted them with grim satisfaction.

She investigated the two hot dishes on the sideboard and helped herself largely to kidney stew and scrambled eggs. Her spirits were low and her head ached, but she was ravenous. If they have to do an autopsy on me, she said to herself, I'll make them work. She took second portions.

Eventually the time came when she couldn't swallow another mouthful, so she stacked the dishes and carried them out to the pantry dumbwaiter. It was a thoughtful gesture and had almost nothing to do with snooping. When she slid the plates on to the shelf, she had her reward.

Somebody was talking to Violet in the kitchen. Her conscience had a brief and unsuccessful skirmish with her baser instincts ; she put her head into the shaft and listened. Violet's voice carried nicely.

" He says the lipstick looks funny," she was saying. " He showed it to me and it did. All squinched down on one side. It ought to be in a point, like."

A man's voice whispered something, urgently.

" Where ? " quavered Violet. " You mean at the dumb-waiter ? "

Beulah ducked and scuttled back to the dining room. She waited there, fussing with the hot dishes, until she felt safe from investigation. Then she relieved her feelings by snuffing out the alcohol flames, insuring disappointment to anyone looking for a second breakfast or a cup of hot coffee. This raised her spirits.

She walked briskly into the library, running an experimental finger over everything she passed, looking for dust. Why was Violet so awed about a lipstick ? Whose lipstick ? Squinched when it ought to be in a point ? Why didn't people tell her these things ? And who was that man, careful not to speak above a whisper ? One of Wilcox's guards, probably, who had no business in the kitchen and knew it. Trust Violet ?

She went over to the French window and looked out. No, they were all there, all four of them. Smoking and laughing, undoubtedly at some coarse joke. It didn't help to open the window a crack ; she couldn't hear a thing. She felt frustrated. Nobody was behaving properly.

By rights, she should have been the household pet this morning, with a rose beside her breakfast plate. Instead, she was being ignored. And after all she'd done, too. She wandered over to the desk, wondering if the Moreys were careless in the matter of leaving mail about, and found a pile of cream notepaper, neatly stacked. At once she was reminded of a duty unperformed, a duty that was both pleasant and unpleasant ; pleasant to herself and unpleasant to certain people who might be surprised to find themselves thrown out on their ears. She sat down promptly and, selecting the best pen, wrote a note to Colonel Davenport.

She told him that he couldn't be more surprised than she was herself to be writing him from his own house. She was sure that dear Mr. Scott had already informed him about the fire—and wasn't that the most terrible thing ? —but there was nothing like a personal note from someone he'd known for so many lovely years. She and Bessy— he remembered Bessy Petty ?—were doing the best they could to help his good friends and even though Bessy would carry the scars to her grave, they hoped, etc., etc. And to think that poor little Florrie as well as that fine Christian, Ruth Lacey, and so on, and so on. It did seem as if someone had been rather careless, but then we mustn't judge, must we ? If he wanted anything done, or any changes made, he had only to command ; she was cordially his, Beulah Pond.

The pleasure she normally derived from licking the envelope of such a letter was slightly dampened when she remembered Mark. Perhaps she should have asked him first. If he'd been around she would have asked ; but he wasn't around. She read it over, decided she couldn't be held responsible for the Colonel's interpretation, and addressed it in care of the American Embassy in London. Then she laid plans for mailing it secretly in Crestwood. If anyone challenged her on the way out she'd say she was going home for fresh handkerchiefs. That had a nice plausible sound, considering the blood and tears of the night before.

She checked the dictograph in the sewing room and as an added precaution hung a few of her more intimate garments in its vicinity. Then she had a look at Bessy, still sleeping soundly, and at Mrs. Morey and the children, who were in the same condition. She hesitated at Mark's door and put her ear to the keyhole. Nothing but silence there. She wrote a note, featuring her need for handkerchiefs, and put it on the hall table. Then, dressed for scaling the Matterhorn, she descended into Crestwood. She ignored the guards and they reciprocated.

Mark, at a kitchen window, watched her weaving down the drive.

" I feel better," he said to Violet. " Sure's you're born, that was our Beulah at the dumbwaiter. I can tell by the set of her shoulders. Or else," he added darkly, " she's up to no good this minute. I wonder if she's running out on me ? "

" The things you have to put up with," Violet sighed.

" I wonder why Wilcox didn't come to me with that lipstick business ? I had an idea he and I were going to be buddies."

" He came awfully early, while you was still asleep. When I asked him about Florrie he showed me that lipstick he took out of her purse. He said maybe another girl would know what made it look like that."

" Did you know ? "

" No, sir. Everything was all right but that. Her money was there and all."

" Nobody ever thought it was robbery, Violet. Now, enough of that. I like your Lacey-Stoneman story better. If you and Florrie had only waggled your tongues a little sooner and a little more ! Why didn't you tell me the day Mrs. Lacey died ? "

" We didn't know you so well then. And she made us promise on the Bible. She said if we told anybody something terrible might happen. She said she was going to try to fix it so nothing would. But now that Florrie's gone, I don't care. "

" That's the spirit. And if it'll make you feel better, Florrie told me some of it herself. You're just filling in the bare spots. Now, let's see if I've got it straight. About a week before I came, Mr. Stoneman fell down the cellar steps. It was late at night. He told Mrs. Lacey the next day that he'd been going for a bottle of Scotch. Right ? "

" Yes, sir. And there should of been almost a full bottle in the library because I put one in there after dinner and nobody had more than two drinks out of it. But he claimed the bottle was empty. And Mrs. Lacey told us that if it was empty he wasn't the one that did it because he was cold sober."

" Odd, if true. . . . So, when he came down for a fresh bottle, Mrs. Lacey was in bed with her door closed and her lights out, but she wasn't asleep."

" It was her neuralgia. She was laying there figuring if she should take a pill when she heard a funny noise. So she opened her door just wide enough to put her head out. It was that dark. She thought whoever it was forgot to turn the light on, but the next morning she found out the bulb was gone. And she found out that two cellar steps was hanging down loose, right at the top. And broken glass all over the cellar floor. It would of killed anybody that fell all that way, the glass and all. Big chunks. I helped sweep it up the next morning."

" I see. Now back to that night. She put her head out of the door. Did she go to help him ? "

" Mercy, no ! She didn't know who it was or if it was human. Then all of a sudden the quiet came, quiet like when you're waiting for a soul to pass. She just stood there in the dark, holding her breath and praying. That was when she heard the other one."

" Ah ! This is the part I could hear over and over ! . . . She heard the other one ! "

" Yes, sir. I'd have died in my tracks. She heard the one, which was Mr. Stoneman, groaning and crawling back. He'd only fell part of the way, poor man. And she heard the other one right at the top of the stairs, breathing. She could of reached out and touched it."

" Why do you say ' it,' Violet ? Are you absolutely sure Mrs. Lacey didn't say ' he ' or ' she ' ? "

Violet shifted uneasily. " She never gave it any name but that. . . . Mr. East, do you think it was somebody she knew ? "

" Could be. Tweeds have a distinctive odour, so do furs. And there's always perfume. Now go on from there. She shut her door and got back in bed, didn't she ? "

" You see ! You know it as well as I do ! I don't see why I have to tell you time and again."

" Because you may remember something new. Go on."

" Well, in about five minutes there's a knock on her door and it's Mr. Stoneman. He's using his cigarette lighter to look at her by. His face is terrible. He says he's had an accident and did she hear anything. She was so scared she lied and said she didn't. He's all dusty and his hand is bleeding where he skinned it on the rail. That's how he saved himself, grabbing the rail. He keeps after her, saying she must of heard or seen something and if she didn't, why not ? So she tells him she was just dropping off on account of taking her pill. That made two lies she'd told, and it worried her. But I don't think they'll be counted against her, do you ? "

" No. They won't be counted at all."

" Then," Violet looked happier, " then he told her he'd had a little accident and don't want it talked about. And he tried to give her five dollars to keep her quiet."

Mark drummed on the table. " And then he went upstairs and wrote to me," he murmured. " Sure you haven't left anything out, Violet ? "

" No, sir. Except how she asked Florrie and I the next morning if we'd taken the bulb and we said certainly not, what would we do with a bulb ? And then she said she knew it was a sin to even think such thoughts as she was thinking and she hoped she'd be forgiven for what she was going to say. She said we was to tell her on our honour did we sneak anybody in that night, and she wouldn't punish us if we did. She looked like she was going to faint when we said certainly not. That was when we dragged it out of her."

" And Stoneman kept nagging ? "

" Every time he thought she was alone. Always asking the same old questions, did she see or hear anybody. And had she kept her mouth shut. It used to make Florrie and I wild, hanging down the you-know-what." She rolled her eyes.

" I still don't see how he kept the thing hushed up. Didn't anybody want to know about the broken glass and the steps ? "

" If they did, I never heard about it. We swept up the glass and Mrs. Lacey told Perrin the steps must be rotted off and would he fix them."

" Where was Perrin that night ? "

" Sleeping in his room over the garage. He slept there until after the fire."

" Did you or Florrie ever hear Mr. Stoneman mention his accident to the Moreys ? "

" No, sir. I've told you every last thing I know. . . . Mr. East, what does it mean ? "

" I wouldn't tell you if I knew. In this house knowedge pays off in bloody dividends. And speaking of pay, would you kick me upstairs if I gave you ten bucks for a new hat ? "

" Mr. East ! There's such a thing as friendship ! "

" There is indeed. But friends can eat together can't

they ? After this job is over I'm going to buy you a dinner, with orchids. And we'll invite all your little brothers and sisters. And champagne for you, if you have a good head. Have you ? "

"There's only one way to find out," she carolled as if she were talking to angels.

His face was grim when he returned to his room. He opened the door without ceremony and stalked in. Stoneman, pencil in hand, turned with annoyance.

"I expect you to knock when you enter," he said shortly. "Even if it is your own room. You startled me."

"I hope to startle you even more." Mark picked up a chair and set it facing his employer. "Once more, why did you hire me ? "

Stoneman threw up his hands. "Did you come bursting in here to ask me that—again ? "

"I did. And don't tell me the same story—again."

"Dear me, you have something on your mind. It's almost too obvious. Well, out with it, but for both our sakes, be brief. There is typing to be done."

"Who pushed you down those stairs about two weeks ago ? And why did you want it kept quiet ? And why did you hire me immediately afterward ? "

"I wasn't pushed," smiled Stoneman. "I fell. And as for not talking about it, when a man reaches my age he doesn't discuss his infirmities. Those same infirmities made me realize that I needed help with my book, so I sent for you. I'm bored with this. I hope that's all."

"It isn't. There were two steps removed from the top and if that didn't break your neck the glass at the bottom would have done for your brachial artery. You were lucky."

"You seem to know a great deal about it." The old man slid a pencil into the sharpener and ground it carefully. "I can't imagine where you got your information,

One would almost think you had been there yourself. But that's impossible, isn't it? You were in New York, weren't you? . . . Weren't you?"

"Hey!" Mark glared. "Hey, what are you getting at?"

"Nothing. But I'm not an absolute idiot. You're trying to connect me in some way with these tragedies, are you not? Very natural, considering your background, but I do wish you'd confine yourself to the work you're being paid for. If you don't, I may be forced to draw some conclusions myself. . . . After all, we led uneventful lives before you came. Barring my little vertigo, of course. When you look at it that way, it seems odd, doesn't it? I wonder if Mr. Wilcox has noticed? I imagine he has."

"Save your breath, Mr. Stoneman. My life is an open book, very clean and very dull. That's why I'm not rich. And I'm not accusing you or anybody. But don't you see how that cellar business may be a link?"

"To what, in heaven's name? Cellar stairs have broken before this and will again."

"All right. What about the glass?"

"I'm afraid we're unpopular in the neighbourhood. Last night's performance is a piece of the same cloth. And you recall the stone I was so unfortunate as to intercept? Young vandals, a commonplace in country villages. They got into the cellar and amused themselves."

Mark held his breath before he asked the next question. "Last night when you came into the nursery you didn't think it was vandalism, did you?"

Stoneman looked out at the snow. "I had no thoughts beyond indignation," he said slowly. "Children—and elderly women——It was ugly. . . . But all that is over now. We really are leaving. Arrangements are being made for crating our own things. Our lovely and extremely valuable things. Jim and Laura came to a decision last night. What should have been a pleasant country idyll has turned into a Grand Guignol. Laura has finally seen the light."

"Wilcox says you can't go."

"My dear boy, we will wait for his blessing and full permission. I fancy they will come soon. Someone has come forward with the story of a tramp. Wilcox is inclined to believe it."

"That's more than I am. What about your trip to New York?"

"It all—depends. My little windfall, the one I need so urgently, is on its way. How would you like to try Greece with me, after the war? Look—I've been checking this chart. If we go down the Dalmatian coast——"

"Mr. Stoneman!" Mark rose in fury and desperation. "There is something hellish in this house and I stay right here until I dig it out!"

"You'll have plenty of time for that. We won't be leaving for several days." His eyes twinkled as he turned back to his papers. "But in the meantime, would you mind getting on with these pages?"

Mark used his final shot, the one he was saving for Wilcox. "If you won't talk to me," he said, "I'll go to Morey. I'll tell him who I am. And I'll tell him about the cellar business and how you gave Mrs. Lacey five dollars to keep her mouth shut."

It scored. Stoneman turned slowly. For a fleeting second his eyes held the look of cold rage Mark had seen for the first time the night before. Never again would he think of Stoneman as a bishop-ridden little curate.

"I wouldn't," he said, and he measured Mark from head to foot.

Mark shivered. He met that steady gaze with all he had and held it. Stoneman broke first, and the old effacing smile returned.

"How very amusing that you should know about that little transaction. Who told you?"

"Florrie," Mark lied.   Florrie was already dead, and safe.

"I was sure the good Lacey would keep her word. Florrie must have eavesdropped, though I can't imagine how. But it's of no consequence to anyone but yourself. I gave Mrs. Lacey five dollars for two reasons ; first, I had frightened the poor woman, and, second, I couldn't have Jim jumping at conclusions. I used to drink rather more than was good for me and I'd promised to retrench. You must admit that falling downstairs at eleven-thirty with an empty bottle clutched to one's bosom has a suspicious look "

"The bottle was really empty ? "

"I see you know the whole story. I'm surprised at Florrie. I'm also beginning to suspect Mrs. Lacey. And spare me any discussion about the light bulb. Someone started to put a new one in and was called away before the job was finished. Afraid to admit it, of course. Now, can we get on with this work ? "

"In a minute," Mark said calmly. "One more thing on my mind.   Did you know Mrs. Lacey took sleeping pills ? "

"Certainly. That was brought out at the inquest." He waited. "Is that all ? " he added plaintively.

Mark uncovered the typewriter and shuffled papers. "That's all," he said cheerfully. "Here we go."

Stoneman stood at his shoulder for a minute and then went quietly out of the room. Mark tapped the keys faithfully and carefully, but part of his mind stayed with the recent conversation. One evasion stood out. Stoneman had known about Lacey's pills before the inquest. Lacey had invited death, standing in that dark little hall, telling her desperate lies.

It was twelve-thirty when Stoneman came back suggesting lunch. Mark said he didn't want any. Stoneman counted the typed pages.

"Good work," he said. "I didn't expect it. You looked like a man who had better things to do."

Mark grunted.

"Come now," Stoneman continued, "you were rather impertinent, you know. But that's the fault of your dreadful background. Have lunch with me and I'll cajole a bottle of claret out of Perrin." He closed one eye in a brotherly wink. "I'll even let him go down for it."

"Cajole it for yourself," Mark winked back. "I want to finish this, and then I'll go up and annoy the invalids."

"As you say, as you say. But do keep one corner of your mind for Greece. Think of it—a Grecian spring, with flowering carpets on the bones of kings!" He left the room, humming.

Mark went back to his typing. "Damn sure he's going to dig up a king," he murmured. "So his little windfall is about ready to drop. If I have any luck I'll be far away from here when that happens because I have a hunch something else will drop with it. Maybe my head." He jumped like a cat when Violet walked in.

"Well?" he grinned foolishly.

"Nothing," she said. After a quick, mysterious look around the room she began to whisper rapidly. "Miss Pond called up about fifteen minutes ago and wanted to talk to you, but Mr. S. said you wasn't to be disturbed. So she said to tell you not to go out anywhere and she's coming back as soon as she can. I was to tell you when nobody was around. She says to keep Miss Petty in her room. She says to lock her in if you have to."

"I think Beulah's acting up," Mark said. "And I'm not the man to lock Bessy in."

"I already did it."

"It won't do any good. If she wants out, she'll out."

"No she won't. I put a pill in her lunch soup. The doctor give me an extra one in case."

He sat back. "I'm not going to Greece with my Mr. S. I'm going to a South Sea isle with you."

" Pardon ? " said Violet.

" Get along. I'm busy. See you later, and thanks. I'll keep an eye on Miss Petty. Leave the key here." He returned to his work with a smile. Beulah, he decided, had discovered that the legless Bittner was a werewolf.

He finished another page. There was no getting away from it, the old man loved his ancient dead with passion. The tarnished comb of a mouldering little princess could turn him into a lyric poet for—let's see—three pages. He was almost as good as Omar ; well, in a way he was. The same weeping over forgotten hyacinths and dusty courtyards.

He punched down a period, shifted, and reached for a cigarette. At that instant Morey strolled in.

" I was just going over to check on the infirmary," Mark said.

" No need. I've done it. All took nourishment at noon and feel fine. Violet's looking after them now. The Petty, though, has locked herself in."

" She would," Mark said easily.

" I tried her door. I think she's afraid of old Joe. I wonder what we hired those women for ? When I came by the station a while ago I saw the other one—the Pond— sitting inside with Partridge. Gabble, gabble, gabble. I thought she was off him."

" On again, I guess."

" Well, I waved my hand like a gentleman and she ducked as if I'd thrown a bomb. Partridge just looked silly. I wonder if she's taking over where Lacey left off."

" Maybe. He's got the house and chickens."

Morey looked over the typed copy. " Is this stuff really any good ? Do you think he's got anything ? "

" He's wonderful," Mark said honestly. " He's as good as the best. It's got soul."

" Has it now ? " Morey marvelled. " Well, I'm not surprised. . . . I've got some news for you. Wilcox is releasing Florrie's body for burial. They've got a tramp locked up. So we're all right."

" Are we ? "

" Sure. Wilcox says we can leave now. If they can't prove it on the tramp they'll call it person or persons unknown. Wilcox says they had a case just like it in Minnesota last week."

" What's a case in Minnesota got to do with Florrie ? "

" Search me. Proves the thing can happen, I guess. You're going to keep on with Joe, aren't you ? "

" I don't know."

" Well, I'm off to hunt packing cases. If anybody wants me I'll be in the garage." He turned back before he reached the door. " Wilcox asked about guards for tonight. I told him I'd let him know. What do you think ? "

" That's up to you," Mark said.

" That's where you're wrong. It's up to Mrs. Morey. She says they make her nervous. I have a feeling they're going to go."

Mark heard him clatter down the hall. " Then why ask me ? " he said to nobody. He typed his last page slowly and closed the machine. So it was going to end like this ; Florrie in her mother's parlour for a day or two, then out in the snowbound little cemetery with Ruthie Lacey for company through the long winter nights. He suddenly felt cold.

He was standing by the window, shivering, when Beulah came in. Her lips were blue and her face was ashen. " If you have a drink up here I wish you'd give it to me," she said quietly.

Something in her bearing alarmed him. He poured a drink from the bottle Stoneman kept in the desk and closed the hall door. " Take it easy," he said. " What's happened ? "

She took a soiled white envelope from her purse, opened

it, and handed him the contents. "There are two pieces of paper," she said mechanically. "Read the top one first. . . . Florrie."

It was a page torn from a pocket notebook, covered on both sides with crowded lines of block printing. Red lines.

"Isn't this——?"

"Lipstick," she said. "She used it to write with. That's what bothered Wilcox. Read it."

Mark looked up. "Then it was you at the dumbwaiter while I was talking to Violet about the lipstick."

Beulah said impatiently, "What's the difference! Read that."

He read, bitterly : I CAME YOU SAID I COULD COME BUT YOU ARE NOT HERE. I WILL TRY TO FIND YOU AT MRS. LACEY'S IF NOBODY CATCHES ME. SOMEONE IS BEHIND ME. I FOUND THIS IN THE TRASH BAG. IT'S WHAT THEY LOST BUT MAYBE THEY DON'T KNOW ABOUT THE LITTLE PIECE TORN OFF. I CAN'T FIND THE LITTLE PIECE. I GUESS THEY THINK I FOUND IT BUT I DIDN'T. MISS POND I AM AFRAID. WHO IS DEAD ?

Mark looked at Beulah. "Where was this ? "

"Under the rug inside my front door. She must have slipped it there that night. I always told her she could come to me for help. And when she did come, when she needed me, I was——" She looked out of the window, seeing nothing. "I'm afraid too. I wouldn't have come back except for Bessy."

"She's all right. She's locked in. Beulah, what did Florrie find ? What does she mean by 'Who is dead ? '"

She pointed to the other piece of paper. It was a newspaper clipping, faintly yellow but carefully preserved except for one ragged tear at the bottom. It bore no date and no identifying marks beyond two capital letters at the top left. They were obviously the end of a name, either of the sheet itself or the place of its origin. To kill time, he fingered the paper. Poor quality, small town. He was afraid to read it. He knew that once he did, things would never be as they were then. She saw what he was thinking.

"Go on," she said. "You've got to."

He read in a whisper. "*We regret to inform our many readers that the party responsible for the crime which occurred on Saturday night a mile west of Citrus City is still at large. Owing to lack of witnesses and due to fact that no description of hit-and-run car is available, our efficient young constable, Mr. Roy Graybar, don't look for an early arrest. But there is one bright ray piercing the sad gloom. Our citizens will be happy to know that the poor soul who met his death in our midst has been identified by a friend who was passing through town. The dead man is Mr. J.——*"

That was all. The tear was a recent one. He noted the two letters at the top. DA. Probably the last two letters of the paper's name or, and he thought this more likely, the name of a state. Citrus City,—— Easy to check in an atlas.

"Would somebody kill to get possession of that?" Beulah asked.

"Yes. He doesn't know the name is gone. Torn off through handling in the trash, and burned. Apparently it's dynamite. Why was it kept? And who kept it?"

"Can you find out?"

"I think so. If I'm any good I can. . . . Beulah, do you want to go home? I'll take you and Bessy down to-night. You needn't explain to anybody."

"No. I won't leave those children. But we mustn't tell Bessy. She's not strong. Mark, will Bessy be safe?"

"I'll make it safe. But I'll be helpless unless you do exactly as I say. You've never seen this clipping and you don't know Florrie left a note! Did you say anything to Amos?"

"Never! I stopped there because I wanted to see some-body I'd known all my life. And while I was there I gave him a piece of my mind about not coming up here last night with Perley Wilcox. He admitted he was grieving drunk."

" Morey says you didn't return his greeting."

" I—couldn't. His name begins with a J."

" What's Colonel Davenport's name ? "

" Jacob. . . . Oh, Mark ! "

" You see ? You're crazy. Remember, J is dead, run over. I like the sound of his friend better. The friend, male or female, who was so conveniently passing through. Small town, hit-and-run with no witnesses, identification, insurance. And not even an initial to give him away."

" Are you going to tell Wilcox ? "

" Everything. I need his help with some long-distance calls. Did Amos say anything about Florrie's funeral ? "

" To-morrow. Three o'clock. . . . Mark, I left you a note saying I was going for handkerchiefs. But I went to mail a letter to Colonel Davenport. I told him about the troubles we were having. Are you mad ? "

" No. I didn't get the note, though. It's probably kicking around. Now you go let Bessy out and then both of you come down for a drink before dinner. And be gay if it kills you." He gave her the key.

It was then four o'clock, and over in Bear River Mrs. Perley Wilcox was writing on a blackboard.

CHAPTER TEN

MRS. PERLEY WILCOX was listening to her kitchen radio when her brother came to the back door with news from her mother. He was glum. The old girl thought she was dying again ; no use telling her it was too much apple dumpling and the new batch of beans she would eat before they were half done. She was holding out for fallen stomach and, by Harry, it ought to fall.

She'd carried on like a child until they promised to drive in
and fetch Pansy. Would Pansy come ? The old girl was
lonesome for another woman, that's all. Nothing wrong a
pinch of soda wouldn't cure. Like as not she took the
soda herself the minute she heard the sleigh drive off.

Mrs. Wilcox, Pansy, pushed a kettle of soup to the back
of the stove, got into suitable clothing, and trotted over to
the family blackboard. This was fastened to the wall
between two windows. There was one message on it
already : POP. LEAVE ME A QUARTER. URGENT. FLOYD.
She drew a line under this and wrote her own : I AM CALLED
TO MAMMA'S EATING TOO MUCH AGAIN BUT THE POOR THING
COUNTS ON ME. FLOYD DO YOUR LESSONS GOOD. PERLEY
DON'T STAY LATE AT LODGE. SOUP ON STOVE WITH GOOD
CHUNK MEAT IN AND BISCUITS AND PIE IN PANTRY. DON'T
LOOK FOR ME BEFORE TEN. MAMMA.

Young Floyd Wilcox came in shortly after four, found
his quarter in the chalk box, read his mother's announce-
ment, and threw his cap in the air. He cut a slab from the
good chunk of meat, making a mess of the stove, and con-
verted it into a sandwich. While he ate this he added a
third message : POP I AM OVER AT A FELLOW'S HOUSE DOING
MATH. IF I GET ASKED TO STAY TO SUPPER I'LL STAY AND
DO MORE MATH AFTER. FLOYD. THANKS FOR QUARTER.

He took his gun out of the closet and went next door to
tell Chester Green they had the chance of a lifetime.

Chester was considered a lucky boy by his friends. His
mother was dead and his father worked for the railroad
and never got home before midnight. Ever since the first
tragedy at Crestwood, Floyd and Chester had longed to
view the scene. This was morbid and not to be thought of.
But morbid or not, to-night was their chance. They'd
ride both ways in the bus with their faces hidden in their
mufflers, and if they were caught they'd take their lickings
like men. The guns were pure chicanery. They might

meet small game in the woods, and parental wrath was
known to soften at the sight of something for the pot.   At
quarter after five they had started up the mountain and
they had one rabbit.

At five Mark entered the library to cast an experimental
fly into a fast-darkening stream.

Stoneman was alone by the fire.   " Drink ? " he asked.

" Later," Mark said.   He walked over to the book-
cases and ran a finger along the titles.   " Travel," he said
over his shoulder.   " I'm looking for travel books."

" You don't need books," Stoneman said.   " I've got it
all in my head."

" This is something new."   He came back with an atlas
and a volume extolling Florida.   " Did you ever do any
research among our native Indians ?   Burial mounds ? "

"No,"said Stoneman after a pause. "And I don't want to."

" You have a closed mind.   That's bad.   And it's
getting worse and worse.   Take that plan of yours for
switching our operations to New York.   Trading the
mountain blast for the city slush.   That's narrow.   I
don't like it.   I like the southern sun."

" I think," Stoneman said surprisingly, " you have a
touch of it already."

Mark laughed loudly and returned to his books.   " Now
back to the Indians," he said.   " I've worked out a wonderful scheme.   You'll get your name in the papers and you'll
like that, won't you ?   Don't answer ; I know.   And now,
get this : while you're waiting for a chance to increase
your prestige in foreign parts, why don't you make a
pretty gesture with the bones of the original American ?
A sort of patriotic warmup ? "

Stoneman reached for the bottle and spiked his drink.
" I'm not offering you any . . . more," he said.

Mark seemed not to hear.   " Florida," he said, stabbing
a page with his finger.   " Florida.   I like places that end

in *da*. Of course you can have Canada or Nevada, but they're cold. Florida is warm, and it sounds nice and soft. Nice and soft, like driving along a road in the dark and— oh, well, that's another story. Florida, lovely climate and full of Indians. If you won't go, I'll go alone. Now all I need is a nice little town for headquarters. Something with a quaint name." He put the travel book aside and picked up the atlas, never once looking in Stoneman's direction. His hands were sweating, but he knew what he was doing. He'd checked the books earlier and found what he hardly hoped to find so soon. Citrus City in the state of Florida. Population fifteen hundred.

"I'm going to my room," Stoneman said.

"No, don't!" He stabbed a page again. "Just when I've found the perfect place. . . . Citrus City!"

Perrin came in with a bowl of ice.

"Thanks," Mark beamed. "Mr. Stoneman needs that. And you'd better bring a fresh bottle. What's your first name, Perrin?"

Perrin looked at Stoneman, but Stoneman had turned his back. "George, sir," he answered quietly. "Is there anything else?"

"Yes. Are these the Colonel's books or the Moreys'?"

"We brought no books, sir." He took another bottle of Scotch from the cabinet, placed it beside Stoneman, and left the room.

"I just wondered," Mark said. "Somebody's checked the name of that town. You know, Citrus City. I guess Davenport went there." He carried the book over to Stoneman and held it before his eyes. "See?" The check was there; he'd seen to that himself.

Stoneman answered in a furious undertone. "Control yourself, you fool! The ladies are here."

Beulah bounded into the room, followed by Bessy leaning sedately on Morey's arm. Mark winced when he saw the gaiety in Beulah's eye. It was the glittering kind that expressed itself in little screams, flounces, and slaps with a fan. Thank God she didn't have a fan. He put the atlas beside the travel book and returned to his chair. He was still sweating. Had Citrus City meant anything to Stoneman? He couldn't be sure.

Morey, pouring drinks, gave Stoneman a long look. " What's the matter with you, Joe? Are you cold? "

Mark pounced. " I'm worried about him," he said. " He's driving himself too hard. He needs a rest, and a warm climate. I've been telling him so. If ever a man needed Florida, he does. Look at him—he's shaking!"

Stoneman was shaking; he'd gone back to his old trick of hiding his hands.

" You need a drink, Joe," Morey said. He filled the glass. " But why Florida? "

" Why not? It has everything." Mark indicated the books. " Just before you came in I was trying to sell him on a little town that seems to have been a favourite of Davenport's. At least, it's been checked by somebody, Citrus City." He raised guileless eyes and swore under his breath. Morey wasn't even looking at him. His eyes were on the door. Laura Morey, rouged and perfumed, was joining them.

The only people in the room who reacted normally were Bessy and Beulah. They made affectionate noises and plumped pillows. Nobody ever looked less in need of a pillow than Laura Morey. She was hard and brilliant, perfectly poised. The three men stared. Mark felt a new kind of cold, this time around his heart.

Her husband spoke first. " You're wonderful," he said. " I always knew you could do it. But why didn't you tell me? I'd have had cocktails for you."

" I'll try Joe's Scotch," she said. She smiled at Mark and Stoneman and took a seat between Bessy and Beulah.

" I feel I haven't been quite fair to you good people. There are only a few days left now, and I want to know you better before I leave. You know we're going ? "

Bessy patted her bandaged face. " I don't blame you. I'm sure the Colonel won't blame you either. I'll be glad to get home myself."

" You've been amazingly helpful," Laura said softly. " If you can only stay with me until——"

" We will," said Beulah. " We'll stay until you're safely on the train. . . . You're taking your time with those drinks, young man," she called to Morey.

Morey winked at her. " How about Miss Petty ? "

" I told her she could have two," Beulah cackled. " One for each pill she took. We'll drown 'em out."

" And we'll carry her upstairs feet first," Mark murmured. He absently took the glass Morey handed him. Things were moving too swiftly and evenly. If he didn't move fast himself he was going to be left on the station platform, holding two suitcases. Stoneman's belated chills were the only good sign. Later on, if Beulah could arrange to take over the dictograph. . . . He stared into his drink and thought furiously about his next move. It came at once and it wasn't what he planned.

A shot rang out, clean and clear. Silence fell like thunder. Stoneman's glass crashed to the marble hearth and he slumped in his chair.

Morey ran across the room. " Joe ! "

" He's all right," Mark cried. " It was outside. It didn't come in ! " He herded the three terrified women into a corner. "Stay here a minute. You'll be safe. Perrin!"

But Perrin was already beside him, looking ready to kill. " What was that ? What was that, Mr. East ! "

" Somebody shooting outside. Don't worry about Stoneman ; get these women upstairs and lock them in with the children and Violet. Then come back here."

He saw them leave, mute and stumbling, and then followed Morey through the French window out into the black night. They stood side by side on the terrace, tense, uncertain, panting.

"Which way?" Morey asked. "Where did it come from?"

"I don't know. Pretty close, though. Shall we divide up?"

" You go right and I'll go left." As Morey spoke, the entire front of the house blazed into light, flooding the snow and the encroaching trees. Perrin came through the window.

" Who turned on those lights ? " Morey snapped.

" Miss Pond, sir. She thought you'd need them. I left her in charge."

" Turn them off. We're targets. Wait, I'll take care of it. Got a gun on you ? "

" Yes, sir."

" Use it. You ? " to Mark.

" No. '

" Neither have I, damn." He spoke rapidly. " East will cover the right, I'll take the left, and, Perrin, you go straight down the drive. Yell if you find anything and shoot anybody you see."

Perrin slipped quietly away. Mark moved off to the right. Morey stepped back to the window.

" Joe ? " he called. Stoneman's thin, frightened voice answered. " Get Wilcox on the 'phone and tell him what's happened. Then you go upstairs with the others. Miss Pond will take care of you. And turn off those lights, all of them ! "

Mark plunged through laurel and rhododendron, cursing the dark. He heard Morey thrashing around on the other side, then the sound grew fainter. It was useless and he knew it. He couldn't see a foot ahead. It would have been better to leave the lights on. Once he thought he saw two figures running down the drive and he nearly shouted. He remembered it was Perrin's territory and

Perrin had a gun. That was something to remember—Perrin had a gun.

The cold was frightful. He could see better now, enough to know that there were no tracks in the snow. Nobody had come that way. He sat on a boulder, panting. He figured he must be half a mile from the house. He looked back. Nothing in sight—not even a start to prick the blackness.

The marksman, whoever he was, was safe. They'd never get him in this wilderness. He could easily be hiding behind a rock, laughing to himself; but he wasn't shooting. Not now. Maybe he didn't want any of the three who were, hunting him; maybe he wanted one of those who hadn't come out. Stoneman, Violet, Beulah, or Bessy, Mrs. Morey. That rock last night . . . the kids. Had last night been a warning and was this the real thing? Had he known they'd come dashing out like idiots and leave the house open for him to walk in? A house that held one old man, four women, two children.

Mark looked at the luminous dial of his watch. They'd been out there for twenty minutes. Ten more minutes to get back if he ran. They'd given the nameless devil a good half-hour. He could wipe out a regiment in that time.

He ran back the way he'd come, falling over the same bushes. When he reached the terrace he saw a small light moving up the driveway. It was Perrin, with an electric torch. So he had that as well as the gun.

" I went down on one side and came up on the other. There's nothing," Perrin said.

" No," Mark said. He told him what he'd been thinking. They moved quickly to the window, still dark and unlocked. Mark wondered about Morey. They heard him coming almost at once, swearing and stumbling. They went into the house together, and Mark walked wearily. There was dead silence and the smell of spilt whisky.

Morey switched on the lights in the empty room and went immediately to the fire. "If I ever get my hands on——" He took up the poker and prodded the coals furiously. "I suppose you didn't see anything either?"

Mark told him what he'd told Perrin, watching them both. Morey looked white.

"O.K. up there?" he called.

Beulah's voice came back, faint but reassuring.

"That's that," he said. "I hope Joe got Wilcox. Go ask him, Perrin, but don't let anybody hear you. And see what Violet can do about dinner. You might tell the ladies I'll be up shortly. I'll have to think up something to tell them."

Perrin left.

"Poachers!" Morey snapped his fingers. "That's what I'll tell them. Poachers. They always sound good. We saw their tracks but they got away. Will that go down, do you think?"

"Not with me," Mark said, pouring himself a drink. "And not, I think, with Wilcox. I have a hunch he'll bring his guards back."

"I wish he would. They never should have gone. But that's Laura. Do you think Wilcox is good enough for this thing? What do you think yourself?"

"I think you'd better get out while you can."

"I've got to." Morey prodded the fire again. "This is the last straw. . . . Well, Perrin?"

"Mr. Stoneman isn't upstairs," Perrin said from the doorway.

"Did you look as well as ask?"

"Yes, sir. I looked in his room and in Mr. East's room. The ladies have locked themselves in the nursery and they say Mr. Stoneman was never with them. I suggest you speak to them yourself, sir. They appear to be nervous."

" Right away."   He paused at the door.   " Get along
with dinner, Perrin, and, East, you might try the cellar
for Stoneman.   Joe takes to the cellar like other people
take to prayers."

Mark went down with Perrin, but Stoneman wasn't
there.   Suddenly he knew he wouldn't be.   He didn't
know what Stoneman had feared, but whatever it was, it
had caught up with him.   Mark waited in the kitchen until
Violet came, then returned to the library.

Morey was trying to get Wilcox on the telephone, but
the operator told him there was no answer.   She said he'd
taken a call nearly an hour ago, from Crestwood.

" Stoneman seems to have reached him all right,"
Morey said.   " But where is he now ? "

" Not in the cellar," Mark said.   " Perhaps—somewhere else in the house."

" No.   He'd be creeping out now, full of apologies and
long explanations. . . . What's that ? "

Brakes squealed outside.   " The law," Mark said.
" And about time, too."

Wilcox was furious.   He'd left a hot dinner and told
them so.   And who was the idiot who babbled over the
'phone that everybody was being killed ?   Where were
the corpses ?   He looked sourly at the crackling fire and
the table with bottles and empty glasses.

" Wait," advised Morey.   " Let me tell you."   When
he finished, Wilcox looked serious.

" You mean the old gentleman is—gone ? "

" Vanished in thin air," Mark said.

Wilcox swung into action.   He spied Perrin in the
hall.   " Get everybody in this room, including yourself
and Violet ! "   He opened the French window and bawled,
" Harry ! "   A blushing farmer lumbered in.   " Take all
the boys and cover the grounds.   Go in the woods if you
have to.   Look for prints.   Look for an old man—he's

probably fallen down somewhere. Bring me anybody you find, dead or alive, with or without guns." Harry withdrew.

"I'm afraid you'll have trouble with prints," Mark said gently. "Three of us have been out there already and the snow's pretty well churned up."

Perrin came back with the people from upstairs, and Morey retreated to the fireplace while the interviews went on. Wilcox learned nothing. There had been a shot close by and Mr. Morey had sent them all away and asked Mr. Stoneman to telephone. Then the men had gone out.

"What made you think you'd need me?" Wilcox asked Morey.

Morey sent a shower of sparks up the chimney. "Past history," he said.

Violet, with flour on her hands, was frightened to the point of impertinence. "I've got dinner to get on," she said. "People got to eat. And somebody ought to be with those children upstairs. I don't know where Mr. Stoneman is, but if it was me I'd look under his bed. As for shooting, the way I feel I don't care if they shoot me next." She burst into tears and went back to the kitchen.

Wilcox organized a search of the house, Mark to do the first floor, Morey the second, and Perrin the cellars. He dismissed the women with a wave. Beulah hung back nervously.

"There's nothing in the nursery quarters, Perley," she said. "Oh, excuse me, I mean Mr. Wilcox. We've been locked in there."

"Omit the nursery quarters, Mr. Morey. Partridge is on the way and he'll help. Don't count on him too soon, he's got a train coming. I'm going to stay right here in case my boys bring in something."

The search went on. From all quarters of the house came the sound of banging doors, moving furniture.

They were back in half an hour. There was no sign of Stoneman.

"His room is in order," Morey said, "and all of his clothes are there." He turned a listening face toward the terrace. "Somebody's coming!"

They all stood up.

Harry stumbled through the window, followed by two men and two blinking boys carrying guns and dragging a sack. Harry was grinning broadly and the two men were carefully looking at nothing. "Here's your gunmen," Harry said. "Big-game hunters." He pushed the boys forward.

Wilcox turned a rich red. "My—my son." He cleared his throat. He turned on the smaller boy. "There's a no-trespassing sign on these premises, and you know it. Open that sack, sir!"

The smaller boy looked ready to cry. "Pop," he began, "Pop——"

"Open it!" thundered Wilcox. "Not on the rug! Get a newspaper! Is this the way you do your mathematics?"

The older boy got a paper and spread it carefully. Then they emptied the sack. Six fat rabbits fell out.

Wilcox counted them with a calm voice and a heavy foot. "Six rabbits is six shots," he said to Morey. "You told me one."

Floyd tried again. "Pop," he said desperately. "Pop——"

"One was all we heard," Morey said.

Mark gave the boys a conspiring grin. "They're beauties. Where did you get them?"

They grinned back like reprieved men facing the governor. "I tried to tell Pop," Floyd babbled. "I tried to tell him. We got 'em over back of the hotel right after we hit the woods. We weren't anywhere near here when we got 'em. We weren't even on this land."

Chester cleared his throat and winked rapidly. "I fired the one they heard, Mr. Wilcox. I thought it was all right. I mean I could see lights in the dining room and all and it was dinner time and I aimed downhill. I knew nobody would be outside to get hurt. I—I only took a crack at that guy's hat."

His audience recoiled. "Hat!" Morey repeated sharply. "He wasn't wearing a hat!"

"The snowman. I couldn't help it."

Wilcox sighed. "How long have you been here?" he asked heavily.

"How long, Chester?" asked the miserable Floyd.

"Since after five. We were just going home."

"Did you see anybody?"

They looked uneasy. Floyd was struck dumb by a sudden seizure of coughing, and Chester took it up.

"Come, now. You were near enough to the house. Did you see anybody before or after that shot?"

Chester quailed. "We saw that man, and that man, and that one." He pointed a sure finger at Mark, Morey, and Perrin. "They came out of that glass door and run all over the place. After."

"What did you do then? Floyd! Cat got your tongue?"

Floyd rounded off his seizure with a small artistic hack. "We—we sort of guessed it was our shot that brought 'em out, so we hid. And we watched."

Mark drew a deep breath. "Were you out there all the time?"

"Yes, sir. Behind some bushes."

"That's what I call a thorough search," Wilcox said grimly. "Two big strapping boys with guns and a sack full of rabbits! What about fresh tracks, Floyd?"

"Nobody been through there for hours, Pop."

"You know what's happened, don't you?"

Harry had been quiet too long. He stepped forward. "I told 'em, sir. To impress 'em with the severity. They say they'd like to help, but I dunno."

Morey advanced, wallet in hand. "Can't you put them on a cradle roll or something, Wilcox? They look smart to me. And they cleared up the shot angle; now we know where it went."

"His mother will kill me," said Wilcox, eyeing the wallet.

"Five dollars each retaining fee." Morey handed it over. "You chaps know this place better than I do. You may find something."

"W-well," said Wilcox "Take off your caps! Where are your manners!"

"I'm very fond of rabbit pie," Morey went on. "That is, if you have no other plans?" More money found its way to mackinaw pockets and was buttoned in.

"Get along home now," Wilcox ordered. "And you'd better make it before your mother does. And if you have any conscience left, which I doubt, you'll rub out that bit about mathematics and urgent quarters. You can come back to-morrow if we haven't found him by then."

Mark had kept in the background as much as possible. He'd begun to form a theory, but Floyd and Chester had knocked it into a cocked hat. Hat. He'd have a look at that snowman to-morrow. He wondered if Chester's aim was as good as Anne's.

Morey and Wilcox went into a huddle at the window; Harry and his silent partners refreshed themselves at Morey's insistence; Perrin left for the kitchen with his reluctant hands full of dangling rabbits. Mark went upstairs and found Beulah.

"What do you think?" he asked her.

"I think Mr. Stoneman went out to help you and that Green boy shot him by mistake and buried him. You'll find him when it thaws."

" Talk sense ! . . . He was alive when we left him.   He
telephoned Wilcox. . . . Beulah, is Stoneman out there
now ?   Did he follow us, in a panic, and lose himself ? "

" I've told you what I think."

There were only three of them at dinner, Morey, Mark,
and Beulah.   The others ate upstairs.   Morey took a cup
of soup, drank it hastily, and excused himself.

" We're going out to make another try," he said.
" Partridge sent lanterns up from the station.   He'll come
along himself, later ; so will Perrin."

" You ought to eat more," Beulah said.

" Violet's filled some thermos bottles.   East, I'd rather
you stayed here, if you don't mind.   I don't like to leave
the women alone, and we all know the grounds better than
you do.   If you'll stay in your room, I think my wife will
feel easier.   Man within reach, you know."

Mark nodded and followed him into the library.

" Better lock this after we go."   Morey indicated the
window.   " I've got a key to the front door."   He stepped
out, trailed by Harry and the two speechless deputies.
Wilcox had gone earlier.   Mark went back to Beulah and
finished a dinner he couldn't taste.

" Did you have a chance to do anything about—Citrus
City ? " she asked.

" Yes.   I found it, and I mentioned it.   I think I got a
reaction and I wish now that I hadn't. . . . You know, we
ought to cover that dictograph to-night."

"Why, for heaven's sake?   There's nobody here but us."

" Somebody might come back."

" Perrin or Morey ! "

" Don't jump at things.   I imagine even Amos and
Wilcox could get admission to my lady's boudoir if they
had a good story.   And—somebody might telephone."

" That would be plain foolish.   You could listen in and
they know it."

"Not in my room. That's the beauty of it. No 'phone there."

"I'll do it. As soon as I get Bessy to bed."

He patted her hand. "I don't know what I'd do without you. . . . You look dead. Why don't you go up now and rest before you take over? There wouldn't be a cot in that sewing room?"

"There would."

"The whole thing's too perfect. Go on—I'll bring Violet when she's ready. Lock her in with Bessy. I give you the usual warning; if you want me, yell. I'll be around somewhere. When Wilcox comes back he and I are going to have a heart-to-heart talk. I want him to do some fancy official telephoning."

He delivered Violet to Beulah an hour later, when Perrin left to join the hunt. In that hour he had thoroughly searched Stoneman's papers and found nothing. There was not even a postcard. There was very little clothing. Except for his bulky manuscript, Stoneman had travelled light. Too light. A dinner coat, but only six handkerchiefs; toilet articles in small sizes, such as a man buys hastily when he finds himself obliged to spend the night in a strange town.

At ten o'clock Morey called up the stairs. He said he and Amos were going to the cellar for wood to build fires. Mark didn't go down to help them because they didn't ask him. He heard them both leave fifteen minutes later.

He was restless and a little angry. It was Perrin's job to stay with the women. He belonged outside with the others. He patrolled the upper and lower halls and even went down to the kitchen. Everything was in order. Once he stopped at the nursery door, prudently left ajar by Beulah. She heard him and came out. Nothing, she told him. Mrs. Morey had moved about earlier but now she was quiet. She'd cried, too. He went back to his

room and looked out of the window, but there was nothing
to see. The trees were too thick. He tried a window at
the front end of the hall and that was better. For half an
hour he stood there, watching the moving lights and stooping
figures. It was like a gallery view of an old-time spectacle.

Someone came and stood beside him in the dark. He
thought it was Beulah and started to say something about
the dictograph. He caught himself in time. It was
Laura Morey.

She didn't speak, so he said nothing. Looking out of the
corner of his eye he saw she was intent on the scene below.

Finally he said : " Pretty picture but confusing plot."

" Yes." She didn't turn her head. Then, " Do you
think he ran away ? "

" Why would he do that ? " he answered carefully.

" I don't—I don't know."

They stood in silence, watching the lights. There were
fires along the driveway.

" He was a very old friend, I know," he said. " This
must be a shock to you. But—I'll get him."

" G—get him ? "

" Yes." He nodded to the panorama spread below.
" They won't find him," he said softly, " but I will."

" No ! " she said. " No ! "

He let her go without comment. Then he went back to
his room and read about Stoneman's dead kings.

At midnight the searchers came back, unsuccessful,
and dumped their ropes and lanterns in the hall. Morey
was staggering with fatigue and went directly to bed.
Harry and the deputies had already gone home, but
Wilcox declared his intention of staying. He would sleep
on Stoneman's bed with one eye open and maybe he'd see
something.

Perrin moved soundlessly from room to room, checking
on doors and windows. Before he went up to his own room

he said there was food and drink in the kitchen for anyone who wanted it. Mr. Morey's compliments. Amos, ostentatiously counting his lanterns, set them down with a clatter at the mention of drink. He reminded Wilcox that the mail train wasn't due until six and said he felt as gay as a lark.

That gave Mark his opportunity. He led them both downstairs and brought out the cold meat and beer. Then he began to talk.

At the same time, over in Bear River, the Fates tossed a monkey wrench. Mrs. Wilcox telephoned that Mamma had it bad this time and nobody was to look for her until after breakfast. And water the ferns. Next door, Mr. Green crawled into his blankets without washing and was off on the first lap of his favourite run. The Cradle Roll, released from supervision, moved like an army down the snowy midnight streets, ducking and crouching and weaving toward Crestwood.

Mark began with an admission of his own identity. If he hoped for a sign of dropped jaw or even a demonstration of bated breath, he was disappointed.

Wilcox calmly opened another bottle. " We thought you were too interfering for a secretary," he said. " And Violet noticed how you typed with two fingers. This is what I've been waiting for. Go on."

" First, what about that tramp you've got locked up ? "

" I haven't got a tramp. I gave that out to see if it would please anybody. Go on—you tell me, then I'll tell you."

He told them about Stoneman's fall and gave the details as he had them from Violet. He was sure he'd been hired as a bodyguard, although Stoneman denied it. And he was sure Mrs. Lacey had recognized Stoneman's assailant. That recognition had been a shock she couldn't hide. She'd tried to get away to New York, but the murderer couldn't afford to let her go. She'd been given a dose of sleeping pills and her room was deliberately fired. There'd been opportunity. She'd gone out to the stables, or garage, for a piece of rope to bind her luggage, leaving her customary thermos jug of tea or cocoa beside her bed. And her little box of pills. Lacey knew too much.

Florrie. Florrie didn't know anything definite. Her trouble was curiosity and pique. He told them about the trash baskets. He pictured Florrie being questioned, perhaps too harshly, and her growing resentment. She must have made a second, surreptitious search before the trash was burned. She found a newspaper clipping and decided it was important. " Nobody knows what made her decide that. We can only guess. She may have over-heard, at some time, a scrap of conversation and uncon-sciously remembered it. The clipping may have brought it back with terrifying clearness and significance. She may have tied it up with Mrs. Lacey's death. She lost her head. She had to tell somebody. Then she remembered how Miss Pond had offered to take her in if things got bad. She was too frightened to wait until morning, too frightened to think of anything but her own skin. She got up in the dead of night, put the clipping in her purse, and crept out of the house. I think she tried to conceal her destination because she took the footpath through the woods. We found her hat there. But somebody was watching her, waiting to see what she would do. She was either followed or met. Anyway, when she reached Miss Pond's she knew she wasn't alone. Miss Pond wasn't home. She stood on that icy doorstep and wrote a little note. She slipped the note under the door. I think her murderer was under cover then because he missed that. Then she ran for her life, towards Mrs. Lacey's house, where there was sanctuary. But death caught her. I'm so sure that's the story that I'm going to put it in a report. Unless something changes my mind.

Wilcox put out his hand.   " Got the clipping ? "

Mark handed it over, with Florrie's note.   " Read the note first."

Amos edged closer to Wilcox.   They read together.

" Dear me," said Wilcox.   " So that's what happened to the lipstick."   He read the clipping next, slowly and carefully, and handed it back.   " You don't seriously think she was killed for a thing like that ? "

" Why not ?   She was killed for something.   That thing came from this house.   It fits in somewhere, either with the owner or the tenants."

Wilcox shook his head.   " It might have been a bit of wrapping paper, tied around some old shoes or such.   It might have been here for years, lining the bottom of a drawer, and just got thrown out.   Florrie could have imagined it meant something.   She always was kind of high-strung.   Why, all it says is that somebody got run over.   It don't say who or where or when.   I don't attach any importance to it."

" Then what was Perrin looking for ? "

" Money, maybe.   These folks could have mislaid a large sum of money and thought they dropped it in the trash.   Naturally they'd speak sharply to her, asking if she found anything.   They found it later themselves and forgot to say anything about it.   As for her being followed and killed——"   He scratched his head thoughtfully. " It could have been a tramp.   It could have been—anybody.   This is a lonesome kind of place."

" Do you think a tramp pushed Stoneman downstairs and murdered Lacey because she saw him do it ?   Did a tramp throw that rock through the nursery window ? Did a tramp make off with Stoneman to-night ? "

" Anybody could get in this house," Wilcox said helplessly.   " There's an old coal chute in the cellar."

"Fine time to be telling me that.   Who knows about it ? "

"Everybody."

"I'm going crazy," Amos said flatly.

"Better not," Mark said. "I'm going to work on the crazy angle in a minute. Do either of you know Colonel Davenport?"

"I do," said Amos. "Perley don't know him at all. He's tall, white hair, about fifty-five, and kind of gay. Married money but has plenty of his own. Inherited this place from his wife, who was older'n him. Don't spend much time here, runs around with swells. Over in London now for the government."

"Mrs. Davenport have any relatives who might be sore about the will?"

"Nope. None that I ever heard of."

"Has he ever rented this place before?"

"Nope. And he ain't renting it now. The Moreys are invited guests. Perrin come along here late in August with a note to Ruthie from the Colonel. He asked her to help out these friends of his that he was lending the place to. Then the freight boxes come along and Perrin got things in order. The family come later. Just like that."

"Has Davenport written to Ruthie or the Moreys since then?"

"Nope. . . . Now this here is going to kill you, Mark. Nobody writes to the Moreys or to Stoneman either. The only mail they ever got was the letters you wrote Stoneman. And some bills from New York stores that come for Perrin. Bills for fancy food and flowers. He does all the ordering. The Moreys don't even write to stores."

Mark whistled softly. "Wilcox, did you know Perrin had a gun?"

"Yes, but nobody's been shot yet that I know of. He showed it to me last night, very frank and open. I said he could keep it. . . . I don't like this."

"I don't like it either. I feel cold in my bones and I

can't warm up to your tramp. How does this sound to you ? Suppose somebody wants these people out of the house ? Don't ask me why, just suppose that's the case. We'll call it a campaign of terrorism. Would that explain the rock through the nursery window and Stoneman's attack on the stairs ? "

" Yes. But it won't explain Florrie and Lacey. People who go around scaring other people are likely to stop short with scaring. They haven't got the guts, excuse me, to murder,"

" Wait. Suppose our terrifying friend got frightened himself ? Suppose Mrs. Lacey got wise to him and he knew it. Suppose he also knew that if she gave him away it would mean—the asylum. Wouldn't that be a motive for murder ? "

Wilcox brightened. " Can you tie that up with Florrie and her clipping ? "

" How's this. Suppose that clipping hides a sordid little crime that got by in a small town but wouldn't bear scrutiny by wiser eyes ? The hit-and-run business being one of our ugly friend's little jokes. I've already said it apparently clicked somewhere with Florrie. I don't think she had any positive information, but I do think she had a strong suspicion—not of an individual, but of a situation. Suppose, before she went to Miss Pond's that night, she confided in someone, here in this house ? The wrong someone. Suppose she telephoned a friend, the wrong friend ? She had to be stopped."

"Stoneman's disappearance," Wilcox said. "Fit that in."

" Maybe he got wise too, and ran away. Or was put away. He was smart. He could spot a—looney."

" I know I'm going crazy," Amos said.

" Stop that ! " snapped Wilcox. " You make me nervous. I'm beginning to see things. . . . Where do we go from here, Mr. East ? "

" How do the neighbours measure up in the way of—
nerves ? Has anybody got a queer relation living in the
attic ? You know, the kind you carry trays to and never
mention. Any old men who have to be watched ? Widows
who've never stopped crying ? Peculiar bachelors ? Lovelorn spinsters ? "

" Amos, you take that one." Wilcox gave Mark an
apologetic look. " My family came from downstate.
We've only been here thirty-five years."

" Bessy is a lovelorn spinster," Amos said. " She
writes to Jimmy Cagney every week and Beulah tears
the letters up. Beulah'd cut your heart out and laugh
while she was doing it."

" If you're right about that we're likely to finish this
case on the other side of Jordan. What about the others ?"

" Nobody here now but the Bittners. They're crazy
all right, but not enough for the asylum. The Canes,
man and wife, normal, went to Florida. The three Caldwell girls, believed to be drinkers, went to Florida with the
Canes. The Tait twins, plain lunatics, are in Bear River
with their sister. There used to be some horse thieves over
by Baldwin, but they died. That's all."

" Tell me more about the Taits."

" Seventy-five years old, sculptors. They used to go
to Europe every year. They got a studio back of their
house. Looks like a stable until you peek inside and then,
oh, my. Everybody laughs at 'em. . . . Who got Bessy
and Beulah in this house ? "

" Mrs. Morey asked them. I think it's all right. I've
even put Beulah in charge of a dictograph."

" God have mercy, nobody else will."

" Don't pay any attention to him," Wilcox said. " He's
been fighting with her for years. . . . Dictograph. I
don't think they're decent, if you don't mind my saying so
Like looking in keyholes. . . . Did you hear anything ? "

" No. It's only been operating a few hours, but I'm hoping. It was on for an hour or so before that rock business, but nothing came over." He didn't say where it was.

" That rock business. Very peculiar. You looked at me kind of funny when I was working on that. I figured you knew something and meant to ask you about it."

" It wasn't much. Just that Stoneman was the only person in the room who acted as if he were—surprised."

" Was he surprised to-night when he heard that shot ? "

" Dropped his glass, and it was a full one, too. But he was in a bad way shortly before that. I'd been working on him." He held up the clipping. " Now we stop guessing and start detecting."

He told them how he'd located Citrus City in Florida and how he'd tried it out on Stoneman. " I think I touched a sore spot but I can't be sure. Every time I got to a crucial point, somebody walked in. He ended up shaking like a leaf, but that could have been nerves. He has them."

Wilcox frowned. " So that thing came from a Florida paper."

" Florida." Amos said bitterly. " Everybody's in Florida this minute. Everybody's been going to Florida for years. Davenport used to go himself. Fishing. Preachers go and priests go and I bet even nuns. Florida ! If I was you I'd forget about Florida before I made a fool of myself—or worse."

Wilcox continued smoothly, " What do you plan to do, Mr. East ? "

" I'm not going to do anything. You are. I haven't the authority. I want you to get the Citrus City sheriff on the 'phone and have him dig up this accident. If he doesn't have the records himself he can get all we need from the newspaper. I don't know its name but there's probably only one. I'd say this clipping is about two years old, maybe three. Ask him to mail you a copy, he can get it from the back files, and—this is important—telephone the details as soon as he has them. I want the date and the names of the dead man and the friend who identified him."

Amos had been struggling and now he emitted a bleat. "Long distance to Florida ? Who's going to pay for that ? The county won't like it. And what are you going to do when them names turn out to be John Jones and Bill Smith, respectable people with nice families ? You can't trace no Jones or Smith, anyway. The county's going to be mad ! "

"If the county gets sordid about a little money I'll pay the charge myself. Put that call through the first thing in the morning and ask the sheriff to call you back when he has the dope. Make him understand it's important. Tell him to call after nine p.m. I want to be in on it. Now, what 'phone can we use ? Bear River's too far. And we want to avoid a party line. Amos—what about the 'phone in your office ? "

"Help yourself. I can't stop you. It ain't no party line, but it's got Lola."

"Lola," explained Wilcox, "is the day operator and she writes social items for the *Bear River Examiner*. Sometimes people read in the paper that they're asked to a party before they get their invitations. I expect I'll have to threaten Lola with arrest. Been wanting to do it for some time."

"What about the night operator on the return calls ? She's the important one. Is she reliable ? "

"She's my own sister. She wouldn't listen to Churchill. She'll do what I tell her and go on with her knitting. Well, that's that."

Mark stirred uneasily and avoided Amos' eye. "Not quite," he admitted. "There's another call. The same procedure as the first. Call back after nine. . . . Get Washington and arrange to talk to Davenport at the American Embassy in London."

Amos stifled a shriek and buried his head in his hands.

" I don't care if it is a week end," Mark went on. " Get him. Tell them it's a matter of life and death. And when you get him I'll talk to him myself."

" I think I'll send Lola for a long walk because she looks pale and work the board myself," Wilcox said heavily. " What are you going to say to Davenport ? "

" I," began Mark, and held up his hand for silence. " Somebody's outside the door," he mouthed soundlessly.

They stiffened and sat without moving. The kitchen clock ticked on. Then Mark rose and walked softly to the door and jerked it back. Beulah stood blinking in the strong light.

She rushed at Mark and seized his hand. " It's happened," she babbled. " It's happened." Her uppers gave a warning clack and dropped spitefully to her lower lip. She parried with a savage thumb.

" What's happened ? " Mark asked.

" Somebody talked, but I don't know who it was ! I couldn't hear him speak ! "

Amos watched her coldly.

" Begin at the beginning, Beulah," Mark said.

She collapsed in a chair and leaned heavily on the table. " It was like this. Mr. Morey came up quite a while ago. I heard him say good night to her, and he said there wasn't any news of Stoneman but she wasn't to worry. And she said she wasn't worrying at all. Then he went back to his room. I heard the door shut. Then, maybe half an hour later, she began to talk again. It was the most awful thing. I couldn't see into that room and I couldn't hear any voice but hers, but I knew she wasn't talking to herself. I can't explain it but I could feel—feel somebody else, standing there, with his fingers on his lips."

" What did she say ? "

" She said—I memorized it—she said, ' We've got to get to Willie Foster. That's our only chance. We've got to get to Willie Foster. You've got to do it. Right away. Right away."

" And then ? "

" And then the other person must have left. But I didn't hear any doors shut. When Mr. Morey was there he banged the door just like he always does. . . . This one —this one came in and out like a—like air."

Mark turned to the others. " Ever hear of Willie Foster?"

Wilcox looked blank. Amos grinned from ear to ear.

" Sure," he said. " Three times." He put back his head and shook with silent laughter.

" Amos ! " Wilcox said sharply. " Get on with it ! "

" Willie Foster," said Amos, " is the name of an old sailing vessel. It's the name of a town too, down on the eastern shore of Maryland. The town was named after the boat. The boat was named after a girl. Miss Wilhelmina Foster, dead about a hundred years. It's a small place, Willie Foster is, mostly fishermen and crabbers live there now. But it's got one prominent native son. Name of Colonel Davenport."

Mark turned to Wilcox with a long sigh. " You started to ask me what I was going to say to Colonel Davenport. Well, I was, and still am, going to ask him what he knows about his neighbours in Crestwood. And what he knows about Stoneman. But chiefly, I want to find out if he's really—there."

CHAPTER ELEVEN

FAT lazy flakes sifted out of a dull sky and clung to the dining-room windows. Mark and Beulah loitered over breakfast. They had the room to themselves.

" I don't mind saying this is one thing I'm going to miss," Beulah said, rattling the silver covers on the dishes. " Just like those movies of English country life."

Mark watched the gathering storm. " Florrie's grave was hard to dig too, but nobody seems to care."

" Want to see me act like a duchess ? " Beulah asked.

" No."

" I'm going to, anyway." She pranced painfully across the room with her nose pointed to the ceiling and a sausage impaled on a fork. An arch backward look told her he wasn't watching. She returned and sat down. " I thought you'd laugh," she said quietly. " I don't know what a duchess looks like, but I wanted to make you laugh."

He stretched his face into a grin.

" Don't," she said. " That's worse. You thought I was listening at the door last night, didn't you ? I was, but not because I wanted to hear anything. I only wanted to know who was with you. . . . Mark, you could have used the 'phone in my house for those calls. You could have made a fire and been comfortable while you waited."

" Party line," he said. " Ella May. Beulah, are you going to Florrie's funeral ? "

" No. I won't leave Bessy and she can't go out in this weather with her face. . . . Where are you going ? "

" Out to watch the men. They're working in that ravine under our windows, the one Violet calls the precipice. Looking for Stoneman."

" Then I'll go up and pack," she said. " We're starting with the children's things."

She went with him as far as the door and helped him into his coat. He didn't even notice what she was doing.

Morey stood at the edge of the ravine, scowling down at a group of men toiling with shovel and pick-axe. He greeted Mark with relish.

"They wanted to know if there's a reward," he said, pointing a scornful finger. "That's the backbone of America down there; the flower of democracy, the lad with the hoe. He tills his own few acres and asks nothing of any man. Except a reward."

"Do you think they'll find him there?"

"No. But Wilcox wants to try it. I don't care what they do. Too bad Joe can't supervise the job himself. He'd love to tell them they were unscientific."

Mark looked up at the windows; from where he stood they seemed to overhang that deep and rocky trench, "Who put those spikes in the sills?" he asked idly.

"They were there when we came. One of Davenport's little whimseys, I suppose. Don't ask me what the original purpose was. I don't know. But they're too high to fall over."

"Not too high to jump over, though."

"Jump! Joe? Joe wouldn't jump over a mud puddle. He might fall in and drown. No, he loves himself too much to deprive himself of his own company."

"You talk as if he were alive."

"He's got to be. How can he be anything else? He isn't in the house. We'd have seen him if he'd tried to follow us. I don't know how he did it, but he simply— got out. He always was a slick one."

"Well, suppose he did get out. How did he do it and why? There weren't any trains at that hour, and if he'd hidden and waited for one Amos would have seen him."

"Amos didn't see you," Morey reminded him. He kicked at the snow. "Joe got the wind up over Mrs. Lacey and Florrie. Every time anybody died, Joe always thought the dark angel was aiming at him and muffed the shot. If they had a tidal wave in South America Joe would pitch a tent for himself on Pike's Peak. No, Joe was scared, wanted to get away, and was ashamed to admit it. I gave him a little money the other day, not much. I have a hunch he hit out for New York."

" But I thought you said his clothes were all there ? "

" I've been thinking it over. He could have had some cached away. Then when those blasted kids popped off with their gun and everybody ran around howling, our Joe seized the opportunity. He said he was going to New York, didn't he ? "

" Yes. In a vague sort of way."

" You can bet that's where he is. Spending his money on equipment and talking big. Then when he's broke he'll come back with a sad story. It's happened before. He knew I'd stop him, that's why he skipped. I'm through."

" Will this business hold up your own departure ? "

" No. Wilcox is a decent guy. Says all I have to do is leave my new address. . . . Well ! Who told you to come out here ? "

" Nobody. I wanted some fresh air. It's snowing harder and harder. Will the snow stop the trains ? "

" Nothing can stop the trains. How's your packing ? "

" Miss Pond and Miss Petty are doing it. Miss Petty says we have too many clothes."

" She's right—for once. Which reminds me, I've got to nail up crates for Perrin. He seems to be afraid he'll smash his lily-white fingers. See you later." He moved off toward the house.

" I'm going down to look at the snowman," Mark said to Anne. " Some boys put a bullet through his hat last night, or say they did. I don't believe them. Want to come along ? "

He felt flattered and paternal when she slipped her hand through his.

" I heard about that," she said. " Violet told me secretly. Ivy will be furious."

Chester hadn't been boasting; the hat was neatly

drilled. Mark and Anne regarded it with awe.

" You and Chester ought to join up with a carnival show," he said. " You both have the eye and the hand."

She flushed. Then she gave a little cry of dismay. " Ivy will be in a rage. They shot his eyelashes off too."

" Get out ! " Mark scoffed. " By golly I believe you're right." The broom-straw lashes were scattered far and wide. " That boy is a devil—I beg your pardon, Miss Morey."

" Put them back," she begged, giving him a handful. " I can't reach. If they aren't there when Ivy comes to say good-bye she'll have a tantrum."

He put them back, one by one, while she patted more snow against the base.

" She simply adores him," she said fondly.

He worked on silently and after a minute he touched her bent shoulder.

" I'm cold," he said. " I'm a sissy."

She laughed up at him. " You ! " The snow was falling thick and fast, clinging to her red cheeks.

" Yes. Look at me. I'm shivering. How's about you and me going back to the house and having a drink ? Elevenses. Cocoa for you."

" Have you finished ? " she asked doubtfully.

" Yep. Come along. I'll race you." They dashed through the gathering storm and he let her win.

He was drinking a stiff whisky and writing in his note-book when Morey came into the library, followed by Perrin. Perrin carried a large wicker basket which he proceeded to fill with the room's choicest ornaments.

Morey shook his head dolefully. " Don't you know you'll stunt your growth if you drink before sunset ? . . . What's the matter with you ? You look green."

" Chill." He slipped the book in his pocket. " What

are you doing ? " Morey was standing on a chair,
unhooking the Renoir and his wife's portrait. " We're
going to crate these down in the cellar. I'll try not to
put my foot through them, but I can't promise anything.
What about that mirror, Perrin ? "

" That is ours, sir."

" You take it. I should invite seven more years like
this one." He climbed down and picked up the paintings.
" Looks queer in here without this stuff, doesn't it ? "

It did, Mark noted. The richness was gone ; all that
remained was a large, comfortable room, a little shabby
and faded. It was hard to remember that Laura Morey
had ever sat on that sofa or that Stoneman had ever
crouched over the fire. The rugs stood out like stained-
glass windows.

" They go too," Morey said. " We'll take them up
to-night." Perrin was moving toward the door, and Morey
followed. " Perrin and Violet are going over to the
funeral. I'm going along too. Want to come ? "

" Yes. Yes, I want to very much."

" Meet me here after lunch, then." He edged himself
carefully through the door.

Mark poured himself another drink and opened his note-
book. He stared at it for some minutes before he began to
write again, rapidly.

Upstairs, Bessy and Beulah staggered about the nursery
with their arms full of clothing and their eyes bright with
the occupational dementia that attacks all packing women.
They dragged heavy trunks into the middle of the floor and
dove headlong into dark closets. They got down on their
creaking knees before small suitcases, when only two weeks
before they had told dear Dr. Wrenn that genuflection was
for the very young and converts.

They worked for some time in what for them was silence,
like two small girls with new dolls and wardrobes to match,

smoothing, folding, buttoning, and unbuttoning. Beulah hummed like a motor that is audible only when it approaches breakdown ; Bessy emitted monosyllables at regular intervals.

" Oh," said Bessy finally, withdrawing her head and shoulders from the depths of an old-fashioned trunk. " Do you know something funny, Beulah ? Ivy's clothes have Saks-Fifth Avenue labels and so do some of Anne's, but Anne's old things, like that fur cape, haven't any labels at all. Ripped out. You can see where."

" What of it ? " Beulah said coolly. " Don't start romancing."

" I won't," said Bessy. " Look at this, Beulah." She held up a small nightgown. " Isn't this the prettiest thing ? Imagine wearing it to bed. I'm sure I couldn't sleep. . . . I wore flannel."

" Um," said Beulah.

" Anne's. It's French. I can tell. You can't beat the French on underwear. It's even got a French laundry mark. You know, that red cotton and the funny little one that they use for a seven. Laundered in France ! . . . Well, I'd have those marks on mine too, but you always made me do them in the washbowl."

Beulah went on grimly folding clothes. Once Violet came in to collect the empty cocoa cups, announce the imminence of lunch, and complain about the food.

" There's that rabbit pie for lunch, but I'll have to open cans for dinner unless they'll eat rabbit again, which they won't. Everybody's in such a hurry to get away they don't order nothing from the store." She was fighting back tears. " I don't care for rabbit myself." She went slowly from one heap of clothing to another, fingering the silk and linen frocks, the small furred jackets, the little bathrobes that were so obviously one hundred per cent. pure wool. She made an inarticulate sound and stalked out.

"Everybody's so cross to-day," said Bessy. "Even best friends."

When the lunch gong rang at one o'clock Beulah began an elaborate detour around the room. "You go on down," she said to Bessy. "Tell everybody I've got a headache. And keep quiet about those labels. They don't mean a thing. If Violet comes up to feed the children, tell her I've locked myself in the sewing room for a little nap. She can save me a leg, if she will. No crust."

After lunch Mark drove to Bear River with Morey, Perrin, and Violet.

A sober little group of about thirty people gathered about Florrie's grave, their heads bent to grief and the storm. At the foot of the winding path that led up from the road several hundred more stood quietly. There were no ropes to hold them back, only a streak of delicacy that none of them knew they had. The wind tore at the decent black of Florrie's mother's veil and bit into the bare and knotted hands of her stooping father. The tall, thin rector of St. Michael's couldn't keep the human misery from his eyes, but his voice never doubted, and though he spoke softly and the words were old they outrode the storm as they had always done.

Mark stood with his arm around Violet. He knew some of those present, and could place most of the others Morey and Perrin, standing erect and hatless. Wilcox. Two of Wilcox's men. Florrie's parents, her brother, and an unhappy youth who didn't seem to know or care that tears ran down his face. A girl with swollen eyes who was certainly a best friend next to Violet. Elderly people who might be uncles and aunts, youngsters who might be cousins. Floyd and Chester in their Sunday clothes. Two old men in capes who looked as if they'd strayed from a third-rate opera company. All weeping softly or staring straight ahead. He drew a deep breath when it was over. There couldn't be a murderer in that lot. There couldn't be unless——

Violet murmured something through her tears and he bent to listen.

" I'm going to set out some violets in the spring," she whispered. " For her to remember me by."

They moved down the hillside to the road.

" I want to talk to you privately," Mark said to Wilcox. " At your house. Arrange it, will you ? "

Wilcox went ahead and spoke briefly to Morey ; then he came back.

" Violet," he said. " Mr. Morey and Perrin have some shopping to do and they want you with them. I'll drive Mr. East home in time for dinner."

She left them with her usual reluctance and they walked on. Suddenly Wilcox stiffened.

" You, Floyd ! " he bellowed. " Cut that out ! "

Mark jumped. Startled mourners turned to stare and then smiled faintly. Floyd and Chester were acting up.

A wild reaction had taken them bodily and was heaving them about in the snow. Something, it could have been Perrin's long black coat and black bowler, had set them off. Whatever it was it made no sense to the horrified Wilcox. To Floyd and Chester, however, it was convulsingly clear. They crawled on their stomachs like Indians in a Western film, they sized the lower branches of one tree and swung to another. They dropped to the ground and pounded each other on the back. Then they did the whole thing over again.

" I gave thirty dollars for that coat," muttered Wilcox. He delivered a second bellow.

Floyd and Chester looked back with broad grins, took in the situation, and subsided into a decorous walk.

Wilcox led Mark around to the kitchen door, to save the hall runner, he explained. Pansy was probably home by now, and if he knew her she'd have a pot of coffee ready.

The boys scampered in ahead of them and fled up the back stairs. Pansy was indeed home. She still wore her hat, but there was coffee on the stove and a fresh batch of currant buns from Mama's. She fluttered like a plump bird and ran into the parlour to light the oil stove.

"No, Pansy," Wilcox said. "Not in there." He turned to Mark. "I boarded up an old shed off the summer kitchen and made myself a real nice little den. Take the coffee there, Pansy. Mr. East and I want to talk."

"What a mercy I built the fire in there," she glowed. She led the way, carrying her tray. "I'm sick because I couldn't go to that funeral, but Mama held me back." She wanted to talk about Mama, but her husband gently blocked her way.

"Better take a look at Floyd's coat," he advised. "He was swinging on trees like a monkey." She departed with little cries.

"Now," he said to Mark, indicating an old Morris chair. "What's worrying you? You don't look as happy as you did last night."

"Did you put those calls through?"

"No trouble at all. Sent the operator out to buy flowers for the funeral and worked the board myself. That Citrus City sheriff sounded right pleased. New fellow. From what he said I gather his biggest job is trailing tourists who help themselves to oranges. He didn't remember about the accident himself but he promised to get it all straight for me and let me know, as per schedule. Now, Washington was different. I had to be a little firm there." He stirred his coffee with relish. "Made me feel good to talk back to those fellows, but I managed to convince them. I didn't give an inch. They'll do their best and if we don't get London to-night we'll get it to-morrow." He radiated Scotland Yard.

" I want it to-night. I'm afraid of the next twenty-four hours."

" Huh ? " said Wilcox, startled.

" Listen. On the day of Mrs. Lacey's funeral Morey, or somebody, told me that Mrs. Wilcox was going to look after the Morey children. How come ? "

" That's Pansy's heart. She's all heart. When she heard the whole family wanted to go, out of respect, she offered."

" Will she offer again if the need arises ? "

" God Almighty, Mr. East ! Not another one ! "

" Not if I can help it. And even if it did happen again, I don't know who it would be. That's—that's what I don't like. . . . No, we may want the kids out of the way on general principles."

" She'll take 'em. All you have to do is ask." He looked worried. " You know something new, don't you ? "

" Yes. Morey thinks Stoneman is alive."

" Where is he then ? "

" Morey thinks he ran away—to New York."

" In a blizzard ? No coat and hat ? No luggage ? And how did he do it, fly ? "

" He could have laid his plans in advance. Hidden his things on the mountain. . . . I'm afraid you don't believe it."

" I don't."

" Neither do I. . . . Where was Amos to-day ? "

" Amos was working at the station. He can't get a substitute unless he's sick. And what's more, he's my deputy. You can't accuse him of—these things. He couldn't do—these things. So help me, I can't even say the word murder in the same breath with Amos ! "

" I'm not accusing him," Mark said mildly. " I'm only trying to place people. By the way, did I see the Taits at the funeral ? "

" You did, and you could have knocked me over with a
feather ! I never knew that pair to show up at a funeral
before. I'd sort of forgot they knew Florrie right well at
one time. Seems to me I heard they made a little statue
of her when she was a child, a fountain piece or something. Very bare, it was. People talked."

" I may look them up. I'd like to see it, if they still
have it."

" They'll have it. They never throw anything away.
Look at their clothes. . . . Mr. East, I don't feel so good
about all this. The way you're talking and the way you
look. Are you holding something out on me ? "

" I have been, but not any more. I know where Stoneman really is."

" Alive ? "

" No."

" Can we identify—the body ? "

" Yes."

" Do you know who did it or was it an accident ? "

" It wasn't an accident."

" I'm going to get my car. You can tell me as we drive
along."

Mark followed him to the back yard and waited outside
the garage. Floyd was there, indulging in hopeless argument. His mother had found a fresh tear in his mackinaw
and put her foot down on further search parties.

" I even told her I'd make five dollars again, but she
says money ain't everything. Can't you make her, Pop ?
Pop, can't you ? "

" No," Wilcox said heavily. " Get out of my way, boy."

" Come here, Floyd." Mark drew him aside. " The
search is practically over now, but I know how you can
make another five." They moved over to the snow-capped
fence.

Wilcox heard the low murmur of their voices. He

saw his son cross his heart and spit over his left shoulder. He heard Mark's low, long whistle. He backed his car out of the garage and waited.

They walked toward him, deep in conversation. " You say it's in here ? " Mark asked.

" Sure. I'll get it." Floyd ducked into the garage and came out with a sledge. " You won't do nothing to hurt it ? " he asked anxiously.

" I'll treat it like my own," Mark said. " Here, put it on the back seat. Got an old sack or something to cover it up ? " The sack materialized, smelling of rabbits.

Wilcox looked on silently. Then he broke loose in a disgusted falsetto. " Belly-whopping on the hill to-night ? Kin I come, kin I come ? "

Mark grinned. " To-morrow night, and you'll be there. . . . By the way, Floyd's going to stay in the house to-night and all day to-morrow too. He's not even going to church. You'll have to make that clear to his mother. He's not to leave the house. Got it ? Even if you call him up or send a message asking him to meet you somewhere, he's not to leave the house. The same thing goes for Chester."

Wilcox shivered. " Get back in there, Floyd," he said. " You heard." He waited until the small bouncing figure slammed the kitchen door. " Ready ? " he asked Mark. They drove off slowly.

Mark walked up from the station to the house. Violet was in the hall, augmenting the dinner gong with vocal invitations. He covered his ears.

" Such goings-on," he reproved. " If we weren't so busy, you'd get fired for that performance. Want to wake the dead ? " The words hadn't left his mouth before he started to apologize.

" Don't mind me," Violet said. " I wouldn't wake 'em if I could. They're better off." She noticed his white face and softened. " You're tired too, aren't you ?

This is a terrible place.   One minute my heart's broke and
I don't want to speak to a living soul and the next minute
I could kill somebody I'm that mad."

" Have I got time for a drink before dinner ?   I guess
not, huh ? "

" No, they want it early.   They're crating in the cellar.
I got to wait at table too because Perrin's busy.   Well,
you'll get a nice long sleep to-night anyway, and I'll sneak
you one of them dusty bottles from the wine bin if you'll
tell me what year you want.   I can't get fired, I'm leaving.
Say, you know what ? "

" What ? "

" That shopping they wanted me to go with them for.
It wasn't at all.   All they bought was nails and lumber and
I was begging for eggs.   They just wanted me along for the
sake of appearances for when they went to see Mrs.
Simmons."

" Mrs. Simmons ?   Florrie's mother ? "

" Yes.   Mr. Morey gave her a cheque for five thousand
dollars from Mrs. Morey, and a note of sympathy, but
Mrs. Simmons wouldn't take it.   Five thousand dollars,
and she said no thank you but I'm glad to have the note.'

" Good," said Mark, softly.

" Good ? " repeated Violet.   " Well if I——"

He took her wrist as she reached for the gong again.
Morey was coming down the stairs, followed by Bessie
and Beulah, Bessy's bandage was slightly askew, giving
her a look that was not entirely out of character.

" Dear boy," she said to Mark.

" Port," whispered Beulah.   " She was getting out of
hand, and I let her have all she wanted.   Now she'll go
to bed without any argument."

Violet moved around the table, bearing a large chipped
platter.   " The china's packed," she said.   She offered
the dish to Beulah.   " I don't know if you can eat it," she

warned. "Canned beans and this other stuff here. I
found it away back on a shelf. It come in a tin box with
foreign writing on it and a picture of a steeple or something.
Come from a country called Check. There's English on it
too. Ham, it says in English. Praygew ham."

"Unhappy little Praygrew," said Morey. "Betrayed
again."

"I don't know what you're all laughing at," Violet said,
"but if you was me I bet you'd be crying." Her eyes
filled. "And on top of everything Mr. Wilcox's men sneaked
in the kitchen while I was to the funeral and ate the rest of
the rabbit I was saving for to-morrow's stew."

"Never mind, Violet," Morey soothed. "I won't
forget how good you've been. What—what did you give
Mrs. Morey and the children?"

"Milk toast and eggs and now I haven't got any eggs.
I asked for eggs this afternoon, but you wouldn't listen."

"I'll get some to-night," Mark promised. "I've got
to see Amos and I'm sure he has plenty. Mrs. Lacey's
chickens, you know."

In the face of this outspoken sympathy her simple soul
struggled back to the surface without much trouble. She
also saw an opportunity for gentle reprimand.

"I couldn't touch them myself," she said, "I mean after
all that's happened, but if nobody else has any tender
feelings I don't mind cooking them."

"Just coddle them, Violet," Morey said seriously.

She nodded. "I'm going after the bread pudding now.
It hasn't got any raisins in it and there's nothing to pour
over it to kill the taste, but I did my best." She vanished
into the pantry.

"Why didn't Mr. Wilcox come in with you?" Beulah
asked. "Didn't he drive you home?"

"Dropped me at the station. He had to see Amos on
business."

"Are they keeping up the good work?" Morey took a mouthful of the pudding. "Violet, you're crazy. The only thing wrong with this is the name."

"I think they're giving up the search, if that's what you mean," Mark said carefully. "He didn't say so, but I got that idea. I told him about your theory."

"He didn't believe it, of course. I wouldn't, in his place. . . . I don't suppose I can coax you into helping Perrin and me to-night? We could use an extra man. Or are you still working for old Joe?"

"I'm still working for old Joe. He paid me two weeks' salary. Besides, I've got a date with Amos and Wilcox. They're drawing up a report—you know, what happened and what they did about it. They want me to help them make it sound pretty. How about to-morrow?"

"Sure. If we have any luck we ought to finish early in the afternoon. I'd like to get Mrs. Morey and the kids off on that New York train that leaves Bear River around eight in the evening. I'd like to get on it myself. Miss Pond, have you ever had any traffic with truckmen?"

"Certainly," said Beulah. "Mr. Bittner has trucks as well as buses. He moved you in, in case you don't remember that far back."

"East, will you drop in on Bittner on your way to your date and ask him to have a couple of trucks here at three to-morrow afternoon? How about you ladies? Can you be ready to leave to-morrow?"

"Certainly," said Beulah again.

"Wish pleshure," said Bessy. Beulah shook her out of her chair and propelled her to the door with a flaming face.

"I wouldn't believe that if I didn't see it with my own eyes," Violet said. "It's a good thing I'm not one to talk. You don't need to worry about me, Mr. Morey, I can stay until everybody's out and lock up. Turn the water off and all. I'm glad to oblige."

" This sounds like commencement day," Mark said.
" Good-bye, good-bye, don't forget to write. I'll stick
around with Violet and turn off the gas. Then "—he
made sure Beulah had rounded the bend with Bessy—
" then I think I'll spend a few days with Miss Pond."
He looked at his watch. " I've got to run. See you later."
He got out of the room before anyone could call him back.

Beulah signalled wildly from the top of the stairs.
" Got to run," he said again. " See you later." He took
his hat and coat from the hall table and slammed the door
behind him. It was quarter after eight.

The Saturday night train had come and gone. The
lamp was burning dimly outside the station, but the
little building stood dark and forlorn. Not until he
reached the platform did he see the pinpricks of light
through the curtain at Amos' window. Wilcox opened
the door.

" I don't mind saying I'm glad you're here," he admitted.
" I told Amos some of what you told me and he's ready to
call in the FBI."

Amos crept out from behind the stove. His face was
ashen. " I don't like it," he said. " It's plain murder."

" It's been plain murder three times, Amos. Don't
worry. We can handle it."

" Why don't you take the poor old gentleman's body to
the undertaker and telephone the governor ? Tell him
what you know ? It's—safer.

" Don't you want your picture in the papers ? I tell
you we can handle it. And I haven't got enough to give
the governor. Not yet. I haven't any proof."

" Proof ! " shrieked Amos. " Proof," he said again in a
hoarse whisper. " You got three corpses."

" And not one witness. Only a theory. I can't prove
Mrs. Lacey didn't die by accident. I can't prove Florrie
wasn't strangled by a tramp. I can't prove a thing about

Stoneman—yet. I haven't even got a motive. That's what gets me. No motive. It's all so—smooth. No motive, no reason. In short, I haven't got a case."

"He's right," said Wilcox. "A good lawyer would laugh us out of court."

"You got Stoneman's body, haven't you? Florrie and Lacey are—embalmed, as you might say. But you got Stoneman. Was he shot or poisoned?"

"Neither. Yes, I've got Stoneman but I haven't got a single soul who saw the thing done. If there were a bullet in his body, that would be fine. But there won't be. Still, Stoneman's our trump card. Nobody knows we've found him. Nobody knows we're wise. So—we use him, dead as he is, to get a confession."

"Confession!"

"Sure. With lots of witnesses. Don't worry. It's all set—I hope." He looked at Wilcox, sitting rigid in his chair. Wilcox nodded.

"Don't let me forget to order Bittner's trucks before I leave. Morey wants them at three to-morrow."

"When they going? What train?"

"To-morrow night, from Bear River. . . . We'll all be going then."

"Some to some places and others to others." Amos shook. "I don't feel like I ever want to see——"

The 'phone rang shrilly. Wilcox lunged across the table. "Yes?" he croaked. "Oh—it's Miss Pond. She wants you, East."

"Cover that mouthpiece. Tell her I've gone out. Ask her what she wants."

Wilcox turned back. "She says Miss Petty won't go to bed. What shall she do?"

"Give her two of those pills. Violet has the bottle. And lock her in."

Wilcox spoke and hung up. His face glistened with sweat.

Mark looked uneasy. "I wonder if I ought to go up there. I wonder if I'm gambling——"

"No," said Wilcox. "You stay here and get those calls. You can't do more than you're doing now."

"She's been nipping, Bessy has," Amos said. "I know. Her father was the same way."

"You know what I feel like?" Wilcox said. "I feel like I did a long time ago, when I was a young fellow in the last war. We used to go into a village at night, to get that *vin rouge*. Every night we'd walk along that road, under the stars, with trees and country smells all around. Every night the same—but one. It looked the same then too, same trees, same stars, same everything, only it was different. You could feel something waiting for you in the dark. You couldn't see anything, you could only feel it. Pressing in, watching you, like. That night they blew the village up. . . . I feel like that now."

"Perley," quavered Amos, "what did you do with that bottle you took away from me? I want it."

The 'phone shrilled again. Nobody moved.

"This ought to be one of them," Mark said. "Go on, Wilcox."

Wilcox took the 'phone. "Yes?" he said. They saw him square his shoulders. "Yes Sheriff, I'm ready for you. Will you wait just a minute, please? I want somebody to take this down as you give it to me." He turned to Mark. "Sheriff Hancock, from Citrus City," he said formally.

Mark nodded. "Go ahead. Repeat what he says. I've got a pencil."

Wilcox began to talk. "Tell it in your own way, sir. Just give me time to repeat. We're all set here. . . . August, 1939. That's the date, eh? You're mailing a copy of the paper? Good. Now, August 15, 1939. Hit-and-run. Yes. Body of poorly dressed man, about thirty-five years old. Hard to tell what he looked like. Yes."

" For God's sake, Wilcox, get the names ! We can't hold that wire too long ! "

" Yes, sir," Wilcox went on. " Now if you don't object I'd like to get the names. You see we can't hold this wire too long. We're waiting for an overseas call. Yes, sir, it does look like a big case, and I'll appreciate it if you say nothing until I give you the word. Yes, sir. I will. George M. Hancock. I'll see it gets in the same as mine. Yes, sir. I'll write you in a day or so. Now—if you don't mind, Sheriff, those names. Yes. The man who identified the victim was——"

Mark's pencil waited on the paper.

" Jones and Smith," Amos muttered. " Jones and Smith, Jones and Smith."

" Will you repeat that please ? " Wilcox spoke quietly into the 'phone. The other voice came back, rasping, indistinct. " Thank you," Wilcox said. " Good-bye." He replaced the receiver and gave a long sigh.

" No soap ? " asked Mark.

Wilcox cleared his throat. " The victim was identified by a man named Joseph Stoneman."

Mark's fist struck the table. " Smith and Jones, huh ? Who pays for the call now, huh ? I said that clipping would tell us something ! "

" Tell us what ? " asked Amos. " You were looking for a crime angle. Well, it's no crime to identify a dead body. If you ask me, we're just where we were before. You can't tell me that Ruthie and Florrie were killed because one night three years ago a man named Stoneman identified a——"

" Who said it happened at night ? "

" Wait ! " said Wilcox. " Wait a minute." He reached down into the woodbox behind the stove and drew out a bottle, which he handed to Amos. "After you, my friend," he said. "The man Stoneman identified was James Morey."

Nobody spoke until Mark said gently, "To quote Florrie, 'Who is dead?'" Nobody answered. "Who is dead?" he repeated.

"Who?" Amos' voice rose. "I'll tell you who! Ruthie, Florrie. Two women who never saw Florida in their lives, never even saw Stoneman and Morey until this past September! And now Stoneman's dead too, and this sheriff says Mr. Morey, says Mr. Morey——."

Wilcox held up a heavy hand that shook a little. "Easy, Amos. It could be a coincidence, couldn't it, Mr. East? The bank accounts are in the name of Morey. She signs cheques with that name. It's a common enough name. There must be hundreds of them in New York alone."

"But if——" Amos began.

"There can't be any but," Mark argued. "He's Morey. James Morey. He's not masquerading. His toilet articles are marked with his initials and they're not new. Stoneman never hesitated when he talked to him or referred to him. He never hesitates when speaking to or of his wife. That child, Anne, she knows what her name is. You can't train a kid like that to act every minute of her life. She—I don't know! I'm going crazy myself."

"Detectives are funny people," said Amos. "You been counting on that clipping to tell you something and when it tells you a honey you try to make out it ain't so."

"It looks to me," Wilcox said, "like I was right in the first place. We got crimes all right, but they haven't anything to do with the clipping. It's so much trash. Plain trash that they threw out when they were getting ready to move. I admit it's kind of throwing us off our track a bit, but it don't necessarily change our plans. Why can't

it be a coincidence ? Say some friend of theirs saw the
thing in the paper and sent it to them for fun ? A gag, as
they call it. A joke, as you might say."

"Possible, but too smooth. Too honest and open.
There's been nothing honest about this business from the
first day I saw Stoneman."

"All right. Look at it the other way." Wilcox wet
his lips. "The clipping is dangerous. Mr. Morey isn't
—himself. He took a dead man's name for some reason
of his own. Did Mrs. Lacey and Florrie die because they
found that out ?· No. No, because Stoneman died too
and he's known it all along. He'd known it for years.
Had to, because he was a part of it. Why wait and kill
him now ? . . . And why would this—this Mr. Morey
take the name of some poor fellow who got run over ?
Because he was hiding from something ? He don't act
like it. He walks around like you and me, in broad daylight. Buys drinks for the boys in Bear River as friendly
as you please. Did he do it to get money ? No, sir. If
that dead fellow was rich he'd have been missed. Somebody would have hollered."

"Maybe somebody has hollered. A little late, but a
holler just the same. Don't forget that practically everybody in this village has been in Florida for the past ten
winters or more. Some of them have travelled abroad too.
The Moreys have Europe behind them, and not very far
behind, I think."

"Still going to get your confession ? " Amos asked.

"I am. I'm still right on that. It ties up with this,
I don't know how, but it does. The answer is right here."
He indicated the village street, silent outside the cur-
tained windows. "I'm counting on Davenport."

"Might be," admitted Wilcox. "There's that Willie
Foster business." He looked uneasily at the 'phone. "I
wish that call would come."

"Look." Amos took another swallow from the bottle. "Don't anybody tell me I'm going to get drunk. I know it. I want to be numb so I won't hear the next body fall. Mark, do you think it's all right to let that luggage go? Would there be anything in it? Somebody could of sneaked down cellar and hid something."

"No. That's all right. I've got to get hold of Bittner somehow. I've——"

The 'phone rang.

Amos scuttled across the floor like a crab. "I'll go to Bittner's. I'll tell him." He slammed the door behind him.

The 'phone rang again.

"Let him go," Wilcox said. "You take this one. It's yours."

Mark lifted the receiver.

A woman's voice, quiet and undistinguished, asked who he was and seemed satisfied with the answer. Then another voice, shrill and clipped, crackled out in argument with a third person who could not be heard at all but who was evidently determined to call the whole thing off.

The quiet voice returned like a soothing parent and asked him to wait. Wilcox left his chair and hung over Mark's shoulder.

The clipped voice crackled again. A fourth quantity, hardly human, came in with a series of thin mechanical wails. There was a pause and then the quiet voice returned. "Go ahead, Mr. East," it said. "You're through."

Mark said, "Colonel Davenport?"

Wilcox went back to his chair, but his eyes never left Mark's face.

Mark spoke rapidly and clearly. He'd rehearsed like an actor. He introduced himself and said he'd been retained by the local authorities to investigate the death of a guest of the Colonel's friends. No, he could not be more

specific ; Mr. Scott, the agent, had written the details.
So had Miss Pond. Yes, Pond. P-o-n-d. . . . Yes, that
was the one. . . . Yes, he knew that. . . . Now, could
Colonel Davenport tell him anything about a Mr. Joseph
Stoneman, an archæologist ? Stoneman.

Wilcox held his breath. Mark wrote something on the
paper lying under his hand. Wilcox read, " Light me a
cigarette." He did.

Mark went on. Yes, Mr. Stoneman had died suddenly
and they were hoping to uncover his past activities in order
to . . . Yes, Stoneman.

Mark's face grew dark. " Colonel Davenport," he said,
" this call has been made with the assistance of the United
States government. You must realize what that implies.
I needn't tell you that whatever you say will be held in
confidence, as far as possible. We've taken every precaution here. If you withhold information you hamper
justice. I repeat, Mr. Stoneman was a guest of the
Moreys, in your own house."

There was a long pause while Mark listened. Gradually
his expression lightened. A grin, not pretty, stretched
from ear to ear. The minutes clicked on.

" Yes," he said finally. " Morey, James Morey, his
wife and two children. Girls. . . . I see. If I'd had any
sense I'd have seen it before. Will you give me that name
again ? " He wrote rapidly and pushed the paper over to
Wilcox without turning his head. " Give me a description,
a brief one, just for the record, although I don't need it.
. . . That's it. There's a difference now, of course ;
there'd have to be."

He leered happily at Wilcox, who held the paper in a
shaking hand.

" I understand your position," he said into the 'phone,
" and you'll be covered. Under the circumstances, you
couldn't have behaved in any other way. I think I can

lay this ghost without publicly bringing in your name. Thank you, sir, and good night.   Or rather, good morning."

Mark and Wilcox stared at each other.

"Did you have any idea of this?" Wilcox asked. "You couldn't! Nobody could!"

"Only a feeling. It kept nagging at me, but I didn't work on it. It's perfectly clear now, though. Remember the night the rock came through the window?   It screamed at us then and we didn't listen. Now here's the story Davenport tells. And here's how I fill in the empty places——"

While he talked, Wilcox watched and listened like a boy at a magic show. Then he became a man again and clenched his fists.

"I was going to carry a gun to your confession party," he said, "but not now. I want this one to go to the chair in perfect health."

"This one may go to the insane——"

Amos came quietly in and stood with his back against the door. "Bittner'll have the trucks up there at three. Did you get your call?   Jones and Smith?"

"We got it," Mark said, "and the county's paying. You'll be glad to know that Morey is Morey. It's no act. I'll tell you the rest later. Right now, have you got any fresh eggs to sell?   I promised Violet I'd bring her some."

Amos took a lantern and climbed the wooden steps that led to his loft.

"How much did you tell him?" Mark whispered.

"Only what I had to. That you knew where Stoneman was and that you had a suspect lined up. It's not safe to tell him more than that. He'll blow up at the wrong time. Let me handle him."

"Do you suppose the Taits are ready?"

"They said they'd be. Funny thing about artistic people. They're never as dumb as they look. We'll drive up your road, cut through the lower woods on foot, and come down from the other end. Can't afford to have Ella May worrying."

Amos came back with two cartons. "Two dozen," he said. "Jumbo. No charge. Violet's a nice girl and she's been through a lot. She can put them on the grocery bill and keep the money for herself. . . . You ain't going already ! You didn't tell me what happened ! "

"There's nothing new, Amos," Wilcox said. "The Colonel says Morey's Morey and that Stoneman was just what he claimed to be, an archæologist. I'm going to use the 'phone. Want to talk to my sister."

"So that paper was trash. Trash with a coincidence. The county won't pay for that Perley. You're sticking our necks out, Perley, with election coming up."

Wilcox had the operator on the 'phone. "Maudie ? " he said. "Just wanted to thank you. The calls came in fine and you did a good job. But then I knew you would, girl. Listen. Anybody try to get my house to-night ? No ? That's fine. Keep it up. Maudie, I don't know when I'll get home and I sure would appreciate it if you'd send somebody around to tell Pansy. Just tell her not to worry and look for me when she sees me."

Amos followed them to the door and watched them drive off.

"I seen that sledge you hid on the back seat," he called after them.

The wind was howling down the mountain and they didn't hear him.

Some minutes later they felt their way through the shrubbery that screened the studio at the foot of the Taits' back garden. No light showed ; the windows were heavily curtained, by request.

Mark talked to the Taits and gave them a list of measurements. They listened gravely, huddled in their ridiculous capes. When he had finished he turned to Wilcox. "You'd better stay here. I'll walk back home."

He went back the way he had come, still bent on separating Ella May from worry.

Beulah waylaid him in the upper hall. "Where have you been ! It's after midnight ! "

"Midnight ? It feels like next year. . . . Where's Bessy ? "

"Asleep, I'm sorry I had to bother you, but she was crying. She wanted to see you. It was awful."

"That's all right. Violet in bed too ? "

"Hours ago. Look here, Mark. I heard something on the gadget this afternoon and this is the first chance I've had to tell you. Mrs. Morey sent five thousand dollars to Florrie's mother and the woman refused it. I heard Mr. Morey tell her when he came back from the funeral."

"I know. It's unimportant, except for the crown it puts on Mrs. Simmons' head. Run along to bed and lock up. You don't have to listen to that thing any longer."

"You—know ? "

"Practically."

"But listen ! " She told him about the labels and the laundry marks. "Does that prove anything ? I mean does it help ? "

"Honey, I've got French laundry marks myself. On handkerchiefs. And I've heard of unpatriotic people who rip the labels out of their clothes to fool the customs. It's plain dastardly. Now go to bed."

He waited until he heard her key turn. Then he went to his own room. He sat by the window, planning. Once he whispered softly and if Amos had heard him he'd have gone crazy again. He said : "So she bites her fingernails when she—thinks ! "

CHAPTER TWELVE

ON his way to breakfast the next morning Mark met Morey leaving the dining room.

Morey's hands were ringed with silver pots and pitchers. He didn't look happy. " I always say," he said grimly, " if you want a thing done right, do it yourself. We nearly left these trinkets for the landlord. . . . Did you see Bittner about the trucks ? "

" They'll be here at three. How're you doing ? "

" My bones are coming through my skin. That Pond woman sent down seven trunks and a list of more to come. I can travel around the world in a suitcase. Women ! "

" Any plans about Stoneman's stuff ? "

" Sort of. I wanted to ask you first. Do you think it'll be all right if I send it along to storage with our things ? "

" Why not ? "

" I don't know. I just don't want to do anything that might raise a howl. Would you—I mean do you mind getting it together for me ? And what about the book ? "

" Sure. I'll do it after I eat. There isn't much. Two suitcases, one for clothes and one for manuscript ; one typewriter. If it's all right with you, I'd like to keep the manuscript."

" Do you think he'll come back for it ? "

" I'm not guessing. He has my address. If he turns up some night he'll know where to find me."

" According to local rumour, if he turns up you'll hear him coming. Like this." He rattled his silver and wailed like a banshee. . . . " They're getting blasé around here. In the old days that would have started something. How did you and Wilcox make out with your report ? "

" So-so. I think he'll convince his betters that he did all he could. Election coming up next year, and you know what that is."

" I'd put in a good word for him if I knew where to put it. . . . Say, do you know what happened last night ? When La Petty looked for her dear boy and couldn't find him she came down with a crying jag. My good port again. Which gives me an idea. I've got about a dozen bottles left, and she might as well have them. I'll call it a Christmas present and Wilcox'll call it impairing the morals of minors."

" She'll love it, but don't give it to her now ! "

Morey shut one understanding eye. " Bring Stoneman's stuff to the cellar when you can." He clanked down the bare hall.

Mark stood in the doorway and surveyed the room. The rugs and curtains were gone ; it was warm and clean, but at the same time it was cold and cheerless. Davenport's hunting scenes still hung on the walls and his heavy glass decanters stood on the sideboard. It was his room now, his house. He was emerging for the first time.

He snapped his fingers suddenly, swore under his breath, and went across the hall to the library. That floor was bare also, but the heavy red curtains still covered the windows. He prowled around.

" That's more than I deserve," he told himself. He went back to the dining room.

Violet came in with scrambled eggs and muffins. " I heard you stamping around," she said. " These floors. Make a person sound like a horse. Thanks for bringing the eggs. How much ? "

" A present from Amos, but don't start dreaming girlish dreams." He regarded her with pleasure. Her eyes were bright, her cheeks red ; he could almost see a *Love Lyric* gathering in her round young throat.

" Youth," he commented. " It gives me a pain. You can get over anything, can't you ? "

" Our business is with the living, not the dead," she said solemnly. " We're taught that." She poured his coffee from a kitchen pot. " Looks kind of terrible, don't it, but what comes out is just the same." She stood first on one foot, then on the other, swallowed a few times, and burst into speech. "Oh, Mr. East, I got a fur coat ! Mrs. Morey give it to me this morning ! It's a grey Persian, she said, and I look like nothing in this world, you ought to see ! "

" I'm going to," he said. " When we have that dinner. Little green orchids, I think. Anybody can wear purple."

" Where ? " she demanded.

" You'll see. Maybe New York. Chaperoned, of course."

" Of course," she repeated doubtfully. " Of course ! A party, like ! And Miss Petty and Miss Pond ! "

" You'll see."

She fussed with the table, found nothing to do, and started off.

" Holler if you want anything," she said over her shoulder. " I haven't got time for manners." The first notes of " Less Than the Dust " bubbled forth. She choked them back. He watched the struggle in her eyes as she weighed grief with happiness. It didn't take long ; before she reached the pantry door she was on the second line.

Mark went to his own room and packed his suitcase. He knew the dictograph would have to wait until later. He packed Stoneman's few belongings and put the manuscript with his own things. Then, with Stoneman's case in his hand, he went to the nursery. It was bedlam.

In one corner, " Old King Cole " bellowed from the depth of a portable phonograph already tagged for travelling. In another, Anne and Ivy were throwing toys into a wooden packing case, oblivious to warning thuds and pre-monitory crashes. In the centre of the room Beulah was being resisted by a wardrobe trunk.

Ivy, her head and arms swathed in bandages, gave a welcome shriek and dropped a set of dishes.

Beulah ran her fingers through her scant locks and gave him a look.

"Get out," she said through her teeth.

He embraced the trunk and slammed it shut. "There," he said. "Now why don't you sit down and rest."

"Why? Because at my back I always hear Time's winged chariot hurrying near. Meaning Bittner's trucks. If I don't get out of this house soon they'll have to take me in a straight jacket. Look me in the eye, Mark. You and Perley Wilcox aren't up to anything, are you? Because if you are——"

"Nothing to worry about. You may proceed as directed. Where's Bessy?"

"Where I'll be to-morrow—in bed with aspirin. . . Ivy, that doll cost enough money to feed a poor child for a year. Drop it. No! No! I mean——!" She was too late.

Mark drew Anne out into the hall.

"How would you like to go to a tea party before you leave?"

"All of us?"

"No. Just you and Ivy. I might drop in later. Some people I know are having ice cream and cake at five o'clock. You could go, have fun, and be back in plenty of time for your train."

"I'll have to ask Mother."

"Now, Anne! Be your age! Do you want to bother your mother at a time like this? Here I go to a lot of trouble getting you a nice invitation and you turn it down. I thought we were friends."

She regarded him gravely. "You mustn't say things like that, Mr. East. You're much too sensitive. Of course we're friends. . . . Do you think it will be all right ? "

"I give you my word. Just don't say anything to anybody. It's—it's a kind of surprise party. We'll fix the details later." He patted her cheek and smiled into her eyes, and was disproportionately pleased when she smiled back.

His next stop was the cellar. Perrin was there alone, hammering the last nails into the box that held silver.

"Here are Mr. Stoneman's things," Mark said. "They're to go with the storage consignment. . . . Where's Mr. Morey ? "

"In Bear River, sir."

Mark watched while he drove the final nail home.

"You have good hands, Perrin. I've noticed them before. Strong hands. I don't blame you for taking care of them." He left without looking back.

Violet sat at the kitchen table with a battered cook book, desperately scanning the section devoted to eggs. She held up a small piece of cheese.

"I never thought I'd thank God for cheese," she said. "You wouldn't be planning to eat lunch somewhere else, would you ? "

"I would. At Wilcox's. I should have told you before. Listen, do you want to do me one more favour ? It's the last I'll ever ask, honest."

She looked down. "I know. Something else I got to keep my mouth shut about."

"You're learning to read my mind and that's not going to do you any good. At four-thirty I want you to dress the children and take them for a walk down by the garage. There'll be a car waiting for them. Pop them in, make sure the curtains are drawn, and then come back to the house.

I don't think they'll be missed, but if anyone asks you where they are, you don't know."

She drew back. "Where—where will they be?"

"Violet, you little goat, they'll be perfectly safe! Florrie's brother is the driver. Doesn't that make it all right?"

"No, sir." Her voice was unsteady. "I'd have to know more. I like those children."

"I know you do. That's why I picked you for the job. You do what I tell you and you'll save them a lot of nightmares. They're going over to have tea with Mrs. Wilcox. After that the curtain comes down to loud applause and we all go back where we belong. And some of us will undoubtedly get plastered."

"Can't—can't I go with them?" She twisted her hands. "I can get off easy. Nobody's eating here to-night. They're having dinner on the train."

"Sorry," he said carelessly, "but we need you here. At five-thirty Mr. Wilcox is coming up to make a statement. He wants everybody present."

"Not servants? Not me and Perrin?"

"Everybody. After the kids go, you come up to the library and take a nice chair by the fire. Don't talk, just sit. And after it's all over you can go home."

Violet was learning fast. "I know!" she gasped. "It's got to do with—— !"

"It's got to do with something you never heard of and don't know anything about; and after it's over you'll be the most popular girl in Bear River, take my word for it. You may even be asked for interviews, like a movie star. And why not? Haven't you got a grey Persian?"

"W-w-ell. . . . I just sit and don't talk?"

"That's it. But when I say don't talk I mean no heckling from the gallery. You'll answer when you're spoken to, like a little lady."

"Would you wear the grey Persian if you was me—then, I mean?"

"I certainly would!" He made a nonchalant exit.

Up in the lower hall he took his wraps from the closet and opened the front door. He looked and listened before he closed the door softly and started down the drive. To anyone watching from the rows of staring windows he was a young man with an afternoon to kill. He dawdled. He flicked snow from the shrubbery, examined fallen branches, and whistled. He eyed the sullen sky with frank disapproval, indicated by head wagging and shrugs. Halfway down and still in sight of the house he discovered a footpath leading off into the woods. This evidently surprised him. He hesitated, looked right and left, and sidled forward in the manner of a nervous tourist entering a catacomb. Once hidden from view he scuttled like a rabbit who knows a better 'ole.

Sometime later he turned up at the station and had sandwiches and coffee with Wilcox and Amos. He stayed there until four-thirty.

Up at the house Bittner's trucks had come and gone. In the front hall a pile of hand luggage, rugs, and thermos bottles stood waiting.

Beulah got Bessy ready for departure. When that was behind her, she carried their suitcases downstairs and went hunting for Violet and a possible cup of tea.

Upstairs in the morning-glory room, now stripped bare, Bessy huddled in a chair by the window. She had wrapped a knitted shawl about her head, for the house was slowly growing cold. It was growing dark too, inside and out. The current was still on, but someone had taken most of the bulbs. Lights burned in the kitchen and in Mrs. Morey's room but nowhere else.

The house was growing colder and colder. Bessy shivered and tightened her shawl. Suddenly she remembered she hadn't seen the children since lunch. She got up and went down the dim hall to the nursery. There was one bulb there. She pressed the button. The room was empty.

Coming back she met Beulah. "I can't find the children," she said. "I don't think I've heard them either, for a long time. I—I want to go home."

"Violet took them out. Come on and lie down, Bessy. I know how you feel, but we can't go until Mark comes. We'll stay until everybody leaves and then we'll say good-bye properly. Besides, we haven't been paid yet and I think Mr. Morey has a present for you."

"Oh." Bessy brightened. "Just as you say, dear." She let herself be led back to her room. "Beulah, do you think walls can talk?"

"What!" Beulah gave her a sharp look. "You haven't been hearing any, have you?"

"No-o-o. Not exactly. But I've had the queerest feeling all afternoon. As if somebody was saying, 'Go—go—go!'"

"Hush." Beulah looked over her shoulder and shivered. "Here, I brought a bulb up from the kitchen." She screwed it into a socket. "This will cheer you up. I never saw such penny-pinching. Taking out bulbs and turning off heat while the house is still full of people!" She settled Bessy on the stripped bed and covered her with a coat. "Now be sensible and relax. I'll stay here with you." She sat on the edge of the bed and stared fixedly at the door.

Morey entered his wife's room with a sheaf of tickets in his hand. "Here they are," he said. "We've given ourselves too much time. What are we going to do, sit around?"

She was standing at the window and she didn't turn.

"A strange car came in a little while ago. It went in

the direction of the garage. When it left it had the curtains drawn. What was it?"

"I don't know. Probably the man from Scott's. He's going to turn off the water and so on. Lock up."

"He didn't stay more than fifteen minutes. He drove too fast."

"He'll be back, and if he wants to break his neck that's his business. Where are the kids?"

She turned quickly. "Where? Aren't they with Miss Petty and Miss Pond?"

"Calm down. I suppose they are. I only asked because the place is so damn quiet."

"Go at once! Find them and bring them here! I won't have——"

The 'phone rang.

"Just a minute," he said. He went to the 'phone. "Hello?"

She moved over to the bare dressing table and stood there, applying rouge with a shaking hand.

"Another complication," he said, turning from the 'phone. "That was Wilcox. He's on his way here. Says he has to see us."

She moistened her lips. "W-why?"

"Search me. You know how he talks. 'I have to do this, Mr. Morey.' Maybe he wants to seal the house after we leave it. I think they do that—when there's been trouble. Don't worry."

Violet, wearing her good silk and the grey Persian, added a straw suitcase and lumpy bundle to the pile of luggage in the hall. She scowled at the one weak bulb that burned at the foot of the stairs, found a stronger one in the socket of the dining-room door, and stood under it with her pocket mirror. She turned her face this way and that, and liked what she saw.

It was a short-lived pleasure. A sudden grinding of

brakes outside sent her scurrying to the front door. Mark
came in, followed by Wilcox and Amos. She wasn't
surprised to see the first two, but she hadn't expected
Amos. In fact, she thought he had no business there at
all. She gave him a cold stare as she stood back to let
them pass. "The old fool," she muttered. "Hanging
around for a tip, I bet. Leaving the railroad to run itself,
I bet. Who's going to flag the six-o'clock train, I want to
know? Some young kid for fifty cents. I got a good
notion to report it."

Then she noticed a movement beyond the terrace,
between the shrubbery and the trees. Men. The snow
was like a veil, but her sharp young eyes missed nothing.
A lot of men. Moving and crouching. Then she remembered with horror that Amos was more than a stationmaster. He was also a deputy sheriff.

She backed away from the door with a terrified look at
Mark and ran to the library. She snatched a dust cover
from Stoneman's old chair, pushed it up to the dying fire,
and literally fell into it.

She heard Mark go upstairs. Very soon she heard him
return, followed by the others. She knew those footsteps, all of them. Miss Petty, Miss Pond, Mr. and Mrs.
Morey. At the same time Wilcox came from the opposite
direction with Perrin. She sat on her hands and stared at
the fire as if it were the only safe thing in the world.

They all came in. Mark went over to the windows and
drew the curtains like a fussy housewife. He chattered
mildly. "Just like a theatre, isn't it?" He smiled at
Beulah. "All the world's a stage, and so on and so on. I
think we'll have a semicircle; it's cosier. Mrs. Morey,
will you take the sofa, please? No, the other one; the
one with the flowered cover. Leave it just where it is. I
want it there. Thank you. Miss Pond and Miss Petty,
will you join Mrs. Morey? That's perfect."

Violet thawed visibly under this quiet barrage of manners and normality. She tilted her shabby beret to a new angle and folded her hands in her lap.

"Now let me see," Mark went on thoughtfully. "Perrin, will you bring those two chairs over here and place one at each end of the sofa? That's right. Mr. Morey, will you take one? You take the other, Perrin."

Perrin stood stiffly.

"For Pete's sake, sit down," Morey said.

Perrin sat down.

Wilcox stood against the French window, shuffling his feet. Violet began to squirm. They were sitting with their backs to her. She couldn't see what was going on. If Mrs. Morey had one of her creeses, and her shoulders looked as if she might, she wanted to be where she could take it all in. Her mother loved to hear about Mrs. Morey's creeses.

"Mr. East," she piped. "I'm here."

"So you are," he said. "Stay there."

Laura Morey turned to Beulah and whispered urgently.

"But of course I thought you or Violet had them!" Beulah's voice was loud and astonished. She turned to stare at Violet.

"If you're talking about the children," Mark said quickly, "they're all right. Believe me, they're all right. . . . Now, if you please, Wilcox."

He stepped back to the wall at Wilcox's right. Amos stood against the opposite wall, to the left. Wilcox cleared his throat.

"I don't want to keep you people here any longer than I have to," he said. "I know you all want to get away. I do myself. But none of us can go until I clear something up. I have to do it. I've got something I want to say, and I expect I will say it later, but first I want you to listen to Mr. East here. I've got a sort of surprise for you, about Mr. East, I mean."

Mark still leaned against the wall, hands in pockets, smile intact.

"Mr. East," Wilcox went on, "was engaged by Mr. Stoneman to help him on a book. At first Mr. East thought Mr. Stoneman had made a mistake in hiring him, but later on it didn't look that way. You see, Mr. East never was a secretary. He is and always was a private detective."

Wilcox, facing his audience, avoided their eyes. Mark and Amos watched like hawks. There were only two reactions. Morey snapped his fingers and grinned. Violet, who had been hoarding her breath for a full minute, released it with a loud pop. At the same time there was an almost imperceptible change in the atmosphere ; as if pulses quickened and minds began to race.

"So," Wilcox continued, "Mr. East's observations, as you might say, are kind of important. He was right here in the house and he couldn't help noticing some things. I should say, he couldn't help wondering about them. He came to me. Now I'm going to let Mr. East tell you what he told me, and what we did about it." Wilcox stepped back clumsily and tangled with the red curtains. "Mr. East," he murmured.

Mark took a step forward from the wall. "Very parliamentary," he said. "All I need is a table with carafe and tumbler." Beginning with Perrin, he looked long and directly into the eyes of each person before him.

"Most of what I'm going to tell you," he said, "I can definitely prove. A few surrounding details are guesswork ; but if you hear me to the end I think you'll believe me." Once more he scrutinized each face.

"First, and I'm starting with the present. Mr. Stoneman is not alive. He did not run out into the storm when that shot was fired and lose himself by accident or intent. He didn't run away to New York. He was killed that night, in this very room, while we were hunting for him. . . . I see tears in one pair of eyes. He isn't and never was worth that. I admit he fooled me too. Mr. Stoneman was a secondary but vital factor in the events that led to the deaths of Mrs. Lacey and Florrie. I mean, the murders of Mrs. Lacey and Florrie."

"Mr. Stoneman?" Beulah's voice was high and thin. "But how, how——!"

"If you don't mind, no questions until I finish. . . . Mr. Stoneman, as some of you know, had a nearly fatal fall down the cellar steps. It wasn't an accident. It was either an attempt to frighten him into submission, because he was getting restive, or it was meant to remove him permanently. You see, he'd served his purpose and was beginning to be a nuisance. But that little episode of the cellar steps, so carefully planned, wasn't a complete success. It backfired. Stoneman was frightened, all right; that's why he hired me. He thought a stranger in the house would save his own skin. He couldn't afford to go to the police—that would spoil his own plans—so he used me as a bodyguard and said nothing. He didn't care what happened as long as he came out of it alive. During this little reign of terror only one thing touched him. That was the rock business. He liked children, and that made him angry. That's the only good thing that can be said for Stoneman. Mrs. Lacey, burned to death in her bed, was nothing. Too bad, but it had to be done. That's how he looked at it, but he was wrong in more ways than one. Mrs. Lacey was the backfire I mentioned before."

He lit a cigarette, and over his cupped hands his eyes looked far beyond the people in front of him. He knew it was a hammy gesture, but it gave him a chance to listen for sounds behind him. There were none, yet, and that was as it should be.

"Mrs. Lacey," he went on, "knew who pushed Stone-

man down the stairs. Now, someone in this room knows
how dark that passage was. It was so dark that the poor
woman could never have proved she saw a thing. If
she'd talked about it, people would have laughed at her.
Or tapped their heads. Everybody in Crestwood and Bear
River knew she needed glasses and wouldn't wear them.
Everybody knew she was incurably romantic. They'd
have put her story down as another tall tale. Then why
was she killed? Why not let her talk? Because the
murderer, who wasn't a murderer yet, literally couldn't
afford the publicity. So her thermos jug was spiked with
an overdose of her own medicine and, when she was un-
conscious she was drenched in kerosene and—lighted. . . .
Violet?"

Violet opened her mouth, but no sound came out.

"Tell these people what you told me. Mrs. Lacey
left her room that night for at least a half-hour, didn't she?"

She nodded.

"You'll have to say it, Violet. I want it heard."

"Y-y-yes, sir."

"That's right. So the murderer had time to spike the
hot drink she took every night. All he had to do then was
—wait. Now we come to Florrie. She was strangled by
the same hands that poured kerosene over Mrs. Lacey.
Over the still-breathing Mrs. Lacey. Florrie was killed
because she found a newspaper clipping in a wastepaper
basket. Her death was pointless and unnecessary. The
clipping was torn, mutilated. Actually it told her nothing.
But the murderer didn't know that. If Florrie had found
the clipping under ordinary circumstances she'd have
burned it without reading it. But she and Violet were
questioned about the wastepaper, and she got curious.
She searched the waste a second time and found that
dangerous scrap. She tried to take it to a friend. She
was—intercepted. That's all about Florrie for the present.

I want to go back to Stoneman for a minute. Florrie's murder was planned at least several hours in advance. Stoneman's was not. He was probably due for a quick end, but I'm sure no definite plan was set. We were all in this room that night, drinking and talking. Some of us were having a good time. A shot rang out. That's when our murderer, a perfect opportunist, saw his chance. He set the stage for Stoneman's murder simultaneously with that shot. . . . It's cold in here. Does anyone want brandy ? "

" No," said Beulah. Her voice was thin and tired. No one else spoke.

Laura Morey's eyes had never once left Mark's face. She sat between Bessy and Beulah, drawn away from them, rigid. Perrin stared at the bare floor. He'd held that same position from the beginning, except for one brief moment. When Mark was talking about Florrie he had turned and looked over his shoulder at the empty hall behind him.

Morey sat spellbound. " Can you prove that about Stoneman ? I mean, is it on the level or are you guessing ? "

" No questions now," Mark said coolly. " Ask me later or read Wilcox's report. . . . Now, back to the clipping. It was a vague little piece about an accident. There were no names, no dates, and the chances for running it down were pretty slim. Also it looked normal and harmless. But we traced it, just to be sure we weren't missing anything. We located its origin and, as a result, put in two telephone calls ; one to a little town in Florida and the other to London."

Wilcox, standing like a waxwork against the crimson curtains, shifted his weight. In spite of the icy air that crept across the floor, Mark wiped perspiration from his face. He saw Perrin's hands open and shut. He didn't look at anyone else.

"Those telephone calls turned up a story that is and always has been available to anybody curious enough to investigate. Unfortunately, nobody was curious. Probably because until now nothing showed above an apparently calm surface. But the waters parted, if you don't mind a little rhetoric, and three bodies came to the top."

He broke off deliberately and looked over at Violet, shivering in her chair by the dying fire. "Violet, do you want that fire built up?"

She shook her head.

"Well, I'll make the rest of this as short as possible. I know some of you want to get away. I'm only going to give you a bare outline of that story. I wish I didn't have to tell a word of it. If there were any way of clearing this up without bringing in the London end, I'd do it. Some of you know what I mean. Believe me, I'm as sorry as hell. . . . The story begins with the failure of a marriage. There was no open break, no gossip or scandal. Two people simply announced that they couldn't get along with each other and the wife took her child and went away. The husband also dropped out of sight. Then, after several years, the woman met and fell in love with another man. She told him about her husband. She also told him her faith prohibited divorce. . . . Pretty dull so far, isn't it? It gets better as it goes along."

Bessy's round eyes glowed in the shadow of her shawl. Her face began to twitch. Beulah took the cold plump hands in hers and rubbed them gently. She spoke in a soothing whisper. "Hush," she said.

Mark went on. "It won't be long now, Miss Bessy," he said. "Yes, divorce was prohibited. But this was her first chance for happiness, so, af ter a long struggle with her conscience, she decided to go through with it. However, before she made her first move, some inkling of her intention found its way into print. I think some gossip writer got hold of the story. That's a guess, but it must have happened like that. Or it may have been a magazine article, one of those pally chats about well-known people. The man she planned to marry was a big shot and anything that happened to him was news. Anyway, the divorce intention became known. Now I skip a chapter.

" The second marriage took place. The child, who had been kept in an obscure boarding school, hidden from its father, knew nothing about it. But the mother and the new husband made plans for a reunion as carefully as they planned their honeymoon. They told themselves they'd meet the child on their return and live happily ever after. It was a long honeymoon. I even know where they went. Cornwall and Scotland. Then, after six months, on their way to the south of France to pick up the child, they stopped over in Paris. The woman went to her bankers for mail and that was the last happy moment she knew. One of her letters told her she was a bigamist."

The atmosphere in the room was thick. Breath turned to vapour and hung like small clouds. The dying fire sighed like a sick soul stirring in its last sleep. Mark droned on.

" Bigamy. A nasty little crime for nasty little people. A stupid, common, vulgar little crime, living on sex and the bankbooks of lonely women, ending in ridicule and laughter. But there's nothing to laugh at here. This bigamy ended in three murders. Why ? What happened ? Something in this story doesn't make sense. What is it ? . . . Miss Pond looks as if she knew the answer, and I know what she's thinking. She's pretty sure she's found the flaw. She wants to tell me that the woman couldn't possibly be a bigamist because she was legally divorced. Think back a minute, Miss Pond. Did I actually tell you she was divorced ? No. I said she'd considered it. You see, she didn't go through with it after all. She didn't think it was——" He stopped and turned slowly.

"Wilcox," he said, "there's something wrong."

Wilcox stared back stonily.

"Is there anyone in this house, anyone who—shouldn't be here?"

The air in the room was like moving ice. It creaked and crackled; it whispered in the corners and curled around the curtains at the window. Amos twisted his head on his thin neck and made a strangling sound.

No one stirred in that row of still, white faces. Only Bessy breathed heavily. Mark heard his own breath, like a dry rattle. He was frightened himself, now.

He flicked his hands across his eyes as if he were brushing cobwebs. "Maybe I'd better stop here," he said. "Something's gone wrong. I don't like it. I feel as if——" He looked at Amos before he spoke again.

"I don't believe in ghosts," he said quietly, "but something is trying to enter this house. I must ask you not to move. . . . I wonder if the dead do return? Not to avenge or to accuse, but to—gloat? I wonder if——" He turned to Wilcox again.

"Who opened that window?"

Wilcox put his head behind the curtains. When he turned back to face Mark he was trembling. He didn't speak.

"What is it?" Mark took a step forward and put his hand on the cord. "What is it?" he said again. "You look as if you'd seen a——" He pulled the cord and the curtains swung back.

The window was wide open to the stormy night. A faint blue glow hung over the edge of the terrace. It swayed in the wind like a living thing. As they watched with horrified eyes it rose in a column and rolled slowly forward until it was almost in the room. It hesitated and came over the sill. In its heart was a leering white figure.

A thin scream went up to the ceiling and hung there, quivering. A figure catapulted through the air and a knife flashed. A black wave of men surged in through the window and the hall. Amos flung himself at the light switch and the chandelier glared down on chaos.

The blue glow was gone and a plaster snowman lay on the floor, knifed into a hundred shards.

A ring of men stood in close formation at the window. Wilcox snapped on the handcuffs. He mumbled the usual formula. Then, "I have to do this, Mr. Morey," he said. He didn't sound sorry.

Mark turned to Bessy and Beulah with a wan smile and pointed to all that remained of the Taits' hasty sculpture. "I wasn't showing off," he said. "The original is Stoneman's coffin."

Morey wrenched himself erect. He looked beyond Mark. His red eyes burned, his mouth twisted. He raised his shackled hands in a slow, grim gesture.

"Who is that man!"

Mark answered with bland venom.

"You mean the gentleman with his arms around the lady? He's a very distinguished Britisher, a surgeon. Dr. George Edward Perrin Oliver. And his wife, so help me, if I have to go through every court in the land!"

"You!" screamed Morey. He sent his guards crashing as he hurled himself at the man who had been a servant in his house.

"Knife!" shrilled Bessy. "Knife!"

A pistol barked. Morey lurched and went down on his knees; blood streamed from his right hand. He bounded back like a spring and threw one black look of hatred behind him as he ran for the stairs.

They were after him like a pack. All except Mark.

"I know what he's going to try for," he whispered to the woman who wept quietly and bitterly at his side. "I hope he gets away with it, but only because it will make things easier for you." He looked up at the ceiling and listened. " One of the windows, over the ravine." He pushed her gently into a chair.

They all sat without speaking, but the room was filled with sound. Running feet in the hall above, slamming doors, muffled shouts ; a thin cracked voice that they recognized as Amos, crying, " This one ! It's this one ! " Another door slammed. Silence. Then the running feet again, pounding down the upper hall, down the stairs, and a dark wave of men sweeping past the door.

Perrin came in with Amos and the Taits. They were panting. " All over," Perrin said. " Wilcox can manage without us now."

Violet crept out of her chair.

" Come here," Mark said. " Are you all in one piece ? "

She got as far as the sofa before her knees gave way and she collapsed on Bessy's lap. It wasn't hard to see what she was thinking. Perrin, Perrin, Perrin. Possibly, even Lord Perrin.

Mark looked at the man and forced himself to think of him as Oliver. " I'd like to ask you a question, but you needn't answer unless you want to. How much did he get from you ? "

" He's had fifty thousand. He was to get two hundred more when we reached New York."

Beulah pawed the air. " Blackmail ! Bigamy ! Murder ! That good-looking man ! I'm having one of my nightmares. Either wake me up or explain."

" And who is who ? " complained Bessy, shifting under Violet's weight. " You're heavy, dear. Do sit on the floor like a good girl. . . . I can't place little Ivy."

" Ivy," Laura said thickly, " is Ivy Oliver. I'd have fought this thing if it hadn't been for Ivy. You see, according to law, she is illegitimate." She began to cry. " But that's not all. He talked about kidnapping too.

First he'd say how sorry he was for Ivy, how she'd be better off dead. Then he'd talk about kidnapping. He'd ask me if I'd read certain cases, and he'd tell me about them, and I'd have to cover my ears." She raised hopeless eyes to Mark. "I was afraid I'd never see her again. I thought of all the other pitiful babies who have died that way. But you must believe me—if I'd known how Mrs. Lacey and Florrie would pay for my silence I'd have defied him. But I didn't know until it was too late."

Oliver bent over her. "Tell it all," he said. "We've been running away too long. Tell it all and then it can't hurt you again."

Beulah's thin claw fumbled for a handkerchief. "I'm beginning to get the point," she said. "I'm—sorry."

"Go on," Oliver urged Laura gently. "Get it out of your mind. All of these people have helped you and they have the right to know."

"The—children? Mr. East said——"

"They're with Mrs. Wilcox, snug as a bug in a rug." Mark smiled reassuringly.

She straightened her shoulders and a faint colour crept into her face. "My husband wasn't fit to live," she said. "I left him when Anne was two years old and went to live in England. I had no near relatives and I had money of my own. You know what happened there. Just as I was ready to start divorce proceedings I had a letter from Mr. Stoneman. It came from Florida. He was an old friend of my husband's. I'd never known anything against him and had no reason to doubt him. He told me Jim was dead and enclosed a clipping, a clipping that proved I was a widow. Of course I believed it. I dropped the divorce action at once. I married. Then six months later, that day in Paris, I did two things. First I went to a gynæcologist. He told me I was going to have a child. Then I went to the bank. I saw Jim's writing on a letter. He had sent it to my London house, addressed to Mrs. James Morey, and it had been forwarded. . . . Shall I tell what was in the letter ? "

" Go on," Oliver said.

" He told me Mr. Stoneman had made one of his classical errors. The man he had identified as Jim was a tramp wearing clothes Jim had given him. He told me how it had happened. He said he had left Mr. Stoneman in Citrus City and gone on a fishing trip. He stayed away longer than he had planned. While Mr. Stoneman was waiting for him he read about the unidentified man. He said Mr. Stoneman was worried and went to see the body. He said he didn't know anything about it until he returned several days later and Mr. Stoneman told him he had written me. They were both horrified, he said. They decided to say nothing. Then later he changed his mind. He was afraid I might remarry, illegally. He hoped I understood. . . . I understood perfectly ! He waited until I had been married six months before he wrote that letter ! And—he asked me to take him back."

" Where is the letter now ? " Mark asked.

" In my safe-deposit box in New York."

" That's where you should have kept the clipping."

" I know that now. But I kept it with me because it was the only vindication I had. I used to—read it over and over. I was looking at it the day before—Florrie died. He'd just asked me for two hundred thousand dollars. I told him I'd have to think it over. But I knew I'd give it to him. He promised to go away and never see me again. When he left my room I put the clipping on my dressing table. It must have fallen in the basket. I don't know. When I went to look for it, it was gone. And the basket was empty. He was wild when I told him. I know now that he was afraid someone would find it and start talking. But he told me he was worried for my sake."

Mark looked at Oliver. " Did you ever suspect that accident was part of a brutal hoax ? "

" Certainly. And so did Laura. But we couldn't prove it then and I doubt if you can even now. Morey did things too well. I believe there actually was a tramp and that Morey got the poor devil drunk and happy before he deliberately ran him down. Or persuaded Stoneman to run him down, with half the blackmail money as a reward. Manslaughter, and he never let Stoneman forget it. I think Stoneman wrote the letter to Laura with manslaughter hanging over his head and a hundred thousand dollars in his dreams. Morey made a point of ragging Stoneman about his driving. He'd do it while I was in the room. Then when I left I'd hear Stoneman whimper and Morey laugh. But Stoneman always remembered the money and recovered. Morey was insane, but Stoneman was a devil."

Amos coughed unhappily. " I don't like to butt in and I'm not criticizing anybody who's had trouble, but why didn't you call his bluff in the beginning ? "

"Ivy is the reason. At first we could think of nothing but the rotten publicity. But soon we faced a graver danger. Kidnapping. He was too smart to threaten openly. You see he was still protesting his innocence. But he planted the possibility in Laura's mind. He constantly referred to a famous case in which wealth and position were powerless. I told her it was a bluff, but later we both knew he was equal to it. Once he locked Ivy in a closet and we couldn't find her for hours. Twice he overturned her pram. You "—he turned to Mark— " you've seen him knock her about in the snow. When she was a year old her wrist was broken. We never knew how it happened, but we could guess. Laura told Anne she must never leave Ivy alone. We couldn't give her a reason. That was a dreadful burden for a child to carry, but I'll make it up to her someday. . . . Can you understand our terror and silence now ? "

Mark remembered two little girls with their hands in his and grimly smiled his answer. " What did you do after you got that letter ? "

" Laura took Anne from her school and went to Switzerland."

" Wait a minute. Was that school in the Basque country ? "

" Yes." Oliver looked puzzled. " Why ? "

" She was playing a version of the national game with snowballs. I pumped her and she was frightened. . . . Sorry. Go on."

" I went on the same train but in another compartment. We didn't want Anne to see me. We'd already decided that after the baby was born we'd go to the States and try to find a solution there. I couldn't go as—myself, but I had to be with them. So I joined them in New York as a servant."

Violet forgot herself and patted his knee. He thanked her gravely.

" At the Swiss border I left Laura and Anne and went back to London. I told my patients and hospital that I was called away on His Majesty's business. Then I confided in the one person I could trust, Colonel Davenport. My mother was an American and he was an old friend of hers. He fixed me up with a passport in the name of George Perrin. I don't know how he did it and I'll never ask. He also provided unimpeachable references. He got those from his friends by hinting at counter-espionage and swearing them to secrecy. It's an amazing list. One of my most enthusiastic sponsors is an elderly duke who hasn't spoken to me for years . . . In the meantime Laura told Anne she was going to adopt a baby. We had to prepare the way somehow. And she told her they were going to see her father. Anne didn't remember her father. She'd been told he was ill. It's an odd thing, but when she met him she hated him on sight. Then about three months before Ivy was born Laura put Anne in a convent and went away to meet her trouble alone."

Wilcox came in silently and took a chair. Nobody noticed him.

"Once in the States," Oliver went on, "we moved from place to place, always trailed by Morey and Stoneman. They kept up the fiction. Their lives were ruined, they said. Their lives! We made the mistake of paying at first. Then we stopped. Laura told him she was ready to take the case to court. He retaliated with the kidnapping suggestion and proceeded to show us how easily it could be done. I knew then that nothing would stop him. Laura was losing her mind. We dropped the plans for legal prosecution and paid again. At the same time I wrote Davenport and asked him to recommend a secluded place. I think I was subconsciously planning to kill Morey. Davenport offered us this place and a house in Maryland. I chose this, for greater privacy. We still thought we could handle things. We thought we'd find a way out. That others would suffer never occurred to us."

Amos leaned over Oliver's shoulder and whispered.

"Train?" Oliver said. "No, we'll put up at the hotel to-night. I want to see some people to-morrow. Obligations."

"I'm sorry he's dead," Beulah said. "I want to kill him myself. He threatened me with a hatchet once, remember? The day you came here."

"I remember." Oliver smiled. "So—we came here. Morey and Stoneman began to quarrel. I think Stoneman wasn't getting his share and threatened to talk. That's one reason why he was killed. The others were Morey's greed and Stoneman's very open reaction to

Mr. East's chatter about Citrus City.   Morey saw that and
Stoneman knew it.   He figured it was time to play on our
side.   He knew he was the only person in the world who
could prove we had been victimized.   And he'd get more
out of Laura than he would out of Morey.   At the worst, a
reduced sentence for turning state's evidence ;   at the best,
a small fortune."

Wilcox coughed unhappily.   His face was serious and
troubled.

" Plenty of people are going to think you and your wife
are directly responsible for these deaths, Dr. Oliver.   I can
understand why you didn't go to the police in the first
place, anybody with kids can understand that.   But why
didn't you come to me after Mrs. Lacey's death ? "

" The night Mrs. Lacey died I thought of Morey and
Stoneman at once.   But it seemed too fantastic.   I had
no proof, no motive.   Then when you and the coroner
both called it an accident I wrote my suspicions off as
nerves.   When Florrie was murdered I knew she must
have found the clipping, in spite of her denials ;   and I
knew Morey or Stoneman had done it.   I told Laura so.
It was too late to help Florrie, but Laura faced Morey with
it.   She told him she was going to the police.   He told her
it was Stoneman.   He asked her to give him a few more
days, only time enough to get Stoneman away and out of
the country.   She refused.   Then he picked up a miniature
of Ivy and looked at it.   He didn't say anything ;   he
smiled.   But she thought what he intended her to think.
So she agreed."

He reached over and took both of Laura's hands in his.
" When he told my wife about Florrie," he said quietly,
" she tried to jump from her window.   He pulled her back.
She was too valuable to lose.   She is ashamed because
some of you heard her screaming. . . . She tore her
fingers on the window latch and broke one of the panes.

You can see the marks."

He held up her hands. Mark remembered that day.

The Taits blew their noses and huddled in their capes.

"We believed Morey when he said it was Stoneman. And when Stoneman disappeared it looked like a confession. Perhaps we shouldn't have given them those days of grace, but we were bargaining for Ivy's life then. . . . I know that if we had never come here, if we had turned them over to the police in the beginning, Mrs. Lacey and Florrie would be living too. But we couldn't read the future. And if Mr. East had come to my wife with his suspicions about Mrs. Lacey's death we could have stopped the slaughter there. But neither could he read the future and his reticence is understandable."

Wilcox nodded in agreement. He saw too clearly his own signature on Mrs. Lacey's death certificate. It was nobody's fault, he told himself. It was a devil's web. He liked the sound of that and said it over and over in his mind. A devil's web.

"Hmm," he said. "Did you see Mr. Morey heave that rock through the nursery window?"

"No. But he did it. It was a warning to Laura that he meant business and as usual it was successful. She promised him the two hundred thousand that night."

"Didn't he ever suspect—you?"

"No. Laura told him I'd deserted her. He was happy about that."

The Taits came forward to say good-bye. Their courtly bows and clicking heels brought a thoughtful look to Bessy's face. That sister of their's wasn't the only woman in the world who could air flannels. She tore down and rebuilt her house while they cast regretful and admiring looks at their own shattered masterpiece.

"Don't touch!" warned Wilcox. "We've got to photograph it. It's evidence."

Oliver walked with the Taits to the front door. When he returned he beckoned to Mark and Wilcox. Amos trailed them across the room to the window. Oliver drew back the curtains.

Two processions were moving into the drive from opposite directions ; two groups of men, each with a covered stretcher and lantern-bearers. They converged and walked slowly toward their destination. Further down, the lights of a parked ambulance pierced the trees. As they drew abreast of the Taits, the old men stood aside and uncovered their heads.

Nobody spoke.

Oliver dropped the curtain.

They had all drawn their chairs close together. Oliver brought a small table and drinks. Nobody wanted to leave.

Wilcox and Amos were waiting for the photographer. Mark was waiting for them. Bessy and Beulah were waiting for Mark and hoping to hear more. Violet was in a trance and waiting for anything. Wilcox promised to drive her home. The Olivers refused to leave until the house was finally closed.

A surly youth put his head in the door and waved a grimy paper.

" Scott's," he said hoarsely. " You gotta get out and I gotta lock up."

" Listen," advised Wilcox. " We've had a little trouble here and we're late. You begin at the bottom and work up, then begin at the top and work down. When you get to the middle, we'll be done."

The youth vanished.

Bessy plunged. " Beulah says Mr. Morey left me a present. I wouldn't touch it with a ten-foot pole. . . . What is it ? "

" It's too young for you," Mark said. " It's already

been donated to the Orphanage, for medicinal purposes. You can look for an epidemic any day now."

"You have a nasty mind," Beulah said affectionately. "I suppose you're the one who turned off the furnace this afternoon and hid the light bulbs."

"I did it," Mark said regretfully, "but I was only a tool. Wilcox dreamed that one up. He said a dim and chilly atmosphere would provide the graveyard touch. It was nice, wasn't it? Amos yearned to play the harp off-stage, but we sat on that."

Beulah sent Amos a look full of pity and insult and turned to Mark. "I suppose you had to leave that body in the snowman until you could take it out with witnesses."

"You're catching on. We'll make it Pond and East."

Scott's man reappeared, scowling at his grimy paper. "It says horse here," he accused.

"Not here, pal," Mark said. "In the stables."

"Oh." He lowered his voice. "Hey. Is it true what they say out there? They say some feller went crazy and killed twelve people."

"No," Mark said. "Only three. And it wasn't a feller. It was a woman." He pointed to Beulah. She bared her teeth. Scott's man disappeared again, with a look that suggested permanence.

"I don't know yet how you located Stoneman's body," Oliver said.

"The answer to that one came out of the mouths of babes." He told them about the eyelashes. "Anne wasn't watching me, so I dug farther. He was bludgeoned to death. The poker, I think. Morey played constantly with the poker that night, stabbing the coals. Removing the traces. Then the other babe, young Floyd Wilcox, rounded out the story. We couldn't have tied it to Morey without young Floyd. You remember his antics at Florrie's funeral? Crawling on his stomach and swinging from tree to tree ? He was following you and Morey when he did it. I collared him later and asked him why. Then he confessed that he and his pal paid us a second visit the night Stoneman disappeared. There was nobody home to keep tabs on them. They prowled around here from one o'clock on. They had a wonderful time frightening themselves until three o'clock and then they started back to Bear River. Over in that grove where the children play they saw Morey. He was replacing the snowman's hat and patting its face. They were enchanted. They thought he was drunk. Then, to complete their evening's entertainment, he made his way back to the house by crawling on his stomach and swinging from trees. He was trying to make as few tracks as possible, of course, but they just thought it was high spirits. The next time they saw him, at the funeral, they let themselves go. They couldn't help it. I think Morey caught on. We worried about that. The boys have been locked in the house ever since. By the way, the Taits built their remarkable replica on Floyd's sled. That's how it moved so smoothly. Two men with clothes-line poles were behind the hedge, pushing. The lovely blue light, which scared even me to death, came out of Floyd's chemical set. . . . I like to think he was trapped by children's toys.''

"How did Morey get Stoneman ? I can't figure it. We were all there.'' Beulah looked affronted.

" He was a quick thinker. After the boys fired that shot he told Stoneman to call Wilcox. He also told him to turn out the lights. Oliver and I heard him. Then he took one direction and sent us in others. He doubled back. He crept in just as Stoneman completed the call and killed him, and—I'm sorry about this—hid his body under this sofa.''

Bessy screamed and tucked up her feet.

" That's the way we reconstruct it. I found the stains on the floor. Soaked through the rug. He was a good psychologist in some things. He was sure we wouldn't look for Stoneman in this room and we didn't. Even if we had looked and found the body, who could tie it to Morey? Wilcox and I nearly went crazy trying to figure how he got the body out, but we did it. When they all returned from the search that night, Morey went up to bed, carrying a rope. The house was locked up. Oliver did that himself. Then when everything was quiet, Morey climbed out of his window, using the rope. We found fragments on an old awning hook. But—here's where we were stumped. Did he let the body down on the rope too? Hardly. He couldn't risk waking Wilcox, who was sleeping with one eye open down the hall. Then I had a hunch. Earlier in the evening he and Amos had come back for wood. I asked Amos if Morey had left him alone, even for a few minutes, while they were in the house. Amos said yes, Morey had gone to the library for whisky. So that was when he moved the body. He hid it in the terrace hedge, which had been searched. I checked this afternoon and saw the broken branches. So all he had to do was climb out of his window, collect the body, and rebuild the snowman around it. Forgetting the eyelashes." He looked uneasily at Laura Oliver.

She smiled. It was only a faint smile, but it was better than the old one.

"For heaven's sake!" Beulah stared at the door.

A new arrival tottered on the threshold. This was a gnome, with a shining bald head and photographic equipment.

"Come in," Wilcox said. "Mr. Spangler, the photographer. We been waiting for you, Buster. Better take the bloodstain first. Wait till we move the sofa."

They slid the sofa with its quaking burden off to one side.

"There," said Wilcox. "Bet you never saw anything to beat that, eh? Take a real pretty one."

The ageing photographer trod the bare boards as if they were hallowed ground. He wheezed happily as he set up his camera. He wagged his head in joyful disbelief and congratulated the group with a toothless grin.

"Poor lad," murmured Wilcox. "It does my heart good to see him. The biggest thing he ever had before this was a three-legged chicken."

Violet, whose eyes had never left Oliver, now began to wilt. "Are you going to stay here all night?" she whispered to Mark.

"I'm going to let the elderly ladies fight for the pleasure of offering me a bed—I hope," he whispered back. "But I'll take you home first."

Bessy pointed a goloshed foot in the direction of the bloodstain. "It's not very red," she complained.

"He was old," Beulah said. "You know, I had this thing all wrong. I thought Amos killed Mrs. Lacey in a crime of passion. Frustration." Amos spat.

"And," she went on, "I thought Mr. Stoneman killed Florrie."

"Mercy. What for?"

"Oh, you know. Young girls—old men."

"No I don't," Bessy said thoughtfully. "But I wish I did."

The photographer had dragged himself away from the bloodstain and was dancing around the plaster ruins. Amos pointed out the knife, still embedded in a lumpy shoulder.

"Don't take it out," he warned. "Don't touch it either. We got to get the fingerprints." He reached in his pocket and drew out the second knife, carefully swathed in a silk handkerchief. "When you're through with the one, here's the other."

"Two!" Mr. Spangler found speech for the first time. "Two!" He turned to Wilcox. "I'll never forget this," he said humbly.

The knives revived Violet, and she turned to Oliver. "He almost killed you! I thought I'd die! He almost killed you!"

"Rank carelessness," Beulah said in the direction of Amos. "Two knives and the room full of defenceless women!"

"Defenceless!" marvelled Amos.

"That was my fault," Wilcox said. "I never thought of knives. And we couldn't search him. Give ourselves away. When he drew the first one we naturally thought that was all."

Oliver put his hand on Mark's shoulder. "That was an amazing shot of yours," he said quietly.

"Mine? I didn't do it. I don't carry arms. Against the law for me. It was Wilcox."

Wilcox stared. "No," he said slowly. "It wasn't me. It wasn't any of my own men either." He looked at Amos, unbelieving.

Amos returned the look with a leer. "I told you to be careful. I warned you plenty and often. But maybe it was all right this time." They followed his pointing finger.

Beulah was down in the depths of the petticoat pocket. She drew out a revolver.

"I did it," she said. "And I'm sure you're very welcome."

Bessy shook a reproving head. "That was your dear father's favourite gun," she said. "He wouldn't like you to play with it."

Scott's man put his head inside the door. "All out," he bellowed. He saw the gun in Beulah's hand. This time when he disappeared they heard the front door slam behind him.

In the laughter that followed Mark heard one voice above the others, high and sweet. He told himself that Ivy would sound like that when she grew up. And he felt repaid.